LOVING HER LONELY HIGHLANDER

Time to Love a Highlander Series
Book Six

by Maeve Greyson

ARE YOU SIGNED UP FOR DRAGONBLADE'S BLOG?

You'll get the latest news and information on exclusive giveaways, exclusive excerpts, coming releases, sales, free books, cover reveals and more.

Check out our complete list of authors, too!

No spam, no junk. That's a promise!

Sign Up Here

www.dragonbladepublishing.com

Dearest Reader;

Thank you for your support of a small press. At Dragonblade Publishing, we strive to bring you the highest quality Historical Romance from some of the best authors in the business. Without your support, there is no 'us', so we sincerely hope you adore these stories and find some new favorite authors along the way.

Happy Reading!

CEO, Dragonblade Publishing

Additional Dragonblade books by Author Maeve Greyson

Once Upon a Scot Series
A Scot of Her Own (Book 1)
A Scot to Have and to Hold (Book 2)
A Scot To Love and Protect (Book 3)

Time to Love a Highlander Series
Loving Her Highland Thief
Taming Her Highland Legend
Winning Her Highland Warrior
Capturing Her Highland Keeper
Saving Her Highland Traitor
Loving Her Lonely Highlander

Highland Heroes Series
The Guardian
The Warrior
The Judge
The Dreamer
The Bard
The Ghost
A Yuletide Yearning (Novella)
Love's Charity (Novella)

Also from Maeve Greyson
Guardian of Midnight Manor

CHAPTER ONE

Thurso, Scotland
December 1, 2022

"They've drained the mock ale again. Were ye expecting this big a turnout?"

"Not half so much, honestly." Lorna Merriweather tightened her hold on the bright red banister of the raised cashier platform, trying to keep from shouting with joy. Excitement and pride coursed through her. "I wish Miss Agatha could see all this. She wouldha thought it grand for sure."

"She sees it, hen." Gracie, her best friend since forever ago, hugged an arm around her. "I guarantee she is smiling down on all of it." With a theatrical sweep of her arm, she took in the quaint, multilevel bookshop that had squatted on Thurso's primary thoroughfare for as long as anyone could remember. "'Tis a grand day, for certain. Just look at it all."

Customers filled the newly renovated place, browsing through the antique oddities, crafts from local artisans, and collections of used books filling the shelves.

"The way ye spruced the place up. Ye know she wouldha loved it," Gracie said. "After all…" She gave Lorna a teasing shake before offering a dramatic curtsy. "Ye never could do wrong in her eyes, m'lady. Ye know that well enough."

"I dinna ken about all that," Lorna said.

But she knew why sweet old Agatha Crowley had left her the store and all her accounts. Of course, that was a special secret between her and the grand dame. They had discovered a kinship as soon as they met. Sisters in the realms of the forgotten, Miss Agatha always said. Neither of them had any family, so they adopted each other. Memories of their happy times and days of laughter made Lorna smile. She hoped the precious old soul was in heaven now, entertaining the angels. Memories of the grand lady's effervescent cheeriness brought tears to her eyes. The world wasn't as bright without Miss Agatha.

She straightened her spine, standing taller as she forced her grief back into the shadows. "I think we have enough lemonade and cola left to mix up one last barrel of mock ale. Surely that will get us to closing time, ye think?"

"Lonnie can put it together," Gracie said. "He's been standing guard over the refreshments to keep those hooligans from Greer Street out of it. That fool bunch probably thinks it is the real thing." She slowly twirled, modeling her seventeenth-century attire. "Besides, we mustn't stain our rentals, aye? Lonnie's tunic and kilt are his own. If the drink splashes whilst he's mixing, 'tis no great bother. Cybil will scrub it clean for him. A mess on ours wouldna be so easily remedied."

"Aye, we must keep ours spotless or we lose our deposit." Lorna smoothed her hands down the dark gray waistcoat. Its snugness and the stiff embroidered stomacher behind the laces in the front took some getting used to. She had refused the uncomfortable-looking boned stays attached to one of the petticoats the costume clerk assured her she needed. That level of realism for Seventeenth Century Day at the shop was entirely unnecessary. The plain linen chemise, bum roll, and wool skirt in a lovely shade of soft grayish blue were ample for the event. All those layers stopped the winter winds, too. As did the fine, heavy cloak that completed the outfit.

Her pride in the success of the marketing event made her insides all bubbly with daring. "I know it might be risky, but I plan to wear mine out tonight. A bit of a walking advertisement for the shop, aye? I canna wait to see what Patrick thinks of it. Hopefully, I won't spill anything at dinner. He made us reservations at Old Town Road. Verra fancy, ye ken?"

"Aww, hen. No!" Gracie made a face and groaned. "Ye promised to dump that scabby roaster weeks ago."

"I did not." Lorna backed up a step, flinching as she bumped into the new cash register and triggered an irritating alarm that trilled like an annoying bird. "Bloody thing!" She punched in the code and calmed the sensitive new computer. "I am still none too sure about this gadget. The old one was not nearly as complicated."

"Ye are changing the subject." Gracie sidled around and cornered her with an accusing glare. "And ye did promise to break it off with him. I remember it clear as day."

"I said I would think on it." Lorna hated to admit she had a fatal weakness for underdogs, and the man was definitely that. Surely, she could help him. All he needed was a little support and positivity. But a wee voice inside her head mocked her, harping on what she already knew in her heart but refused to accept. It was time to cut her losses and give up. She had wasted enough time trying to reform a man who would never change. "And I have been thinking on it," she repeated without conviction.

Gracie thumped the banister. "How much more of yer life do ye intend to waste on that fool? And why in heaven's name would ye even consider marrying him? Makes me furious the way he pulls yer strings and makes ye dance to whatever tune he fancies." She snagged hold of Lorna's left hand and tapped her ring finger. The ill-fitting engagement ring slid to one side, revealing a green circle staining her skin. "Not only that, his ring is a feckin' piece of shite. Just like him."

Lorna snatched her hand away and hid it in a fold of her skirt.

"It is all he could afford. And besides, the ring doesna make the engagement. 'Tis the feelings behind it." She struggled to sound more certain than she felt. "I am helping him come around. He is a work in progress, ye ken?"

"Ye canna change a piece a shite into anything other than a turd," Gracie retorted. "Once a jobby, always a jobby."

"That's the truth of it!" Lonnie called up from the main level. He yanked open the door to the storage closet in the base of the cashier platform. "I never left Cybil wondering if I would show or not. Never forgot her birthday, either. And I sure as hell never hurt her feelings by insulting her hair. That bloke deserves a swift kick in his arse."

"Ye fight tooth and nail for everyone else," Gracie said. "Why will ye not stand up for yerself with that rat?"

"Can we talk about this another time?" Lorna made a subtle jerk of her head toward their customers. Folks were staring and migrating closer so they wouldn't miss a word. Gossip traveled faster than grass through a goose around here. She wanted the shop well known and talked about in all of northern Scotland, but not because of her rocky love life. Besides, Patrick wasn't so bad most of the time. They just never caught him at his best.

The front door's bell jangled a cheery hello to the newest patron coming in off the street.

"Well, speak of the devil." Gracie offered an elaborate bow. "Yer knight in shining armor has arrived, m'lady."

"Gracie." Lorna fixed her friend with a pleading look. She didn't want this evening to begin with a poor start and put Patrick in an impossible mood. "Be nice, aye?"

"I will not." Gracie took a defiant stance and hiked her nose higher. "I dinna like the way the man treats ye. He can go straight to the devil far as I am concerned."

Patrick made his way to the cashier platform, giving the shop a critical once-over as he sauntered past the displays and sale tables. "Looks nice. Bet all this set ye back a tidy bob or two. Got anything left in those accounts the old lady left ye?"

"That is none of yer bloody business," Gracie snapped. "Did yer mam never teach ye if ye couldna say something nice, dinna say anything at all?"

"Feck off, Gracie." Patrick shot a sneer her way, then turned his attention to Lorna. "We got reservations in thirty minutes, hen. Dinna be dawdling about getting out of that garb."

Lorna forced a smile even though her cheeks burned with embarrassment. She might still save this evening. At least, she hoped so. She tried to overlook his rudeness. Up to a point. He had not had an easy life, and she did her best to keep that in mind. But in the last few weeks, his behavior had gotten worse, and she refused to be abused. This might very well be their last evening together.

With a model's pose, she turned and displayed the gorgeous authenticity of her costume. "I am wearing this. Along with the loveliest cloak that came with it. What better advertisement for how we have made the shop into so much more than merely a store for used books?"

He stared at her as though waiting for the punch line. "Ye are joking, right?"

"I am not, and if ye dinna like it, ye can bloody well cancel on me like ye did last time."

His attitude had worn her last nerve as thin as could be. Gracie's *harrumph* frazzled it even thinner. "Ye are being an arse, Patrick. I deserve better." Her old fears of being alone again squeezed her insides until she couldn't breathe. But she stood strong, refusing to apologize and take it all back to appease him. Being alone was better than being mistreated or taken for granted.

He waved off her criticisms as though swatting flies. "If ye want to dress like a damned eedjit, go for it. Makes me no never mind." He cast another glance around the shop and checked his watch. "We best be about it, then, and at least get some food for my hard-earned money. I had to give that bloke my credit card number when I made the reservations. Stingy bastards charge ye if ye dinna show."

Every customer in the shop stared at them, their browsing through the rare books and antiques forgotten. Their faces told her exactly what they thought. Her stomach tightened with that same queasy feeling of embarrassment he always triggered whenever they were out in public. Gracie was right—she should have broken it off months ago. But he could be so disarmingly sweet sometimes, and anybody was better than nobody at all.

Or so she had thought after being alone all her life. But loneliness might be a better partner than Patrick, after all. She had survived it before. She would bloody well survive it again.

"If ye canna afford the place, we dinna have to go," she said in a hushed tone. She forced a fake smile for the onlookers, wishing they would go on about their business.

He motioned for her to join him. "Come on, will ye? I just said they charge if ye dinna show. I'll be damned if I pay for wasted air. We can share a salad and have nothing but water for drinks. I hear tell the bread's free with it. After that, I thought we could go to the cliffs and watch for yer mirrie dancers ye're always going on about."

"Just go. Ye can have the whole feckin' salad." She held so tight to the banister that her knuckles ached. The reassuring weight of Gracie's hand on her back helped keep her strong. "Besides, ye hate the cold and the wind is up. It will cut right through ye on the cliffs. Go on wi' ye now. I will be staying here."

A change came across him, as if a curtain had dropped to reveal a different personality. He tucked his chin and sheepishly rocked from side to side. "Sorry, hen. Had a hard day stocking shelves, and they told me I have to take the night shift permanent from now on. Canna sleep worth a shite during the day, and they bloody well know it." He resettled his stance and apologetically shook his head. "But none of that is yer fault. Ye know I'm sorry. Come on, Lorna. Ye know I dinna mean it when I get ratty. 'Tis just after a bad day." With the beguiling smile that always doused her irritation with him, he motioned for her to join him. "Come on, hen. We will eat us some dinner, then watch for those northern lights ye love." He shrugged. "And we need to talk over some things. Important stuff, ye ken?"

Gracie tugged on the back of Lorna's jacket, trying to keep her in place. "He is full of shite," she said for Lorna's ears alone. "Throw him his ring and send him on his way."

Lorna turned and rested a hand on her friend's shoulder. "I have to handle this as I see fit, aye?" She wouldn't shame Patrick publicly. When she broke it off, it would be in private.

Gracie's mouth tightened into a disapproving pucker, but she said no more.

After an appreciative nod for her friend's rebellious silence, Lorna hurried down the steps to join Patrick. "I'll be in bright and early to set things right after today's celebration," she called back over her shoulder. As she settled the cloak's heavy richness around her shoulders, she shot her friend a beseeching look, wishing she wouldn't pout. "Did ye hear me, Gracie?"

"Aye," Gracie said. "See ye in the morning." She turned to the register to help a customer.

"Leave the heavy cleaning for me," Lonnie said while glowering at Patrick. "And call if ye need anything, aye? Me and Cybil dinna go to bed till late on Thursdays. Too many decent shows on the telly." He held the door for them, his scowl getting darker by the minute. "Call no matter how late, Lorna. Cybil would never forgive me or herself if we weren't there when ye needed us."

She gave his arm a grateful pat. "I promise. See ye in the morning, aye?"

"Aye," he said with a curt dip of his head, then closed the door.

"What do ye see in them?" Flipping his collar up against the cold, Patrick shot a disgruntled look back at the shop.

"They ask me the same about you." She tried to focus on the colorful holiday lights twinkling in the store windows and strung across the buildings. Their bright jolliness helped lift her spirits—

at least until they reached the restaurant with a *closed until further notice* sign propped in the window. The evening she had held such high hopes for unraveled even more. He had lied. Again. "Do ye even have a credit card, or was that a lie too?"

"I have one. Over the limit on it, though." He shrugged deeper into his coat. "And this week's pay damn sure couldna bear one of their meals. Sorry, hen." With an irritating grin, he tipped his head toward the sign. "All worked out for the best, though. Them froze pipes shut them down with no notice. Canceled our reservations and didna even try to charge me."

"Why did ye not just say that back in the shop instead of blowing hard and loud about eating at an expensive place?" She turned and headed back down the street through the freezing drizzle. Enough was enough.

He caught hold of her arm and stopped her. "Dinna be like that. A man's got his pride, ye ken? What was I supposed to say in front of all them folks?"

"The truth." She yanked free of him, tugged the hood of her cloak farther over her face, and charged onward.

With a sidling hop, he got in front of her and blocked the way. "I got enough bank to get us a few bottles of ale and some chips. We could pack it all to the cliffs with us. Have a right fine picnic while we chat. If ye have a fiver to chip in, I could even get us some of those biscuits ye like."

"Go to the pub and good riddance. I am going back to the shop." She shoved her hand in his face, showing him the wetness filling the air. "Ye need good weather for the northern lights, so once again ye are off the hook for whatever ye promise but never deliver."

"The weather's set to clear. Radio said so." He angled around, doing his best to herd her in the other direction. "If ye dinna believe me, step inside Hagerty's. Old Rob will tell ye." With a nod at her clothing, he winked. "Ye wanted to show off yer outfit, aye? The lads'll love it."

No matter what she did now, she would feel like a pathetic

loser for letting him manipulate her as long as he had. His pals in the pub would laugh and make fun of her, and if she returned to the shop to get to her apartment above it, Lonnie and Gracie's pity would be more than she could bear. Or she and Patrick could stand out here in the weather arguing and, with any luck, he would catch pneumonia. That was the only option that truly offered any promise.

"I am going home," she said, hoping she could climb the fire escape in the back without tearing her costume. At least that way, she would avoid Lonnie and Gracie. "Ye do whatever ye wish."

"But we need to talk." He fidgeted in place like a lad about to wet his pants. "It's important."

"So talk, then." She hugged her cloak closer, fighting to keep it from flapping in the wind. A scowl upward confirmed the mizzling rain had stopped. A starry blanket of blackness chased away the soft gray of low-hanging clouds. Just like he had said it would, damn him straight to hell. Still cold as the dickens and her fingers numb, she wished she had worn her gloves. "Well? What do ye have to say?"

"Rain's stopped. Since ye dinna want to go to the pub, let's just go on to the cliffs."

She studied him, trying to figure his angle. "Why are ye so dead set on going to the cliffs? Ye hate watching for the lights."

He jutted his chin and shoved his hands deeper into his pockets. "Trying to do better by ye. That's all. Were ye not nagging me just the other day that we never do anything ye want to do?"

"I dinna nag." She sniffed and rubbed the end of her icy nose. "I was calling ye out for not showing up when ye said ye would."

"Whatever." He scowled up at the sky, then leveled his glare with hers. "We need to talk about our engagement, and I thought the cliffs would be nice and private." His nose wrinkled as if he smelled a stink. After a disgruntled look up and down the street, he gave her a curt nod. "Ye canna take a shite in this place without everyone talking about it."

That part was true enough. The gossips had already whispered in her ear several times about him and Lucy Hamstead. Gracie and Lonnie swore they had heard about them sneaking around too. But it couldn't be so. Not with him working extra shifts when everyone said they had seen them together. She had even spotted his wreck of a car in the parking lot at the warehouse during the times in question.

But something was off about him tonight. She couldn't quite put her finger on it. An uneasy realization filled her. A premonition of sorts. One way or another, be it good or bad, tonight would forever change their relationship. She felt it in her bones. She might as well return his ring now.

"Well?" He stomped his feet and blew into his hands. "My car's parked just up there. Are ye coming or not?"

"If ye try to throw me off the overlook," she warned, "I will take ye with me. Just so ye know." She was only partially joking. He had never been physically abusive, but with tonight's strange mood, she wouldn't be surprised. Woe to him if he tried. She might tolerate his rudeness, but if he attempted to physically harm her, she would defend herself with ease.

He eyed her as if she had lost her mind, then shook his head. "I canna believe ye would say such a thing." His voice shifted to the tone he always used when trying to make her feel guilty. "Shall I get the car?"

"Aye. Fetch it." While she waited for him to return, she pushed the engagement ring around her finger with her thumb. A nervous habit she had adopted since he first gave her the ill-fitting thing. When she had suggested having it resized, he talked her out of it. When her finger started turning green, she understood why. But none of that had mattered. Until lately.

His rusted-out, beat-up excuse for a ride backfired twice as he pulled up beside her, then motioned for her to come around and get in.

"Chivalry is most definitely dead," she grumbled. She yanked on the dented door with all her might, pried it open, then slid into the seat.

"Gonna take a while for the heat to get going," he said as they pulled away from the curb. "Least we're out of the wind, though."

"I suppose so." She hunkered down into the heavy wool cloak, thankful she had worn the layered costume.

"What's with ye tonight?" The car backfired again, then sputtered and jerked as he shifted gears and gave it more gas.

"I am going to need a little more to go on before I answer that." She had an idea what he meant but wasn't about to make it easy on him. Her patience had taken too long to run its course with Patrick Inverarry. But she had finally reached its end.

"Ye're a right wee snippy bitch tonight." He took the turn that lead to the cliffs just outside of town. "Nearly bad as Gracie."

She snorted. "I will take that as a compliment."

He shot her a quick scowl, then returned his focus to the road. "I've not done a thing to deserve such treatment."

A bitter smile came to her. "Aye. Ye are right. Ye've not done a bloody thing."

The auto's engine groaned as the incline grew steeper. Patrick urged it to where the pavement ended and parked. "I canna leave it running. Have ye seen the price of petrol?"

A heavy sigh escaped her as she stared straight ahead. Such a beautiful overlook. Nothing but the sea and starry sky. And yet here she sat unable to enjoy it because she had caved to her fears and become a coward. Well, no more. Without a doubt, being alone was better than being with Patrick.

She slipped the ring off her finger and turned to give it to him.

"I dinna ken how to say this," he said before she could speak. "So, I'm just gonna say it. I need the ring back. Me and Lucy are getting married next week. She's up the kyte."

She sat there and blinked, shocked into a stupor. Then rage, regret, and an explosive jumble of angry emotions fought for control of her. Slow-burning rage won out. She trembled with its intensity. "What?" She needed to hear it again. Just to be sure.

"Pregnant. Couple months, I think." He shrugged. "That one

time without a condom bit me in the arse, so now I gotta pay. Marriage or child support. Leastwise with marriage, I'll get me house cleaned and meals cooked."

What a despicable, self-centered arse. She truly felt sorry for Lucy Hamstead. "So when ye told me ye were working extra shifts, ye were really working her. Right?" Not that it mattered. What made her angriest was he was breaking up with her before she could break up with him.

He shrugged again. "It's different for a man. One woman ain't always enough."

"Well, I've got news for ye—ye now have one less woman to treat like shite." She shoved the ring into his mouth. "Here's yer bloody ring. I hope ye damn well choke on it."

Without waiting for his reaction, she shouldered open the door and wrangled her way out of the car. The heavy layers of cloak, skirt, and petticoat worked against her, tangling around her feet. Angry tears burst free. How had she let herself believe she could change him? Fury at being made to look like the greatest sort of fool grew stronger. Bitterness at her gullibility made her sob. She didn't look like a fool. She was one.

The sky chose that moment to explode into rippling bands of brilliant green, violet, and red. Shafts of light danced tall and proud across the horizon as far as she could see. The icy wind roared in her ears as it shoved against her back, making her stumble forward.

"I have been such a feckin' idiot," she shouted at the breath-taking spectacle. "Why?" Blinded by tears, deafened by the wind and sea, she dropped to her knees. Or tried to. But the land was gone. She pitched forward, frantically clawing to stop her fall. The colors of the aurora borealis increased in intensity. They swirled around her, becoming so bright she squinted against the phenomenon's brilliance. An eerie humming vibrated through her, making her feel as if her bones were about to shake off her flesh.

She balled up and tumbled faster, bracing herself for the final impact. She just hoped the pain didn't last long. Whether she hit frigid water, razor-sharp stones, or both, death was imminent. Vertigo took over. Or maybe the world was spinning and not her. She couldn't tell anymore. Why was the fall lasting so long? Or was she already dead and hadn't realized it till now? An ear-splitting howl made her slap her hands over her ears. Churning nausea hit, sending the burn of bile into her throat. She gagged and retched in midair, then dry-heaved until her insides felt turned inside out. Everything went black and silent.

Then she hit. Hard.

CHAPTER TWO

THE ABRUPT STOP knocked the wind out of her. Lorna lay there wheezing and struggling to suck in air for what felt like forever. Before doing anything other than trying to breathe, she assessed herself for injuries. Arms and legs were numb with the cold but not hurting or bent to any strange angles. Everything responded when she twitched it, so no paralysis. No taste of blood or loose teeth. Her jaw ached a bit. Stomach still churned, but why wouldn't it after all that? The longer she lay there concentrating on calming down, the steadier she felt. She pulled in a deep breath. No broken ribs. Thank goodness for that.

With her cheek against the hard, frozen ground, she frowned at her fingers laced through spikes of frost-covered grass. What the devil had just happened? She must be dead. That was the only excuse for the lack of pain. Well—she had some pain. But nothing worse than the time she had banged around inside a barrel when rolled down a hill on a dare.

Then she became more aware of her surroundings. Patches of icy grass instead of a rocky beach or the sea. How? Another bout of dizziness hit as she gingerly pushed up to a sitting position. A glance upward bewildered her even more. How had night already gone to the gray fuzziness of a wintry morning? At least, she thought it was morning. She couldn't really tell from the heavy blanket of low-hanging clouds.

"If this is the afterlife, somebody got it all wrong." Of course, if hell was hot, maybe heaven was cold. She eased around, turning in a slow circle, taking in everything. "This is not heaven. I know this place." This was the grassy part of the overlook that led up to the edge of the cliff. The more she studied the area, the more her confusion churned. Where was the road? The wide car park? Everything was familiar, but not.

She felt her head for any knots or bumps. Other than a few sore spots, she had none. But still—the fall must have addled her enough to make her black out for a while. That would explain the disorientation and loss of time. But how had she ended up here in one piece instead of in the water or stabbed by the rocks at the base of the cliff? And where the devil was Patrick? Had he just left her here to die? Aye, he was a selfish bastard, but this was extreme even for him.

A harsh gust of wind stung her cheeks, bringing with it the clean, crisp smell of a snowstorm on the rise. She held out her hand and stared at it. Tiny bits of icy whiteness pelted her skin, melting on contact. Her fingers turned bright red and burned with the cold.

"Gloves," she mumbled, then patted her clothing. Clothing. Wait—she wasn't wearing her winter coat. "Oh, bloody hell. I hope I haven't ruined anything. That pricy costume deposit is as good as gone."

Still unsteady, she made it to her feet and brushed herself off. Near as she could tell, she hadn't damaged anything—neither clothing nor herself. The snow fell faster, large, wet flakes that promised deep drifts in no time. She tucked her hands into her armpits to warm them and shrugged deeper into the cloak. "I should have taken those fingerless gloves and wrist warmers the clerk offered."

The walk back to town would warm her. She squinted up at the sky again, trying to find the brightest spot in the grayness. "I wonder what time it is." She hadn't worn her watch to look more authentic. Increasing her pace, she berated herself with every step. "It is my fault I ended up out in the cold like this. Should have sent that self-centered dobber packing weeks ago."

She soon forgot her irritation with herself as the snow pelted down faster and walking became more difficult. Huddling deep in the hooded cloak to escape the cutting wind, she stared downward, watching her boot tips as the layers of icy, wet whiteness forced her to work harder to clear the drifts. As the incline leveled out, she halted to catch her breath. The intersection at the edge of town should be just up ahead.

"Much more trudging like this and Gracie can go to the gym by herself tonight." She shoved back her hood and squinted through the weather, searching for the brightly decorated windows of Hook's Cafe. It should only be a bit farther. Strange that none of the lights were strong enough to shine through the storm.

An eerie shiver not caused by the weather rippled across her. She looked back in the direction from which she had come, then turned and strained to see through the blowing snow in front of her.

Thurso, or at least some sign of it, should be visible by now. This was the bottom of the hill, the base of the turnoff at the crossroads that led to the overlook. Hook's Cafe, Ferguson's market, Benson Petrol Station, and the shuttered Bits and Bobs shop should be right there. Where were the street signs? The utility poles? She stared at the space filled with nothing but drifts and a few dark, scrubby bushes and trees poking through the glistening white mounds.

"Where the hell am I?" Was she really dead? "Just stop!" This was no time to panic or go barmy with the cold. She just hadn't walked as far as she thought. That was all. All she needed to do was soldier on.

A muffled clattering off in the distance drew her attention to the left. It also filled her with relief. At least she wasn't alone anymore. A steady creaking of wood and leather, along with the jangling of chains, became louder. Something snorted. Or at least it sounded like a snort. The snow made everything muffled.

She retreated a step and squinted to focus on the team of monstrous, hairy-footed draft horses churning into view. They pulled an amazing replica of an antique carriage behind them.

"Feathering," she said, still stunned at the sight. "Not hairy-footed." Her breath fogged in the frigid air as she snorted. "Like that *really* matters right now. I guess I better stop thinking out loud. They might be afraid to help me because I seem crazy." She always talked out loud when alone. Seemed as natural as talking to a friend.

As the beasts drew nearer, the authenticity of the rig amazed her. Why in the world would they be in Thurso on a day like today? Not sure if it was safe or not, she hopped in place and flagged them down. "Help me! Please!"

The driver perched high on the front of the coach jerked to stiff-backed attention and pulled on the reins. "Whoa, laddies!" The magnificent beasts lurched to a stop, seeming disappointed to do so. They stomped and shook their heads, rattling their gear as if signaling this was no time for dawdling.

Fighting the slippery ground, Lorna floundered closer. "Thank ye so much for stopping! Might I get a lift into Thurso?"

"A lift?" The man glowered down at her, his bushy brows and even wilder beard crusted with snow. "Ye mean carry ye to Thurso?"

"Aye. If ye could, I would be most obliged, and once we reach my shop, I'll be happy to pay ye well for yer troubles." She didn't want to insult the man, but surely it cost quite a lot to feed four such enormous horses and keep such a coach in fine working order. Especially in this weather.

"Driver! Why have we stopped?" A man clutching a plaid around his head peered around the partially opened carriage door.

"Got a young miss here," the driver shouted over the blustering wind. "Lost in the snow. Begs for a ride into Thurso. Says she keeps a shop there." The man coughed out a wheezing laugh as he dusted the snow off his tam. "Last I know of, there weren't no shops to speak of in Thurso. St. Peter's Kirk is there, but the town is just a port and a few pubs. Aye, it might ha' grown some, but I think this poor lass is tetched with the cold." He squinted at her. "Unless ye repair nets for the fishermen? I saw that new place last time I came through here. That yer shop?"

"I own Crowley's Books and Things. In the middle of town. Been there for years."

He stared at her as if she spoke a language he didn't understand. Was he making fun of her? And how could he say the town was nothing but a port? Thurso was one of the most significant towns in Caithness, and the church he spoke of was nothing but a ruin.

Lorna sank deeper into her hood and clutched it under her chin, unsure what to do. Her toes throbbed with the cold, spurring her into action. To the devil with the man and his odd sense of humor.

"Sir!" she shouted through chattering teeth. "Please, might I have a ride? All I have on me is a tenner, but it's yers if ye will just let me in out of this weather."

Bloody hell. A tenner should be plenty. She had planned to pay him more for his troubles if he had been more helpful. But now she felt like telling him to kick rocks. If she wasn't about to freeze to death, she would.

She shoved her hand through a slit in the folds of her skirt, fumbled to find the small cloth pouch hanging from the tie at her waist, and fished out the ten-pound note.

Steering clear of the horses and their snorts of freezing mist, she stretched and handed it up to the driver. "Here. See? A tenner to let me inside the carriage and take me into town."

The man squinted down at the bit of paper, then plucked it from her hand. His head tilted first to one side, then the other, as he turned it back and forth, studying it. "What game is this ye're playing at, lass?"

The male occupant inside the coach hopped out and shoved between them. He snatched the note from the driver and scowled down at it. "Bank of England?" He turned to her, his thin face so puckered and drawn that she backed up a step, afraid he was about to vomit. "Who are ye?" he demanded in a croaking voice that matched his pallor.

"Lorna Merriweather. Who are ye?" By this time she could have walked home. The only thing keeping her here was the fear of frostbite. If these two didn't stop blethering like a pair of thoughtless fools, she might still risk losing a few toes.

The gentleman's bloodshot eyes bulged as if about to pop out of his face. "I am Reginald Leckness, Laird of Clan Auchinleck." He acted as though the name should mean something.

She decided to try one last tactic. With a polite nod and the best smile she could manage, she changed her tone to the one she used for calming difficult customers. "It is an honor to meet ye, sir, and I apologize for interrupting yer outing. But please, might ye grant me shelter till we get into town? Once we reach Hook's Cafe, ye can let me out and I'll be on my way and no more trouble to ye."

The snowstorm and her strange fall from the cliff had disoriented her. The cafe couldn't be that far. Dear old Maggie Hook would spot her enough credit for a piping-hot cup of tea. Once she warmed up for a little while, she could easily make it back to the shop.

"Let the woman inside, Reginald! I grow tired of sitting here, and my earl awaits." The order came from within the carriage. The woman's shrill voice brooked no argument.

The thin, sickly laird's shoulders sagged. He yanked the door open wider and tipped his head toward the opening. "Ye heard my sister. Inside with ye."

Lorna hurried around him and climbed onto the step. She perched there for a moment, uncertain which bench to take. Everything looked so—historically authentic. She wondered what era they were re-enacting.

A scowling, yet beautiful woman was buried in a mound of fur pelts and heavy wool plaids. She sat with her back against the front of the boxy carriage. The spot next to her was empty, but Lorna felt certain that belonged to the laird. Opposite the woman sat a shivering young boy staring down at his lap. Beside him was a tiny slip of a girl who appeared frightened, exhausted, or both.

"Are ye coming in or not?" the beauty snapped. Her feathery brows, a shade lighter than her dark auburn hair, slanted to a sterner angle.

That made Lorna's choice easier. She bent and offered a smile to the wee lad. "May I sit beside ye?"

He jumped as though startled, then slid over to give her more room. "Aye, mistress," he whispered with an obedient dip of his head.

Poor dear. He must be afraid of strangers. She settled in beside him, noticing that he and the timid lass had nothing but a single blanket to keep them both warm. That didn't seem right when the laird and his sister were buried up to their eyeballs with furs and wool wraps. "Let's snuggle in and share our warmth, aye? It's cold enough to freeze the bark off a tree."

He risked a shy glance up at her, sharing the tiniest hint of a smile.

"Come on," she coaxed. "It's all right. I promise."

After hesitating a second longer, he huddled closer, as did the girl on his other side. Lorna shared her cloak with them as much as she could, then looked across and gave the woman and her brother a polite nod. "Thank ye both so much. I dinna ken what I would have done if ye had not come along."

The laird acknowledged her gratitude with an explosive sneeze, then burrowed deeper into his mound of coverings. His sister shot him a disgusted glare, then riveted a predatory gaze on Lorna. "Ye are most welcome. Yer name, if ye please?"

"Oh...sorry." Lorna debated whether or not to offer a handshake. Many folks no longer took part in that custom. It spread too many germs. She offered another nod. "Lorna Merriweather. And ye are?"

The woman blinked, staring at her as if surprised. "I am Lady Murdina Sullivan." She slid another repulsed glance at her sniffling brother. "Sister of the ailing Laird Leckness here, and recently widowed." Her feral gaze flickered to the wee lad. "That is my son, Frances." Her nostrils flared as she pulled in a deep breath, as though summoning whatever patience she possessed. "And next to him is Hesther, my lady's maid."

"It's a pleasure to meet all of ye."

The maid managed a trembling smile. Frances stared at his hands and didn't respond.

"Frances!" Lady Murdina barked, making everyone in the coach jerk.

The boy sat bolt upright, his eyes wide and filled with leeriness. "Aye, m'lady—M-Mother?"

Lady Murdina rolled her eyes, then returned her attention to Lorna. "Ye must forgive him. He has not been the same since the passing of his father."

Lorna's heart ached for the boy, and without hesitating, she wrapped an arm around his shoulders and hugged him closer. "It's hard to lose family. I am verra sorry for yer loss."

"Thank ye, mistress," he whispered, and snuggled closer.

Lorna smiled as he melted into her embrace as if no one had ever hugged him before. She loved children. Always had. She had grown up in a social care group home and been repeatedly passed over for adoption or placement in a foster home. So, she had helped the short-staffed orphanage take care of all the abandoned and abused children with nowhere else to go. Sad thing was, once she turned eighteen, the law required that she move out. And without the proper certification, they couldn't let her help anymore. So she had struck out on her own. Once again belonging nowhere and having no one.

"He likes ye." Lady Murdina appeared thoughtful, but it was her calculating smile that made Lorna hug the child a little tighter. The woman nudged her maid with the toe of her boot, startling the girl. "Do ye not think so, Hesther?"

Without even looking, Hesther bobbed her head and whispered, "Aye, m'lady."

Lorna wondered what sort of situation she had stumbled into here. Were they actors headed for a re-enactment? If so, something was not right, because wee Frances and Hesther were as uneasy as cornered animals. The poor lad trembled against Lorna, and she would lay odds it wasn't because of the cold.

She eyed Lady Murdina. That woman set her on edge. The auburn-haired beauty had a feral quality about her that made Lorna wonder if she sprouted fangs when the need arose.

"Children always take to me," she said, determined to keep the lady talking to find out more.

"Do they now?"

"Aye. Usually."

Lorna wished she could help poor Frances and Hesther but wasn't sure how. Maybe if she found out where they were staying and gave one of her old care worker friends a call, that would help. From the general ill feeling permeating the coach, this odd little group needed an interview as soon as possible. Hesther might be too old for social care intervention, but there were labor laws that could still protect her.

"I overheard ye say an earl awaits ye?"

"Aye." The lady sat taller as if settling into a hard-won throne. "The Earl of Caithness. I am to be his countess."

Lorna found that even more confusing. Was that part of their script or real? The Right Honorable Malcolm Sinclair was divorced, but she thought she had read somewhere that he had chosen to spend the House of Lords' Christmas recess in London this year. With his children grown, they probably preferred spending holidays with their father in the city. Or was the woman referring to an earl from a particular historical era that was part of the performance?

"How nice," she hurried to say when she realized Lady Murdina waited for a comment. She made a pointed glance around the carriage. "Quite the rough ride, but I suppose it adds to the romance and realism, aye?"

The woman eyed her with a befuddled expression. "Aye, it has been long and trying," she said. "But we reach Thursa Castle within the hour. I feel certain my prospective husband will see to our comforts after such a dreary trip from Edinburgh."

"*Thursa* Castle, ye said?"

"Aye." Lady Murdina preened like a bird proud of its new plumage. "Ye have heard of it?"

"Of course, m'lady." Lorna concentrated on not appearing skeptical. There had to be a logical explanation for all this. Either the woman and her brother were certified nutters, or whoever wrote their script had not researched the area. *Thursa* Castle no longer existed. Not even in ruins. Hadn't for centuries. However, *Thurso* Castle was still intact. At least in spots. Parts of it had been torn down and rebuilt to house the current Viscount of Thurso. But the site where ancient Thursa once stood was nothing more than a mound of dirt. Maybe the viscount was giving a holiday party, and these actors were part of the entertainment?

More uneasiness threatened to make her stomach churn anew. Why hadn't the driver stopped to let her out by now? They should have already reached the cafe, but she couldn't tell. They had shuttered the oddly glassless windows with blankets fastened tight across them with wooden strips to keep them taut against the wind. This level of authenticity was ridiculous this time of year. Did these folks have no common sense at all? They should've updated the carriage with some concealed heaters and glass for the windows.

A smelly oil lamp that looked like a convincing replica of an ancient brass Roman lamp sputtered on the wall between the covered windows on Lady Murdina's side of the carriage. It spewed out sooty smoke, making the already acrid pungency inside the boxy coach even worse. When had these people bathed last?

"Could we have the driver stop?" Lorna tried to pry an edge of the blanket away from the window next to her.

"Whatever for?" the laird asked before blowing his nose loud and long on a lacy-edged handkerchief.

"We should have reached my stop by now." She loosened a corner of the covering, gathered it out of the way, and peeked outside. "What the bloody hell?"

"What was that?"

Lorna ignored Lady Murdina. Instead, she yanked the blanket the rest the way off the window, knelt on the bench, and hung halfway out of the carriage. "Where is Thurso?" she shouted up at the driver. "Where are we?"

"Thursa Castle up ahead," he bellowed down to her.

She couldn't see much through the swirling snow. The icy wind stung her eyes, making them tear. She swiped the moisture away and squinted harder. Where was town? Where the devil had the buildings gone?

Something yanked on her from behind. "Get back inside here, fool girl!" The laird exploded with another coughing fit. "And cover that damned window! Are ye trying to kill us all?"

Numbed into a heart-pounding stupor, she eased back, crouching on the bench as she stared out the window while gripping the edge of the opening. Disbelief, denial, and rising panic filled her. Even through the storm, a few outlines of the larger structures should have been visible. The town's buildings reached the edge of the sea in every place except for the cliffs. But all she could make out was the ancient pillar, the crude stone obelisk carved by the Picts. And the driver was right—Thursa mound was just up ahead. The obelisk marked the path to the foundation of the old castle.

But it couldn't be so. That stone must be another Pictish monument.

She knew that to be a lie of desperation but clung to it, anyway. They had to have turned off and taken a route farther east to a part of northern Scotland she didn't know. That was all it could be. They just called it Thursa as part of their playacting. What other explanation was there?

"Look what ye have done!" the laird croaked. "We shall freeze to death afore we arrive."

"Reginald!" Lady Murdina snapped. *"Haud yer wheesht!"* She threw off her coverings, rose from her seat, and swayed back and forth to keep her balance. "Cover that window, girl, lest I be forced to kill my fool brother!" She threw a blanket across Lorna's arms. "Cover it! Now!"

Lorna glared at them both, ready to tell them to go straight to the devil. Did they think to force her into their little acting troupe just because she was already dressed for the part?

Then she noticed Frances and Hesther out of the corner of her eye. Both cowered in their seats like pups afraid of another beating. For their sake, she covered the window and secured the blanket as best she could.

"Open the gate!" the driver shouted.

Or, at least, that was what Lorna thought he said. With the wind blasting against the sides of the coach, it was hard to hear anything. As she settled back down onto the bench, the coach shuddered to a stop.

Reginald exited like a shot.

Lady Murdina rose and shook a finger within an inch of Frances's and Hesther's noses. "Remember what I said. Both of ye. Understand?"

They each gave a flinching nod, then recoiled back against the seat.

A raging protectiveness surged through Lorna. She shoved in between them and Lady Murdina. "Ye best leave them alone." She fisted both hands. "There are laws, and dinna think I willna call the authorities for help." She didn't know where they were, but there had to be a landline phone or a cell phone somewhere.

Rather than lash out, Lady Murdina took on a malicious glint in her eyes that matched the cruel set of her mouth. "Dinna try me, lass. Once I am Countess of Caithness, I can order ye stripped and beaten in front of the entire clan."

"So ye are a coward, then? Let others do yer fighting for ye?" Lorna had dealt with bullies before. This poor excuse of an actress didn't know who she was up against. If it came to protecting Frances and the maid, Lorna would thrash Lady Murdina and her stunt double both. Neither of them would be in any shape to continue this re-enactment.

"Sister!" Reginald's croaking shout echoed with warning. "Yer betrothed approaches."

Lady Murdina transformed into a smiling bride-to-be. "We shall continue this discussion later," she said, then stepped down from the coach.

"The two of ye stay close to me, aye?" Lorna locked eyes with Hesther and Frances until they both nodded. "Soon as I get to a phone, I will call Gracie. She'll come for us—wherever the bloody hell this is. I know kind folks in Thurso who can help both of ye. Even offer ye a place to stay if need be or ye can stay with me."

"What is a *phone*, mistress?" Hesther asked in a fearful whisper.

Lorna halted just as she was about to step out the door. She stared at the wee girl who seemed sincere about the strange question. "What was that?"

"A *phone*," Frances said, perking up now that Lady Murdina wasn't around. "She asked what it was?" The lad's pallor had even changed to a healthy pinkness now that he was no longer afraid. "I want to know too. Be it a magical horn to call the angels?"

"A magical horn to call the angels?" Lorna repeated, completely dumbfounded. Why did they cling so fiercely to their roles in this strange re-enactment?

"Aye." The lad bobbed his head with interest. "Is Gracie the angel sent to save us?"

Before Lorna could respond, a large man wearing a shaggy black fur draped around his shoulders ushered forward an older woman wrapped in a colorful plaid.

"Come on wi' ye now," the matron called through the door.

"I be Mrs. Thistlewick, housekeeper here at Thursa. Make haste afore ye freeze or the ague sets in. That laird of yers mustha surely coughed and spewed all over ye during yer trip."

Lorna spared the grandmotherly woman a leery glance, then hurried to help Frances and Hesther exit the carriage first. These two new members of the cast must be part of the re-enactment troupe as well.

Once on the ground, she looked up, and her knees threatened to buckle. Even through the blinding snow, she could make out a dark, towering structure. How the devil had they constructed such an elaborately realistic set out here without anyone knowing?

A large, forbidding keep stood tall and fearsome in the center of a high protective wall. A scattering of smaller buildings surrounded it. What wasn't coated with ice and snow appeared to be stone that their artists had colored to look a weathered, faded gray. The mottling of the blocks was amazingly realistic.

She shook her head. None of this could be real. It had to be a movie set or something. There was no other logical explanation. But the more she saw, the more she doubted her logic. An ominous dread knotted in her middle, making it hard to breathe.

"Uhm…I need to use yer phone, please," she said to Mrs. Thistlewick. "My cell phone is back at the shop serving as a hotspot till our Wi-Fi is installed proper. Or if I could use one of yer cells, that would be grand."

The ruddy-cheeked woman's mouth slowly dropped open before she turned to the young man wearing the furry mantle that made him resemble a woolly mammoth. "Lady Murdina said the child's nurse *was* a mite odd."

"I am not odd. These two need help, and I intend to see they get it." Lorna squared off with Mrs. Thistlewick, ready to argue the point. If she concentrated on the wee ones, it kept her mind off her own worries. "Now, if ye would be so kind as to take them inside where it's warm and get me to a phone, I would appreciate it. Neither of them has been properly cared for during this trip. I must notify the authorities."

"Edmond! If ye let yer gran catch her death from this weather, I swear ye will sleep outside for a year and a day." The shout came from farther down the bailey, near a smaller building built against the barrier wall. All Lorna could make out was a tall, shadowy form through the stormy grayness and blowing snow.

"Will ye come on, then?" Edmond the woolly mammoth begged. "Weather like this gives Sir Jasper a raging case of the red arse." He gave her a pleading look, then bent down and placed himself nose to nose with the old woman. "Gran, go inside. I will bring them in."

They did need to get inside. Neither Frances nor Hesther wore heavy enough clothing to stand out here in the storm. Both stood there hugging themselves, shivering and cowering from the wind. Lorna pulled them in close and wrapped her cloak around them, sheltering them as best she could. "Come on. Let's get ye inside where it's warm. I'll find a phone soon as I can."

Edmond cast a thankful glance to the heavens. "A fine idea for certain. Gran, take them while I help the lads with the trunks, aye?"

Mrs. Thistlewick toddled along beside them, holding her plaid to block the wind off her face. "A good decision ye made, lass. I dinna ken what that *phone* thing is ye want, but I am glad ye chose to come inside." She offered a kindly smile. "My old bones canna abide this cold too long, but I am housekeeper here and have greeted every visitor to Thursa since our chieftain was a wean. Dinna fash yerself. I shall see that ye and the bairns are well taken care of."

"Mrs. Thistlewick." A rich, deep voice capable of drowning out the wind halted Lorna mid-step. "Did ye not trust the rest of us to usher our guests into the keep?"

"I told ye I wasna ready to hand over my duties," the spunky matron replied. "Should ye not be tending to that woman ye sent for?"

"Mrs. Thistlewick." The man's tone became affectionately

scolding. "Remember yesterday's talk, aye?"

Lorna squinted from the depths of her hood and almost lost her balance. Hesther and Frances steadied her even though they peeped out from under her arms like frightened chicks. The man gently admonishing the elderly housekeeper made Edmond the woolly mammoth look like the runt of the litter. This hulking mountain of maleness was the epitome of the famed Viking raiders of old. His long, silvery blond hair snapped in the wind. The shadow of his short beard enhanced the strong cut of his jaw. A white-tipped fur rested across his impressively broad shoulders like a royal mantle. The man's raw handsomeness made her stare and not care if he noticed or not.

He bent and propped his large hands on his knees, offering Frances a smile that seemed a bit sad. "Welcome to Thursa, young Frances. Yer mother and uncle are already inside getting settled in their rooms. Shall I take ye to them?"

The lad wrapped both arms tight around Lorna's waist and buried his face against her.

"He is afraid of ye," she said. The child's fear demanded she be the brave one, even though she didn't feel it. "Ye go ahead. I will see to them." As the wee lad hugged her tighter, she jerked her chin toward the ominous castle that should not be there and forced a prim smile at the man. "Ye can tend to yer guests, aye? If Frances is willing, perhaps ye can get to know him later." Surely, this could not be Lady Murdina's earl?

The Highlander's vivid blue eyes flared wide for a brief moment, then flexed to cutting, narrow slits. Without taking his gaze from hers, he motioned for their elderly escort to keep walking. "Into the keep with ye, Mrs. Thistlewick."

The housekeeper gave Lorna a woeful shake of her head. "Aye, my chieftain. I shall await these wee ones. Dinna be too harsh with her, aye? Lady Murdina said the lass has yet to learn her place, but the wee laddie loves her dear, as ye can see."

"Is that true?" The man's sharp gaze bored into Lorna like a pair of lasers. The iciness of their blue hue laid open her soul.

Lorna stood tall. "If ye wish to scold me, can we do it some-where out of the wind? It is cold out here, and these two are freezing." She refused to be bullied or conned ever again. That was what had landed her wherever this was. She had let that damn Patrick manipulate her like dough. Never again.

The chieftain stood tall and dismissed them with an arrogant glance toward the entrance. "Inside wi' ye. Then we speak."

CHAPTER THREE

G UNN SINCLAIR FOLLOWED the rebellious trio up the steps into the keep. Well, the lad and timid wee lassie were not rebellious, but the tall, comely woman who protected them most definitely was. Neither Lady Murdina nor her brother had mentioned difficulties regarding those serving them in the personal capacities of lady's maid and nurse. Or, at least, he didn't think they had. To be honest, he had not fully listened. However, he never doubted Mrs. Thistlewick's word. The wily old housekeeper missed nothing.

"We will speak here," he announced as soon as they stepped inside the entryway. He shouldered the heavy oak doors shut. The raging storm howled and battered at them, angry at being kept out.

The insolent lass, her boldness both intriguing and irritating, ignored him. Instead of properly giving him her full attention, she brushed the snow off the young lad, then dusted more of the same from the maid's thin shoulders. She gently steered them through the arched entrance into the great hall and pointed them at the nearest blazing hearth. "Go get warm. I will join ye soon, aye?"

The two peered up at her with expressions that reminded him

of lost pups in search of their mother. They both hesitated, as if afraid to leave her.

"If anyone bothers ye, sing out and I will come running," she assured them with an encouraging nod. "Go on, now. I willna let anyone hurt ye. I promise."

"No one will harm either of ye here," Gunn said, insulted that they looked to the nursemaid for protection rather than himself.

Their leery gazes shifted away from him and returned to their self-appointed guardian angel. She removed her cloak and draped it over the arms of the timid lass. "On wi' ye, now. Get warm. Wrap in my cloak, if ye like. It'll help hold the heat close around ye."

That seemed to convince them. Either that or the warmth of the fire had become too tempting to resist.

Watching them walk away, she raked a hand through her tousled mane. Its golden shade, striated with ambers and soft browns, reminded him of rippling fields of ripe barley. Strangely, her tresses barely brushed the tops of her shoulders. Why the blazes would she cut it so short? Punishment for insolence, perhaps?

When she turned and leveled a stern gaze upon him, the unusual coloring of her eyes caught him off guard. They almost glowed an eerily bright blue-green, the same shade as the shimmering spirits that sometimes danced across the night skies in winter. Her hooded cloak had hidden them, as well as her fetching curves.

"I need to use yer phone," she said.

"My what?" He didn't recognize that word. Did she think to delay their talk by speaking gibberish?

A slight frown creased her brow and frustration flashed in her eyes. She resettled her footing and stood taller, as though ready to battle. "What is this place?"

Impressed and slightly amused by her courageous stubbornness, he mimicked her stance. "Thursa Castle."

She hugged her arms across her middle, bowed her head, and

pinched the bridge of her nose. "Thursa Castle. Near Thurso in Caithness, aye?"

"Aye." He noted that the longer she spoke, the tenser she became, even though he had yet to confront her about her brazenness.

"And yer name, sir?" She nervously raked her hair back again, pulled a strange circular ribbon from around her wrist, and secured her tresses away from her face.

"Gunn Sinclair, chieftain of Clan Sinclair, and sixth Earl of Caithness."

"*Sixth* Earl of Caithness?" she repeated.

He gave her an aloof nod, curious to hear what the fidgeting beauty said next.

"I see." She pressed both hands to her cheeks, kept them there as though her teeth ached, then peered at him through her fingers.

"Are ye unwell?"

"I am not sure yet." She swiped a hand across her forehead, then squinted at him. "I dinna suppose ye would ken today's date?" Even though she appeared indifferent about the question, all the color had drained from her cheeks. "The trip has..." Her words trailed off.

"Addled ye?"

"Aye." She nodded. "Badly."

"Second of December," he replied. "Year of our Lord 1622."

She clutched her throat as though about to choke. "That is not possible." She stumbled back into a stone pillar and sagged to one side.

He lunged forward and swept her up into his arms before she hit the floor. "Edmond!" he bellowed.

"Edmond and the lads are still unloading trunks," Jasper said as he strode into the hall. A gust of snow and wind accompanied the trusted war chief before his aides slammed the doors shut behind him. He shook the snow off his fur mantle while grinning at Gunn's armload. "The loud redhead was the one I found for ye. Are ye considering this one too?"

Gunn ignored the man's poor attempt at humor. "This one is the nursemaid to Lady Murdina's son. When I told her today's date, she swooned."

Jasper stepped up beside him and peered down at her. "Comely lass. Maybe she has a bairn on the way?"

"I dinna ken." Gunn turned and strode deeper into the hall, glaring at the kinsmen and servants pausing to eye him with interest. "Back to yer own affairs. All of ye."

"Ye have killed her!" wee Frances screeched. The scrawny pup grabbed an iron from the hearth and charged at him, swinging it like a sword. The thin young maid followed close behind, brandishing a stick of firewood like an ax.

Jasper blocked them both. He snatched the rod and wood away, scooped up the lad, and held him under one arm. He shook a finger in the wee lass's face, walking her back several paces. "Mind yer manners, now. We dinna attack our chieftain."

"He has killed her!" the boy cried, thrashing and kicking to get loose.

"Curse him!" the teary-eyed maid said. "Curse him to die too!"

"She is not dead!" Gunn motioned for Jasper to bring them both closer. "Cease yer yowling and touch her cheek."

Tears streaming down his face, wee Frances bared his teeth and shot Gunn a hateful glare. As Jasper brought him level with the unconscious nursemaid, he finally calmed and looked down at her. His small hand trembled as he barely brushed a finger across her cheek. "Warm," he said, then turned to the scrawny maid. "She is still warm."

"Aye," Gunn said. "She is warm because she still lives. Women do this sometimes." He resettled the lady in his arms, deciding that holding her was rather nice even though a mite unconventional. "Do ye ken her name? She never told me."

"Swear ye willna hurt her." Frances glared at him, distrust and hatred ringing in his tone.

"I willna hurt her," Gunn promised quietly, then nodded to Jasper. "Set him down. Young Frances is a brave protector to be treated with respect."

"Chieftain! What have ye done?" Mrs. Thistlewick pushed into their midst.

"I have done nothing. When have ye ever seen me mistreat a woman?" He returned his focus to Frances and knelt so the boy could better see his nursemaid. "Her name, lad?"

"Lorna Merriweather." Frances stepped closer, slid his hand into Lorna's, and gently patted it. He nodded at the sniffling maid beside him. "And this here is Hesther." After another pat on Lorna's hand, he asked, "When will she wake?"

"Da! What did ye do?"

Gunn clenched his teeth and bowed his head to keep from snapping at his beloved daughter. "I caught the lass as she swooned so she wouldna hit the floor."

Nine-year-old Bella moved closer. She gave Frances a sympathetic nod. "Is she yer mama?"

"I wish she was," the boy whispered.

Lorna's lashes fluttered against her pale cheeks, then she opened her vivid blue-green eyes, blinking rapidly as though confused. "Oh my." The breathlessness of her whisper stirred Gunn, daring him to cradle her closer to hear it again.

He smiled down at her, regretting that now she was awake, he no longer had an excuse to hold her. "Are ye better now, lass?"

She hurried to look away while trying to right herself and put her feet on the floor. "Aye, I am. Thank ye for helping me."

He supported her while she stood, keeping hold of her arm. "Ye still seem a mite unsteady."

"I will be…uhm…fine." She tried to ease free of his grasp but lost her balance.

Frances jumped in and wedged himself under her arm. "I feared he had killed ye for certain."

Lorna flickered a weak smile down at the boy. "Everything is fine." She exhaled a shuddering breath, then added, "I am sure it will be."

"Bring the lass some of the warmed wine," Mrs. Thistlewick said with a sharp clap of her hands that sent nearby servants scurrying.

Gunn led the addled beauty to one of the long trestle tables and helped her sit on the bench beside it. He seated himself opposite her. Her sweet, fresh scent still clung to him, stirring memories of late summer breezes wafting through fields of heather. He opened his mouth to speak, but before he could say a word, his wee daughter jumped in and interrupted.

"I am Bella," the child said with a bright smile. She rested her hand on his arm while keeping her introduction aimed at the slightly dazed woman sitting opposite him. "This here is my da, but ye ken that by now, I am sure. What be yer name?"

"Lorna Merriweather," the lass said, appearing more than a little unsettled. With an elbow propped on the table, she rested her head in her hand. "Sorry to cause such a fuss. I dinna wish to be any trouble."

"I dinna think ye will be the one causing trouble," Bella said, then turned back to him. "That woman ye invited here is nipping at Mary, Janie, and Alice like a herd dog. Nothing in her rooms suits her, and that man who came with her is as growly as a cornered badger."

Gunn struggled not to smile. Bella's information betrayed her latest whereabouts. "Have ye been spying from the tunnels again?"

The youngling ignored his question and continued her rant with a flick of her little hand. "And that woman bleats like a spoiled bairn about any and everything. Saying that a countess needs more than one lady's maid, since hers is so lacking." The child turned and gave Hesther an apologetic nod. "Sorry, lass, but she did say that."

Hesther accepted the criticism with a pitiful curtsy. "I understand, miss. If ye will take me to her, the brunt of her anger will return to me rather than the others trying to please her."

"I have heard enough," Mrs. Thistlewick said with a disgruntled huff. "With yer permission, my chieftain, I shall attend to this matter. I know just the maid to sort the Lady Murdina and help her settle in proper."

"God help that maid," Lorna muttered quietly. Her lovely eyes flared wide when he chuckled. "Sorry. I should not have said that."

"So that is why yer mistress said ye dinna ken yer place," he said.

She squinted at him with a pained frown, as if he had spoken words she didn't understand. "I was not aware I had a *mistress*."

"Interesting." Storing that away for future pondering, Gunn turned back to the housekeeper. "Do as ye wish about Lady Murdina's maids, Mrs. Thistlewick. I know ye will handle everything properly." He leveled a fatherly gaze on his daughter. "And ye, my wee one, need to mind yer manners. As the chieftain's daughter, ye dinna address yer prospective stepmother as *that woman*, ye ken? And dinna be spying on her from the tunnels."

Bella glared at him. "She is not my stepmother yet."

"Perhaps not, but she is our guest." He chucked a crooked finger under her chin and locked eyes with her. "Promise ye will try harder to be a polite hostess."

She glared at him and remained silent.

"Arabella?" He only used her full name when her behavior warranted it.

"Promise," she said in a sullen tone that nullified the oath.

"Good, then." He turned her to face Frances and the timid Hesther. "Take them to yer floor, aye? I am sure they are weary. They can rest in yer sitting room until we sort out the arrangements and get them settled where they belong."

"And is it all right if we go by the kitchens and ask Cook to send up some treats?" Bella asked. She stepped closer and whispered behind her hand, "Dinna they look too thin, Da? I think they need an extra bannock or two."

He nodded. "Aye, my proper wee hostess. A wise plan, indeed."

Bella took hold of Frances's and Hesther's hands and tugged.

Frances planted his feet and shook his head. "Nay. I stay with Mistress Lorna."

Lorna reached over and squeezed his shoulder. "Go ahead wi' ye. I will come up in a bit. Soon as I am a tad steadier."

He caught her hand and held it between both of his. "Ye promise?"

She placed her other hand over her heart. "I swear it, my knight in shining armor."

That made him throw out his chest and wave for Hesther to follow him. After one last glance at Lorna, they allowed Bella to lead them away.

"Lady Murdina was right," Gunn said while subtly motioning for Jasper to make himself scarce and keep everyone else at bay.

Lorna sat straighter, her lovely eyes narrowing to watchful slits. "And just what is it that Lady Murdina was right about?"

"The lad loves ye." He noted she visibly exhaled, as if she had held her breath. "Have ye cared for him long?"

She scowled down at the table, as though troubled and ready to weep. "Actually, I just met him. Only a few hours ago. Their coach stopped when I flagged it down because I was too frozen to plow through the drifts any longer."

"Flagged it down?" He eyed the cut and quality of her clothes. Fine, heavy weaves with no worn seams or patches. Well fitting, as though made by a personal seamstress. He caught her hand and turned it palm up in his. No callouses to speak of, and her nails were as neat and clean as Mrs. Thistlewick's freshly scrubbed floors. Skin as soft and smooth as a newborn colt.

Everything about her stirred his loneliness. Made him wish he had an excuse to tarry with her and touch her even more. He stroked his thumb across the back of her hand, mesmerized by the sensation. She seemed more of a highborn lady than a bairn's nursemaid.

She cleared her throat, ousting him from the spell. "Chieftain?"

He jerked his hand away. "How come ye to be out in a storm like this? Alone?"

Worry returned to her features. She glanced around the large gathering hall as if searching for the answer among the stone columns and Sinclair crests fluttering on the walls. "I dinna ken," she finally said, and gave a defeated shrug. "I woke up this morning, and I was just...here."

Her dilemma presented an intriguing puzzle. *If* she spoke the truth. Since she was fully dressed, no one had stolen her from her bed, and they hadn't appeared to harm her. She seemed to be telling what she knew but held more back. He saw it in her eyes and her nervous fidgeting.

"What do ye remember about last night? Or even before that?" he asked.

She looked away, wrinkling her nose at something in the distance, something only she could see. After a long moment of strained silence, she shifted and gave another jerking shrug. "Last night, I was watching for the mirrie dancers with the man I thought I was going to marry." Anger flashed across her face and made her voice become louder. "But the northern lights waited to come until after he showed me I was a fool."

She stared down at her white-knuckled fists. After a slow, deep breath, she lifted her head. Her jaw went hard and fierce as if she clenched her teeth. "Then I shoved his ring in his face and stormed away just as the sky exploded with a brilliant show of lights." Her expression took on that pained, faraway look again. "I stumbled off the cliff. Or I thought I did." Confusion returned, furrowing her delicate brow. "And when I opened my eyes, it was daytime and starting to snow."

Gunn studied her, trying to make sense of her tale. It was clear she believed every word she said. Her story was her truth. It would be a terrible shame for such a fine woman to be tetched in the head. But what else would explain such outlandishness?

Of course, there was the lore. He remembered his Norse grandmam's stories about the lights. How their gleaming colors were the reflections off the Valkyries' armor as they led warriors to Odin. Old Grandmam also spoke about how the play of colors across the night sky was sometimes the breath of brave soldiers who died in combat. On his Scottish side, his ancestors said the lights were epic fights among sky warriors or fallen angels. Who knew what real magic the wondrous lights held?

"I dinna ken how I came to be here," Lorna said, interrupting his weighing of her story. "I just know I am here and not sure what to do."

The desperation in her voice touched him, and that, he could not allow. He forced himself to harden his heart, and sat taller. "If what ye say is true, then why did Lady Murdina claim ye to be her son's nursemaid as if ye had served her for ages?"

Lorna's expression hardened. "Ye will have to ask her that." Pure disgust registered in her tone.

"Ye dinna like her."

She drummed her fingers on the table and cast another look around. "Did Mrs. Thistlewick not order me some wine?"

"Aye, she did, but I signaled we were not to be disturbed while we talked." He leaned over the table and pinned her with his gaze. "Why do ye not like the Lady Murdina?"

Barely controlled contempt puckered the tempting bow of her mouth. "I dinna like people who are unkind to children or animals." She rose and stood beside the table. "If ye dinna mind, I want to check on Frances and Hesther now. Make sure they are okay."

"Make sure they are what?"

She flinched and shuffled a half step away. "Uhm…make certain they are settling in and have everything they need." She lifted her chin, assuming a protective aloofness. "Besides, should ye not be attending to the Lady Murdina and her brother? According to yer daughter, they are yer guests."

"I am chieftain, and I *attend* to whomever I wish."

He stood and squared off in front of her. This one was high-born to be sure. A regal timbre echoed in her sultry voice, and the subtle stirrings she unleashed within him were concerning. He sensed the heat she awakened within him could become lethal with little or no encouragement.

"I recommend ye mind yer tone with both myself and the Lady Murdina." He took a step closer and gave her a quelling gaze. "At least until ye share the truth of yer plight so I might help ye."

She glared up at him, her face an unreadable mask. "Is that all, Chieftain Sinclair?"

"What is yer truth, Mistress Lorna?"

"I already told ye." Her tone had turned dull and expressionless.

"My lord!" Lady Murdina emerged from the southern stairwell. The trilling pitch of her voice made the hairs on the back of his neck stand on end. She swept toward them, her bright green gown more fitting for an evening ball than midday at a wintry keep. "Our rooms are lovely. Thank ye for settling us in so nicely."

He didn't miss the venomous gaze she shot at Lorna. Stepping between them, he took Lady Murdina's hand. "I am glad ye find Thursa to yer liking." He didn't reveal what Bella had reported. That information would be saved for a later time. "Did Mrs. Thistlewick's tonic help yer brother?" From the amount of whisky the housekeeper had added to the scant spoonful of honey and heated wine, it should have knocked the man on his arse.

Lady Murdina beamed with gratitude. "Indeed, it did. He is sleeping like a wee babe."

Lorna cleared her throat and stepped closer. "Excuse me for interrupting, but if someone could show me the way to Frances and Hesther, that would be lovely."

"I was wondering why ye were neglecting my son," Lady Murdina said, her tone dripping with daggers.

"Were ye now?" Lorna said. "And just when were ye going to

tell me I had suddenly become yer employee?"

Lady Murdina's lips parted, and Gunn picked up on a nervous twitch in the corner of her left eye. He stepped back, stanching a smile while preparing to enjoy the entertainment. From what he had observed so far, he would place his wages on Lorna.

The haughty Murdina flipped a hand and huffed a fake laugh. "Silly lass. Always playing games. How many times must I tell ye to save all that for Frances?" Her smile turned even icier. "After all, without ye, my wee Frances would feel as though I had tossed him to wolves." She arched an auburn brow, the twitching in her eye gone. "Ye wouldna wish poor Frances harmed now, would ye?"

Gunn shifted his focus to Lorna. The communication between the two women went much deeper than words. Had Lady Murdina actually threatened to harm her own son if Lorna didn't do as she wished? He remained silent, waiting to see how the duel played out.

"I will not allow Frances or Hesther harmed," Lorna said through clenched teeth. "Not under any circumstances."

"Good, then," Lady Murdina said in a tone as syrupy as treacle. "We understand each other."

"No one will be harmed here," Gunn interjected. Ill feelings between the two or not, he would not allow Lady Murdina to manipulate anyone in his keep with the use of threats. His instincts bellowed that he had sorely erred in allowing this one into his midst. He wanted a wife he could never love, but not a hateful wretch. He set a stern gaze upon the woman. "I assume the sharpness in yer tone comes from weariness, m'lady?"

Her eyes flared wider, but she recovered quickly and smiled. "Of course, m'lord." With a friendly dip of her head in Lorna's direction, she added a casual flip of a hand. "Mistress Lorna understands me completely. She knows there is no ill will between us two or myself and my son."

"Might I have an escort to Frances now?" Lorna repeated, turning her back to Lady Murdina.

"Aye. Ye may." Gunn spied the perfect maid for the task. "Ebby!"

The gangly lass set down the candlestick and polishing cloth, then jumped when it fell over and clattered to the table. After righting it again and giving it one last dusting off, she came running.

"Aye, my chieftain?" The eagerness in the bumbling maid's eyes made her a favorite in the keep even though she fumbled at everything, often destroying everything in her path. Mrs. Thistlewick shrewdly kept her away from any tasks involving fragile items.

"Take Mistress Lorna to Bella's floor," Gunn said. "See her settled into Freyda's old room."

Lorna's devotion to the children had decided him. He trusted her. At least for now. The entirety of the situation bore watching. He considered himself a fair man and would give Lady Murdina a chance. After all, the contract stipulated thirty days. Perhaps the woman was just a wretch when weary.

"And I wish ye to become Mistress Lorna's personal maid," he added to Ebby. "With this being her first time here at Thursa Castle, she will need yer help in settling in and being at her best for the weans. There are plenty of bedchambers in Bella's suite. See that everyone is made comfortable."

"I will, my chieftain." Beaming a proud smile, Ebby curtsied, then turned to Lorna. "This way, mistress. I shall see ye want for nothing."

"Thank ye, Chieftain Sinclair," Lorna said.

Leeriness and something unidentifiable still flashed in her eyes. This lass needed something. If only she would trust him.

He offered her a polite bow. "Ye are quite welcome, Mistress Lorna." He watched her walk away, finding himself wishing she had stayed so they could talk longer.

Lady Murdina's faint huff made him turn to address what appeared to be petty jealousy. He countered her unreasonable huff with a snort of his own. "I felt sure ye wished the nurse caring for yer son to always be close to him and at her best, aye?"

"Of course, m'lord," she said. "I feel certain whatever ye decide is always best." Her pained expression did not match the tone of her sentiment.

"And that is another thing," he said. "I prefer to be addressed as *my chieftain, the Sinclair*, or by my Christian name, *Gunn*." With a dip of his chin, he added, "I feel *m'lord* distances us too much. After all, we have thirty days to see if we can reach an accord. We shouldna keep ourselves aloof from one another. Do ye agree?"

"Of course. I shall bear that in mind, my chieftain." Lady Murdina's left eye took to twitching again. It fluttered so hard and fast, she pressed a finger to it.

"Are ye unwell?" Gunn hoped she would use that as an excuse to flee back to her rooms. The way their first meeting had gone so far had filled him with nothing but regret. The only bright point was he knew he would never love her.

Well, that wasn't the only bright point. The mystery surrounding Mistress Lorna Merriweather intrigued him. Almost as much as the lass herself.

"Perhaps ye wish to return to yer rooms for a while?" he asked.

"I am rather tired." Lady Murdina dipped a weak curtsy and offered her hand. "Pray excuse me. I shall see ye after I have rested, m'l...my chieftain."

He took her hand and bent over it but chose not to kiss it. He just wasn't in the mood to play the game. "Rest well, m'lady." A calculating smile curled his lip. "Once ye are rested, ye can meet my daughter, Bella."

"I look forward to it." Her eyes narrowed as she slid her hand out of his. Without another word, she flounced away.

Gunn didn't spare her a second thought. He was more interested in discovering more about Mistress Lorna.

"Jasper!" he bellowed. "I have a task for ye!"

CHAPTER FOUR

L ORNA SAT ON the stone ledge, hugging her knees as she stared out the window. Her warm breath fogged the glass, but it didn't matter. She looked within rather than out at the frozen land. Nothing made sense. And she had no clue how to survive or what to do next. The immediate choices that sprang to mind were to laugh hysterically, sob uncontrollably, or simply throw up. Or a combination of the three. Seventeenth-century Scotland. How the bloody hell had this happened?

"Mistress Lorna!" Ebby gently scolded as she chunked another log into the fire. "Ye will catch yer death sitting there. Come here to the fire and see the table I set for ye. And I didna chip a single dish!"

"I am really not hungry." Lorna didn't pull her gaze from the snow-covered landscape. She hated to dampen the friendly maid's enthusiasm, but eating was at the bottom of her agenda at the moment.

"'Tis nothing grand. Just warmed bannocks and soft cheese. Enough to settle yer wame till supper." Ebby sidled closer to the hard ledge of the windowsill and patted it. "Whilst ye eat, I can fetch some pillows for yer seat here. Make it more comfortable. Would ye like that, mistress?" The tall young woman clasped her hands in front of her narrow middle and rocked back and forth from heel to toe.

Lorna bowed her head and covered her eyes. A heavy sigh left her. It took every last shred of control she possessed to keep from crumbling into an inconsolable mess.

"What can I do, mistress?" Ebby asked softly. Her tone echoed with sympathy as warm and caring as a hug. "I will do whatever I can to make things better for ye. Swear it on my grandmam's grave." She perched on the ledge, leaned over, and peered up into Lorna's face. "Do ye wish for someone else to be yer maid 'stead of me? I can run and ask the chieftain or Mrs. Thistlewick. They're sure to send another lass who doesna bumble about as much as I do. She could be here quick as a wink."

That selfless question hit Lorna in the heart. She lifted her head and forced a quivering smile. "Ye are the perfect one to help me, Ebby. No one else would do."

The girl blew out a relieved sigh. "Thank heaven for that. I feared I had done something wrong again." She hopped up and took a few steps toward the table and chair she had carefully angled near the crackling fire. "Mrs. Thistlewick ordered the verra best herbs and spices be steeped in yer wine. 'Tis sure to warm ye from the cold."

Lorna forced herself to her feet. Deep down she understood that grieving the situation did no good. She had never really been one to cry unless angered. A stark childhood had honed her ability to hold back tears to avoid being taunted as weak or a crybaby. And it was time to be strong. Not curl up in a corner and weep. She could do that later. When no one else was around.

"Everything is verra nice," she said, her smile coming easier now as she noticed the coziness of the room. She hadn't paid that much attention to it before now. Avoiding a mental meltdown had consumed all her focus. "Thank ye for everything."

She ran her hand across the softness of the tidy bed in the corner closest to the hearth. A wooden trunk with leather straps sat at the foot of it. A tall wardrobe took up most of the wall on one side of the lone window. Ebby had moved the small table from beside the bed and placed it in front of the hearth, along with the only chair in the room. Centered beneath a tapestry of deer frolicking in a field of flowers was a long, narrow cabinet. A large pitcher and basin, a pile of neatly folded linens, and assorted covered crocks covered the top of it. A small but thick rug woven from scraps of wool covered the center of the small room. Lorna found that surprising, since Ebby had said this was a former servant's quarters.

"'Tis a cozy wee corner, is it not?" Ebby pulled out the chair and nudged it toward Lorna. "Mine is the next one down. So I can be here fast as can be." She smiled and made another coaxing motion with the chair.

"Quite cozy, indeed." Lorna wanted to be seen as appreciative, because she was. Her arrival in the past could have been a great deal worse. She seated herself and stared down at the plate of bread. Maybe if she nibbled at the crust, Ebby would stop hovering. "Where are Frances and Hesther?"

"They are in Bella's solar, having a wee treat that Cook sent up for all of them." The tip of the maid's tongue peeped out the corner of her mouth as she poured a dark, steamy liquid into a cup. Deep concentration furrowed her brow, and she chewed the corner of her lip while edging it closer to Lorna. "Here ye are, mistress. This will help ye feel more like yerself."

Lorna tried not to smile at the lass's herculean effort to keep from spilling. The heady scent of strong red wine and spices met her before the cup reached her lips. A sip confirmed it. She held it on her tongue for a long moment before swallowing, savoring the hint of cinnamon and clove. Expensive spices for this age. "It is verra nice." After another sip, she set it back on the table. Better go easy on that, since she had nothing in her stomach.

"Ye dinna like it." Ebby's dark brows drew together over her worried eyes. "Did I let it get too cold? Like a fool, I forgot the wrap for the pot before leaving the kitchens with it."

"Ebby, it's fine. I promise." The poor maid was so eager to please. Perhaps she could use that sweet trait to her advantage. "Tell me about Thursa Castle, aye? That will help me feel more at ease."

"Happy to, mistress." But she held up a finger. "Beg pardon while I check the sitting room again." She opened the door, peered out, and frowned. "They still havena brought yer trunks. How can I put away yer things if they dinna bring them in from the bailey?"

Lorna inwardly cringed, knowing that what she was about to share would seem strange. "I have nothing but the clothes I'm wearing. There will be no trunk."

Ebby stared at her, slowly blinking as though struggling to process that information. "Nothing?"

Lorna tried to play it off as a common thing. She rose from the table and moved closer to the fire. "Well, there is my cloak. Hesther may be using it to keep warm, though. That poor wee lass needs it more than I." She stretched her hands closer to the flames, reveling in the delicious warmth. "Now, come. Tell me about Thursa. About yer chieftain and what I can expect from him."

"Oh, he is the kindest man, mistress." Ebby's smile brightened like a beacon. "Most wouldha put me back out in the cold, what with my fumble-fingered ways." She hugged her thin frame and rocked from heel to toe again, looking more contended than anyone Lorna had ever met. "But not Chieftain Sinclair. He allowed me to stay here at Thursa."

Lorna decided Ebby's rocking had to be a quirky, self-soothing habit. She turned to warm her backside. "How long have ye known him?"

The maid's rocking shifted to a swaying from side to side. "Ever since he found me and my brother going from door to door, begging for scraps in Inverness. We were nothing but a pair of weans, really." Her swaying stopped, and she twisted her stained apron in her hands. "He brought us here, and Mrs.

Thistlewick took us in." She wiped the corners of her eyes. "She made my wee brother's last days so much easier than they wouldha been."

"I am so sorry." Lorna reached over and squeezed the lass's hand. "I never meant to stir unhappy memories."

Ebby offered a trembling tip of her head. "Those memories were the start of many good and happy times. My wee brother is in heaven now. No more suffering for him. And I am blessed to live here with the kindest folk I have ever known." She smoothed her apron back down and added more wine to Lorna's cup, accidentally sloshing a bit on the table. "Oh, me." As she dabbed at the spill with a rag from her pocket, she bumped the table and spilled even more. "Heaven help ye, mistress. Did ye anger himself to be saddled with a maid like me?"

"I am glad he chose ye for me." Lorna rested her hand on the girl's arm, stopping her vain efforts at cleaning up the mess. "Dinna worry about the table, aye? We can tend to it later." Hoping that everything she had heard about servants knowing the *real* workings of a keep was true, she leaned close and lowered her voice. "But I do have a question. If he is such a kind and generous man, why the devil is he marrying that vicious cow?"

Ebby clamped her mouth shut and shook her head. After a hurried curtsy, she darted out the door, banging into everything in her path.

"Well, bloody hell." Lorna stared at the door Ebby had left ajar. Clearly, she had pushed the girl too far.

Not knowing what else to do, she wiped up the wine spills and sorted the table, slightly disappointed that her closest source of information had disappeared. She wondered if Mrs. Thistlewick had a rule against gossiping.

After cleaning the mess the best she could, she ventured out into the adjoining room and then on into the next, which appeared to be a library or learning area of sorts. Bookshelves lined the walls, and a stringed instrument she wasn't familiar with leaned against a chair. The chieftain had called this Bella's floor, but sakes' alive, how many rooms did one child need? Did she not get lonely up here all by herself? And how in the devil did she ever find anyone to help her? Shouldn't the nursemaid's room connect to wherever the bairns slept?

She found her way to what appeared to be the main hallway and forged onward. After glancing around to ensure she was alone, she paused and listened at the closed doors, hoping to hear the children talking. That method made her search go quicker.

At the third door, she picked up on a muffled conversation that made her frown. That wasn't a child's voice. It sounded like a man. What was a man doing on the children's floor? Assuming the worst, she threw open the door, ready to fight if need be. Quickly assessing the innocent scene, she tucked her fists behind her back.

"What are ye doing here on the children's floor?" she asked, deciding to deflect their befuddled looks with bravado.

The man standing in front of the children's table proffered a polite bow. "Good day to ye, mistress. I am Sir Jasper Sinclair. The clan's war chief." He grinned and added a humble shrug. "Or man-at-arms. Whichever ye prefer. The title makes no difference." He moved toward her, and his grin took on an irritating smugness. "However, once ye have been here a while, ye will find our fine chieftain has granted me the right to go anywhere I wish in this keep."

She refused to be bullied. He might be a high-ranking knight within this clan, but she was determined to hold her own. Head held high, she positioned herself between Frances and Hesther. They sat at a large round table, in chairs made smaller to fit bairns. Bella sat with them, looking as though she had just gotten away with something she should not have done.

"Ye have not answered my question, sir." Lorna rested a hand on Frances's and Hesther's shoulders. "Why are ye here? These are my charges. I have a right to know yer business with them."

"He was asking about ye, Mistress Lorna," Frances said around a bulging mouthful of what appeared to be bread and jam.

"Wanted to know where ye were from and how we came to know ye."

Jasper shot a quelling glare at the lad. "Ye dinna have to tell everything ye know, boy."

"I told yer chieftain all about myself," Lorna said. She sauntered around the table and squared off in front of him. "So, he sends ye up here to intimidate these two because he thinks me a liar?"

The war chief lifted both hands and backed up a step as though surrendering. "I was not intimidating them." He looked to Bella for support. "Did I not speak kindly to yer new friends?"

"Jasper isna mean," Bella assured her, then added, "Unless ye give him a case of the red arse, of course."

Lorna struggled not to smile at the young miss's assessment. "Be that as it may, if yer chief wanted to know more about me, he should have asked." She tipped her chin to a defensive slant. "Since he sent ye to do his asking, I assume he must be a coward?"

"My da is not a coward," Bella said. She hopped up from her seat, rounded the table, and took a defensive stance between Lorna and the frustrated war chief. "He is cautious, 'tis all. A wise chief always confirms whatever he is told by strangers." She resettled her footing while stretching to appear taller. "He knows he must be cautious. Let the wrong person in the keep and it'd be like letting a stoat in with the hens."

The child's love and loyalty warmed Lorna's heart. She gave the youngling an apologetic nod. "Ye are quite right. I beg yer pardon for calling yer da a coward." Then she leveled a hard gaze on Jasper. "Take me to yer chieftain. I would have a word with him."

The man's reddish-blond brows ratcheted to a stormy angle, highlighting the leeriness in his eyes. "What sort of word?"

"Well now, if I wished to have it with yerself, I would have already done it, would I not?"

All the children giggled.

Jasper glared at her, his nostrils flaring like a great, red-headed beastie about to charge. His ruddy jaw set to a hard line, he waved her toward the door. "It appears I have no choice in the matter. This way, mistress."

Before following the irritated man, she turned back to Frances and Hesther. "Are ye both fine?" She hoped they could give her an honest answer. If not, she prayed she could see the truth in their eyes. "Ye are well and feel safe?"

Timid Hesther eased her worries with a genuine smile. It was the first time the young maid had ever appeared happy since they met. "Miss Bella is a kind and generous hostess, mistress." She aimed a shy glance down at the crumb-filled plate in front of her. "And I have never eaten so much in my entire life."

"'Tis verra nice here," Frances added, then shot a fretful look at the open door. "As long as we dinna have to go around the lady, we be fine."

Lorna had a fair idea whom he meant but found it odd that he didn't address Lady Murdina as *Mother*. She offered an understanding nod. "We will try to limit those times to as few as possible, aye?" She joined Jasper, then cast a glance back. "I'll be back up in a bit. My meeting with Chieftain Sinclair shouldna take long."

They both encouraged her with a nod, but Bella rushed toward her. "Dinna ye be mean to him, aye? My da has not had an easy way of it."

Lorna crouched to the petite young girl's level. "I am only mean to those who are mean to me. So far, except for sending a spy"—she shot a withering scowl at Jasper—"yer father has treated me with respect. Therefore, I will return the favor."

Bella cocked her head to the side, her ebony braids swinging like pendulums. "I think we shall soon be great friends, Mistress Lorna."

Lorna accepted the child's comment with relief. She was thankful for any ally, no matter the age. "I hope so, Miss Bella. I would be honored to be yer friend."

"If ye still wish to go, we should go," Jasper said from behind her. Lorna almost laughed. The man sounded as growly as a toddler in dire need of a nap.

Bella leaned forward, cupped her hand to Lorna's ear, and whispered, "Beware the beast. Ye gave him a case of the red arse by scolding him."

"Aye, well…he will just have to get over it—or die with it."

With a last nod at the children, Lorna followed the sullen war chief to the stairwell. "Who watches over Bella now?" she asked. As second only to the chieftain, surely he didn't fear sharing information the way Ebby had.

He clumped down several steps, remaining silent, as if she had never spoken.

Lorna clenched her teeth and stomped harder, making sure her steps were louder than his. The man had no idea how tenacious she could be.

"She is just a wee lass," she continued. "Seems like that floor of hers would be terribly lonely with just her." She trailed a hand along the stone wall of the large pillar that made up the core of the stairwell. Wooden steps surprised her. She had expected the old spiral staircases of stone that filled most multi-floor castles. She liked these better. Someone had carefully crafted them to fill the space with broad and solid steps that were much safer than their stone predecessors.

Jasper still didn't answer her. Well, not actually. It seemed as though the thunk of his boots became louder. The fool was trying to out-stomp her.

"It is verra unmanly to pout," she said, raising her voice to be heard over the racket of their stomping.

That halted him and made him glare back up at her. "Ye belittled my chieftain for sending me to find out more about yerself, aye?"

"Aye."

"And yet ye do the verra same thing by trying to draw out more information about Thursa Castle from me."

"It is not the same thing." Well, maybe it was, but she wasn't about to admit it. "I was inquiring after the welfare of the child—not prying into any personal secrets about Chieftain Sinclair."

Jasper puffed up and folded his arms across his chest. "Ye dinna consider the man's only child one of his personal secrets?"

She shooed him onward. "Just go on wi' ye, aye? I refuse to stand in this stairwell and argue about it."

He snorted a growling huff, then continued downward. His plodding stomp jarred her last raw nerve. By the time they reached the landing he sought, she was ready to strangle him.

He yanked open the door, then stepped aside. "Straight down that hall. The door there on the end."

She stood in the doorway, eyeing the dimly lit corridor. "And what exactly waits on the other side of that door?"

"Himself."

She clenched her teeth tighter, determined not to give the man the satisfaction of getting under her skin. "What room is it, I mean? I dinna want to walk in on the man whilst he is taking a shite, now do I?"

That won her a lopsided grin and a low chuckle. The war chief gave her a smug look that riled her even more. "He doesna make a habit of shitting in his library, mistress. Ye should be quite safe, I assure ye."

"Ye are an arse, Jasper. A complete arse, ye ken?"

"Thank ye for noticing, mistress." After a polite nod, he turned and descended the remaining stairs, leaving her standing in the doorway.

She stared at the door at the end of the hall. "Nothing to do but do it." She charged ahead and knocked.

The fast thumping of a brisk pace across wooden floors sounded on the other side, then the door flew open, revealing Chieftain Sinclair's narrow-eyed scowl. Within a moment, his sternness softened some, but not much. "Aye, Mistress Lorna?"

Bloody hell. She wanted to retreat but refused to let him win. "Ye and I need to have a word."

"Do we now?" He swung the door open wider and waved her inside. "And what word might that be?"

Her steps slowed as the lavishness of the man's library hit her. The plushness of the rugs. Cushioned chairs and couches scattered throughout the area. An impressively large mahogany desk beside the window. The faintest scent of pipe tobacco and whisky wafted through the air. A man's room that vibrated with testosterone and alpha maleness.

She almost forgot what she came to say. Then she caught a glimpse of Jasper as he passed outside the window, trudging through the snow in the courtyard. She turned and faced the Sinclair. "Dinna be sending yer man to interrogate and intimidate Frances and Hesther. If ye want to know something about me, ye can bloody well ask me yerself."

One of his blond brows, the one split by a faded scar, twitched upward. A combination of disbelief and amusement flashed in his eyes. "My war chief is not a cruel man with children. He would never mistreat weak ones such as those two." He moved closer, his gait as smooth and deadly as a predatory cat's. "What did he do? Describe this crime of which ye accuse him."

"His size and presence are enough to strike fear into those wee ones. Neither he nor any other man has any business on Bella's floor." She retreated a step and then another, wishing Gracie was with her. Gracie could argue with a wall and make it believe it was the floor. "And I dinna appreciate being spied upon." She backed into the window ledge and bumped to a halt. "It is a cowardly act."

The chieftain's mouth twitched, making his closely trimmed beard shimmer in the room's soft lighting. It reminded her of golden fur. She ran her thumbs across her fingertips, imagining the feel of those short bristles. This man made it difficult to concentrate and stay firmly on topic. He was so…everything.

"Well?" she said, shaking herself free of the trance.

He stood within inches of her, cutting off any means of escape. His nostrils flared as he leaned forward and sniffed. "Ye smell nice. Like a field of heather just bloomed."

She stanched the urge to sniff herself, knowing her deodorant and body spray had to be on their last legs. "What has that got to do with anything I just said?"

He shrugged. "Nothing. But ye did say I should speak directly to ye about matters concerning yerself, did ye not?"

"I meant if ye had questions." A hint of mirth danced in his eyes, making her flush hot with anger. "Ye ken verra well what I meant."

Chieftain Sinclair took a step back and propped his impressive arse on the lip of his desk. "Aye, mistress. I do ken what ye meant, but I also know if I ask ye the same questions as before, the answers ye give will be just as strange and incomplete. Surely, ye must realize the story ye told was difficult to believe. Ye arrived here with naught to yer name but the clothes on yer back. Two waifs that ye claim to have just met love ye as though ye are their mother, and the lady who brought ye here would rather spit in yer face than say yer name." He gave a theatrical bow. "But I will try it yer way, since ye feel so strongly about it. Where are ye from, Mistress Lorna? The truth this time, if ye please."

She knew her tale was impossible to swallow. She was the one bloody well living it. "I am from Thurso," she said, then remembered what the coachman had said. "Or at least I was…at another time."

"At another time?" He eyed her for a moment, then shook his head. "Ye see? That answer is exactly what I mean. What do ye mean by *at another time?*"

"I canna help it," she fired back. "It is all I know to say." Weariness and frustration threatened to undo her. She should not have come down here. She sagged back against the windowsill and buried her face in her hands. "I dinna ken what is to become of me," she whispered, more to herself than him.

"Ye have a home here, mistress," he said just as quietly. He moved closer, so near that his heat reached out and embraced her. "For as long as ye need it. I dinna make it a habit of ousting the needy from Thursa."

"Could ye please just call me Lorna instead of *mistress*? Just plain Lorna." She lifted her head and met his gaze. "I am not used to all these titles and such, and it just doesna sound right when ye say it."

"I dinna wish to be disrespectful." He gave her a lopsided grin, then appeared to be studying her. "Ye need a dram, I think. In the worst way."

After pulling in a deep breath and letting it go, she found the strength to return his smile. "That would be lovely, Chieftain Sinclair."

"Gunn," he corrected her as he turned and headed toward a cabinet loaded down with decanters.

"Beg pardon?"

"Gunn," he repeated as he filled a pair of round-bellied glasses with an unmistakable golden liquid. "'Tis my Christian name. My mother was from Clan Gunn." As he handed her a drink, he lifted his in a toast. "If I am to address ye as Lorna, then ye should address me as Gunn."

"Will that not upset everyone else?" She sipped the whisky and breathed it in to increase its heady richness across her tongue. After the day she had, the water of life hit the spot.

"I am chieftain. If I say it is so, then it is so. *Everyone else*, as ye put it, will adjust accordingly."

"And what about yer betrothed?" Lorna knew that Lady Murdina would unravel at the seams when she heard her future husband addressed by his first name by someone other than herself. Not that Lorna cared, but she didn't want innocent folk caught in the crossfire.

"Lady Murdina is not my betrothed just yet. We must reach an accord before that happens. If we canna foresee a bearable alliance in thirty days, the agreement becomes null, and there will be no union."

As the whisky warmed her, it also loosened her tongue and

made her braver. "Which brings me to my next question—why the devil would ye even think about marrying that woman? She is a hateful cow."

All joviality left him. A quiet somberness took its place. "My reasons are my own, lass, and I prefer not to share them. They are quite practical, I assure ye." After fetching the decanter, he joined her at the windowsill and leaned back against it beside her. He held the whisky higher and arched a brow. "More?"

"Aye." She held out her glass. "But no more after this one. I have not eaten today and already had a sip of mulled wine. I dinna want to get silly."

"Did Ebby not bring ye any food?" A concerned frown furrowed his compelling features as he poured a generous amount.

"She did. But at the time, I didna think I could keep it down. It has been a verra troubling day." There was no other way to describe all that had happened. And she feared if she went into too much detail, he would either have her locked up for madness or torched for being a witch. "Ebby is verra sweet. Thank ye for assigning her to me." She huffed a bitter laugh. "Although I may have run her off. She ran like her skirts were on fire when I started asking questions about ye."

That made him smile and reveal a dimple that was almost hidden by his neatly trimmed beard. "Mrs. Thistlewick keeps a strict rule in place with all the servants. They are not to repeat details about me or my daughter."

"I figured as much." She sipped the whisky, breathing it in again to draw its heat deeper. "A good rule, actually. Gossip can be a verra dangerous thing."

"Aye, it can."

She became increasingly aware that the windowsill seemed much smaller with him in it with her. He brushed against her every time he topped off her glass, appearing oblivious to the fact that the rock-hardness of his muscles pressed against her. Not that she minded. In fact, she rather enjoyed it. He gave off a pleasant warmth and somehow smelled better than the other males she had encountered so far. His manly scent reminded her of warm gingerbread.

She leaned closer and inhaled deeply. "Ye smell verra nice too, by the way."

He chuckled. "Thank ye, mistress."

"Lorna. Remember?" She held out her glass again. "Just this one more, and then that is it." It had been a terrible failure of a day, and she deserved as much whisky as she wished. But she needed to keep her wits about her.

The look he gave her sent more warmth racing through her than any swallow of whisky ever could. "Ye can have as much as ye like, lass." Before filling her glass, he rose, caught hold of her wrist, and tugged her along behind him. "But let us move to the couch, aye? More comfortable."

She allowed him to lead her to the sofa angled in front of the hearth. A contented sigh slipped free of her as she sank into the upholstered cushions and wiggled her rear like a hen settling into her nest. "Aye, this is much nicer than that cold, hard seat at the window." With the crackling fire to her right, and the warmth of the whisky soaking through her, she found herself relaxing to the point of being boneless. And friendly. And not giving a rat's arse about a single worry in the world. A fleeting notion that maybe whisky had been a poor decision crossed her mind as a jaw-cracking yawn escaped her. She hurried to cover her mouth and blinked hard to force her eyes to stay open. "Oh dear. Forgive me. I am so sorry."

Gunn settled down beside her and filled her drink to overflowing. "Ye have nothing to apologize for. I ken ye have had a trying day. The coachman told Jasper about finding ye in the snow. How long had ye been wandering in the storm?"

She took a hearty sip, then lifted her glass and admired the flickering firelight through the golden liquid. "Seemed like forever walking in that snow. Never made it to Hook's Cafe." She finished the drink and held out it out again. "Just this one more, aye?"

"Aye, lass, just this one more." With a smile that deepened his irresistible dimple, he sloshed another generous dram into her glass.

"I do think a lone dimple simply makes the man, ye ken?" She ached to brush her fingers across it. "'Tis so hard to resist a handsome devil with a dimple."

She stanched the urge to touch him by taking another drink. The way he stared at her with so much mirth dancing in his eyes gave her pause.

A brief moment of clarity shoved through her carefree whisky fog. She pressed her fingers to her mouth in delayed panic. "Bloody hell—did I just say all that out loud?"

He grinned, making that damn dimple even more beguiling. "Aye, lass. Ye did."

She cleared her throat. Nothing to do but press on in the hopes he would forget it. "Ye said Jasper talked to the coach-man?"

"Aye."

"I will have ye know that sorry git took my last tenner then didna even stop and let me out when we went through Thurso."

"Yer last *tenner*?" He stared at her as though confused.

"Aye, my ten-pound note. I gave it to him for a lift to Thurso." She downed the rest of the whisky much too quickly. "Bloody hell." She wheezed in a deep breath and thumped her chest, trying to cool the burn trailing down her gullet. "That one set me on fire." She resettled back into the pillows and found herself snuggled very nicely against Gunn.

Without thinking, she rested her head on his shoulder. She just needed to rest her eyes for a bit. It had been such a terribly long day. Surely, he wouldn't think badly of her. All considered, he had been very nice so far.

"Ye dinna mind if I rest here a wee bit, do ye? I promise to be quiet as a wee mousie and not bother ye."

He wrapped an arm around her and gathered her more comfortably against his chest. "Rest ye well, wee mouse." His voice rumbled beneath her cheek in the nicest way. "Rest ye well."

She patted his chest and nestled closer until she was just right. "Ye are a kind man, Gunn Sinclair. I thank ye for yer understanding and hospitality." She hitched in another deep yawn and patted his chest again. "Ye have no idea how much I appreciate ye being as good as ye are."

"Ye are quite welcome, lass. Quite welcome, indeed."

CHAPTER FIVE

T HE LONGER HE sat in front of the fire with her sleeping against him, the more at peace he became. His weary heart hadn't enjoyed this much ease in quite a while. He controlled his breathing so as not to disturb her. She felt very nice against him like this. Dangerously nice. Her softness made it difficult to sort through everything she had said when the whisky unleashed her tongue, as he had hoped.

Gunn sipped his drink, then cautiously tipped his head and rubbed his cheek across her hair. Not a wise choice. He clenched his teeth to bite back a lonely groan. Mistress Lorna's clipped tresses were as silky as they looked.

Nay, not *Mistress Lorna.* Just plain Lorna, as she had requested. That almost made him laugh. There was nothing plain about this unusual woman.

He thought back over all she had told him. Lived in Thurso at another time. What the devil did that mean? *Another time?* He had been to Thurso many a time over the years, visiting his ships and warehouses. If a lass such as herself had taken up residence there, he would have known it. And she behaved as if she didn't know anyone here or anything about Clan Sinclair. But how could she not if she had lived in Thurso?

He took another wee taste of his whisky, making the drink last. Poor lass. He was ashamed to admit that he had only refilled his glass once to however many times he had filled hers, hoping to grease her words. And the ploy had worked. Somewhat.

He smiled and scratched his thumb across his dimple. So she thought him a handsome devil? A subtle aching bloomed in the center of his chest, then surged downward and became an uncomfortable throbbing in his crotch. Damned if he wouldn't love to enjoy her right now on this very couch. But he knew better than to succumb to that temptation. Something deep inside him knew this lass would never be anything as simple as an idle tumble. And while he would welcome a friendship with her, never would he make the mistake of allowing anything more. He could not risk it.

A light scratching on the door made him tense and glance down at her. She barely stirred, rubbing her nose as if it itched, then returned to the slow, steady breathing of her dreams.

The door eased open. Mrs. Thistlewick tiptoed inside, glancing all around until she found him. Her sparse gray brows shot to her frizzy white hairline and her eyes went wide and round.

He pointed his glass at her and gave her a warning scowl to go along with it.

She puffed up with the haughtiness of a nesting peahen. "Dinna be giving me that look," she scolded in a harsh whisper. She marched over and snatched the glass from his hand. Before returning it to the cabinet, she bent close and sniffed Lorna's slightly open mouth. When she straightened, she fixed him with a damning glare. "Shame on ye, my chieftain. Plying the lass with whisky to get her talking."

"I did not *ply*." He made a shushing motion as the lovely miss stirred again. "I merely offered, and she accepted. Poor thing has not had an easy time of it. She needed a dram or two."

Mrs. Thistlewick rolled her eyes. "Aye, and I feel sure the Lady Murdina will give her an even easier time of it when she discovers she drank herself into yer arms."

"She nay drank herself into my arms," he argued. "She was weary from the start."

As if to back his claims, Lorna shifted again and started snoring.

"There. Ye see?" He nodded down at her. "Weary to the bone." When the housekeeper failed to budge, he glared at her. "And the reason ye came in here, Mrs. Thistlewick?" The efficient matron rarely interrupted him when he closed the library door. In fact, no one in the keep did. It was an unwritten law.

With her hands primly clasped in front of her thick middle, she pursed her lips as though choosing her words carefully. After another pained glance down at the lass, she shook her head and rolled her eyes again. "Wee Bella not only wishes for Master Frances and poor wee Hesther to stay on her floor, but she now claims that perhaps she does need a nursemaid after all but doesna wish it to be Freyda again." She aimed a curt nod at the woman sleeping against him. "She wishes for Mistress Lorna to tend to her along with the others."

"Does she now?" He scrubbed his jaw line, scratching his fingertips through this beard. The more he thought about it, the more he liked the idea. Besides, if the agreement between Lady Murdina and himself resulted in a union, it would be as such anyway. He nodded. "Tell her it shall be so."

"And Ebby got yer weary mistress there the clothes from the trunks. As ye ordered." She cleared her throat with a disapproving *harrumph*. "As soon as Mistress Lorna feels more rested, I feel certain Ebby can get them altered to better fit her."

"Ye seem more fractious and judgmental than usual, Mrs. Thistlewick. Ye might as well speak yer mind and be done with it." He braced himself for whatever tirade was about to ensue. The dear old soul had always been more of a grandmother and guardian than a housekeeper.

Her sternness melted away, and she bowed her head. "I understand why ye decided on this plan of yers to wed a woman ye would never love, but I dinna agree with it."

"It is for the best," he quietly replied. "I must do as I see fit, ye ken?"

"Aye." She cast another lingering glance at Lorna. "I pride myself on being an excellent judge of folks. That wee lass there willna be pleased with herself when she awakes. It would be the gentlemanly thing to do to ease her down onto the pillows and move yerself to the desk. Lessen her embarrassment that way when she comes to."

While he knew the housekeeper was right, he loathed the idea of moving. But he supposed it was better for both of them. He waved the matron closer. "Dinna let her fall too hard when I slide out from under her."

After a coordinated effort, Lorna soon lay curled on the couch, hugging a pillow under her head. Gunn already missed her warmth, but Mrs. Thistlewick was right, and he didn't wish the lass embarrassed.

Then he realized the housekeeper still stood there, frowning. "Now what ails ye?"

"Perhaps I should wake her and help her to her room." She nodded. "That way, if she remembers how she fell asleep with her head on yer chest, the both of ye can pretend it never happened."

"I never realized women could be so calculating." He moved to the whisky cabinet, poured himself another, then waved it in the couch's direction. "By all means, do whatever ye see fit."

"Dinna be growly with me, my chieftain."

He threw up a hand and strode to the window, staring out at the frozen courtyard and not seeing a thing. The housekeeper had destroyed the rare peacefulness of earlier and replaced it with resentment.

A slight groan from the couch made him turn. Lorna curled into a tighter ball, hugging her stomach and holding a hand over her eyes. "Idiot." She gave another pained groan, clapped a hand over her mouth, and floundered to her feet. She stumbled a few steps, looking wildly around the room while both her hands sealed her mouth shut.

"Merciful heavens!" Mrs. Thistlewick said. "Hold on, lass. I shall fetch a basin."

"No time," Gunn said. He threw open the window and waved the lass toward it. "Over here!"

Lorna charged forward, hung out the window, and vomited. As she retched with a violence that shook her clear to her toes, she slid farther out over the ledge.

Gunn caught hold and held her around the waist to keep her from toppling out into the snow. As she convulsed in his arms, he rubbed her back, trying to bring her some ease. "There, lass. Get it all out." He looked back at Mrs. Thistlewick. "Water for her, aye? And a wet cloth to soothe her."

The housekeeper didn't move, just stood there with a self-satisfied smirk plumping her rosy cheeks.

"Mrs. Thistlewick! Now, if ye please." What the devil was the old soul plotting now?

Lorna heaved hard and fast for a bit longer, then went limp and just hung there out the window. "Kill me now, aye? Just shove me out and make sure I break my neck when I hit."

Gunn massaged her back, alternately rubbing and patting while still hugging an arm around her waist and holding her steady. "Now, now, wee mouse. None of that talk. Once ye rid yerself of all that fine whisky, ye will feel better."

"No. Just shove me out into the snow and let me freeze to death," she rasped. "I have heard it's peaceful. Ye just go to sleep and there ye are."

Since her retching appeared to be at an end, at least for now, he eased her back inside and held her in the crook of his arm. He sat with her on the windowsill in case she had more to purge. "It appears ye canna hold yer whisky."

"I know better than to drink whisky." She slumped against him, covering her face with her hands. "Bloody hell. This is worse than last Hogmanay."

"Here ye are, lass." Mrs. Thistlewick appeared at their side with a tankard of water and a basin. "Rinse yer mouth. It will help."

Eyes squeezed nearly shut, Lorna swished the water around her mouth, then spat. "Thank ye," she whispered, then sagged back against him.

Mrs. Thistlewick shot him another smug nod, then toddled to the door. "Take care of her, my chieftain. I have much to attend to with the feasting scheduled for tonight. Off I go." She latched the door firmly behind her.

Lorna dove back to the window's edge and retched again with hard, dry gagging.

"Ye need to drink water to keep from turning yerself inside out. Hold fast while I fetch more, aye?"

Still gagging, she waved him away. He hoped that meant she agreed.

When he returned with the tankard refilled, she took several deep gulps, then held her breath as if determined to keep it down. "I know better than to drink whisky," she said in a hushed voice, as if speaking hurt her head. "Wine, I can handle. Ale? I can down it by the gallons. But whisky?" She closed her eyes and shuddered, making him wonder if she was about to hang out the window again. "I know better. But it has been such a bloody awful day."

"It didna take the drink long to turn on ye. That's for certain." He offered her the damp cloth he had fetched along with the water. "Here, my fine wee mouse. To help ease yer suffering."

"Thank ye." She wiped her face, then pressed the rag to her throat and squinted at him with one eye barely cracked open. "And why is it ye have dubbed me *mouse*?"

Unable to stop himself, he grinned. "Because ye promised to be quiet as a *wee mousie* right before falling asleep on the couch." He brushed her hair out of her face, the motion seeming as natural as if he had done it all his life. "And it fits ye, I think. Mice are survivors and protective of their families. Both traits remind me of ye."

She dipped the rag in the water and pressed it to the back of her neck. Closing her eyes, she leaned her head back as though reveling in the coolness against her flesh.

"Ye dinna even know me," she said without opening her eyes.

"I know enough." And were he a wise man, he would run like hell from this woman who had landed in his midst. But it was the dead of winter, this was his home, and the possibility of his arranged marriage loomed near. He had to manage this with care.

With movements that were stiff and careful, she gingerly slid off the windowsill and stood. "I am sorry I made such a spectacle of myself." She paused and forced both eyes fully open, cringing at the effort. "Thank ye for yer kindness. And yer patience." She swallowed hard and took a deep breath, obviously still on shaky ground. "Please forgive me if I dinna make the feast tonight, aye?"

The thought of her not there pained him, and that reaction troubled him even more. Even though he had just met this woman, he hungered for her company. Instinct and past experience warned him that nothing good would come of that. And yet he shoved the warning aside. He was wiser this time. He could manage it.

"Ye must come to the feast. The children will need watching over."

With a hand covering one of her eyes, she squinted at him with the other. "It is not as though they are wee bairns. All three are old enough to cut their own meat, ye ken?"

"But they need ye there," he argued, sounding desperate even to himself. "Both Frances and Hesther will be too timid to eat without ye there to shield them from Lady Murdina."

"Well, bollocks." Her mouth puckered as though she was about to vomit again. She eased down into a chair, bent forward, and held her head in her hands. "I wish they had as much pluck as Bella. That wee lass will put old Murdina in her place."

A sense of pride filled him, threatening to burst his seams. "Aye, my precious Bella is fiery as she is canny. Does me proud."

Lorna lifted her head and offered him a smile. "With that dark hair and those big eyes, she is already a beauty. Ye will soon be beating the lads away with a stick."

"Aye." An old, familiar aching settled back across him. "She is the image of Mariella, her mother."

"Forgive me. I can tell by yer expression her loss is still a fresh wound. I didna mean to stir it." She leaned back in the chair as she rubbed her temples.

With a slow shake of his head, Gunn seated himself in the chair opposite her. For the first time in the longest while, he felt the need to speak of his pain. "Mariella died five years ago. A fever took her." He shuddered at the memory. "It took many in the clan." He leaned forward, propped his forearms on his knees, and stared down at his clasped hands. "Then two years ago, my second wife, Corinna, died while trying to bring my son into this world. He died a few moments after she did."

"I am so sorry," Lorna whispered.

"I loved both my wives," he added quietly. "And I loved my wee son as well." He lifted his gaze to hers, yearning for her to understand. "I am a weak man and a coward, lass. I canna bear that kind of loss again." After pulling in a deep breath that turned into a despairing sigh, he continued, "But I need an heir to protect this clan and see after Bella once I am gone."

"So ye chose an arranged marriage to a despicable woman ye have no danger of loving," she said, as though reading his mind.

"Aye."

Lorna slowly shook her head. "A sad fate for such a fine man who deserves so much more."

"But a fate I embrace." A bitter smile came to him. "For the good of my clan, my daughter, and my weary heart."

She pulled her feet up into the chair and hugged her knees. With her chin propped on them, she studied him. "I agree Lady Murdina is a beauty, but as heartless as she is, do ye really think she would make a good mother to yer future heir? What if it takes a few tries to get a son? Can ye really see her mothering a brood of bairns?"

Her questions bored into him like well-aimed arrows. Their

logic stirred knots deep in his gut. "Perhaps she is not as heartless as she seems. Could be she is merely jealous of the lovely young woman in her midst. This is only her first day here."

Lorna made a face as if she thought him ridiculous. "Doubtful. I think ye found yerself a full-on witch with that one."

He offered a rueful smile. "I have known men married to worse, and they lived to tell about it."

She frowned. "And how does Bella feel about all this? Have ye asked her?"

"It is for her own good."

"Okay, that means ye either have yet to ask her opinion or ye have and she disagreed with yer barmy plan, aye?"

"There is that *okay* word again. What the devil does it mean?" He leaned closer and fixed her with a teasing grin. "Perhaps ye are the witch?"

She rolled her eyes. "*Okay* means the same as *all right*. Sort of. Anyhow, that is not the point. Ye should listen to Bella. It is important to a daughter for her father to listen."

"Did yer father listen to ye?" As soon as he said it, he wished he could pull the words back because of the change that came over her.

"My father left my mother before I was born." Her jaw flexed to a hard line. "Or so I was told when I was old enough to ask where I lived before the orphanage."

"Nuns raised ye, then?"

"Something like that." Her voice had gone dull and emotionless. She scrubbed her face with both hands and rose from the chair. "I should go check on Frances and Hesther."

"And Bella."

She smiled. "And Bella." Her gaze locked on him, and her expression shifted to one of befuddlement.

"What puzzles ye, mouse?"

"We have only just met, yet here we are chatting like old friends. I came down here to scold ye about sending spies, and we end up drinking together." She pressed a hand to her chest and rumbled out a very unladylike belch. "Oh my, pardon me. And heaving, well, I heaved with ye as if we were old pub mates. Ye even gave me a nickname. That is rather odd, do ye not think?" She pinched the bridge of her nose and rubbed the corners of her eyes. "I mean, it's nice and all, but strange that we find each other's company so comfortable, ye ken? Like the fit of a favorite old shoe that's good and broken in?"

"It is nice." He refused to acknowledge the strangeness of the situation. Instead, he was just relieved that she had noticed the ease of their connection as well. He offered his arm. "I shall escort ye back, aye? The halls can be confusing."

She took his arm, leaning on him as if almost too weary to walk. "It is rather mazelike," she said. "But I suppose that would deter an enemy from being able to find ye. Are there hidden passages too? Behind the walls and such?"

He chuckled. "I am sure if ye ask Bella, she will be more than happy to give ye a tour of the tunnels, even though she is not supposed to use them."

"Are they dangerous?"

"Somewhat. And also a slight invasion of privacy. The passages provide spy holes into several of the rooms, and my wee daughter is often too curious for her own good." As they entered the stairwell, he eyed her. Even in the torchlight, her coloring still seemed a mite pale. "Are ye certain ye can manage the stairs?"

She squared her shoulders and lifted her chin. "One step at a time. All I have to conquer is one step at a time."

Her determination impressed him. He waved her forward. "Onward, then."

With slow, plodding steps, she climbed, supporting herself with her left hand against the center pillar. As they passed beneath a sputtering torch, he made out a strange marking on her ring finger. A greenish line. "What is that on yer hand, lass?"

She halted and looked back at him. "What?"

He pointed at her left hand. "What is that mark?"

Her face hardened into a scowl, and even in the dim lighting, he made out the flush of red flooding her cheeks. "That is the green my engagement ring left behind."

"Ah yes, I remember ye saying ye gave the ring back to the man after he angered ye."

"He did not just *anger* me. He made me a fool of me." She resumed climbing the stairs, faster this time.

A protectiveness flared within him. "Give me his name. I shall send for him and see that he receives justice."

She didn't reply. Just kept climbing as if he hadn't spoken.

"Lorna?"

"His name is Patrick Inverarry," she said. "I doubt ye can find him, and it doesna matter anyway."

"It does matter. No one should mistreat ye." He took the steps faster to keep up with her.

She halted at the landing and gave him a sad smile. "I appreciate the offer. But trust me, he is not worth the effort." She rested her hand on the door. "Is this the right one?"

"Aye." He moved up beside her and pushed it open. "After ye, m'lady."

She snorted a laugh. "Ye best not call me that in front of yer future wife." She halted partway down the hall and frowned at the doors. "I dinna remember which room I found them in."

"Come, I will show ye a way to remember." He pointed at a small image carved in the upper left corner of the door. "What do ye see there?"

She moved closer and studied it. "It looks like the sun."

"Aye, it is. And this room is the solar for this floor." He moved to the next door and pointed at its upper left corner. "Just as this carved rose shows this to be one of the doors to Bella's room."

"One of the doors?"

"Aye. When we built the keep, I wanted to ensure that many of the rooms had more than one way out. Lives could depend on it." He never wanted those he loved trapped anywhere.

The solar door flew open, and a grinning Bella joined them in the hall. "I knew I heard ye!" She caught hold of Lorna's hand and smiled up at her. "Did Mrs. Thistlewick tell ye?"

Lorna didn't answer, just turned to him with a confused look.

"Bella wishes for ye to look after her as well as Frances and Hesther," he said.

Relief flooded Lorna's face, and she smiled down at the child. "I would be honored, but ye will have to explain what exactly a nursemaid does. I've taken care of wee ones before, but none so as mature as yerself."

"I am no trouble at all," Bella assured her with feigned innocence. "Is that not so, Da?"

Gunn eyed his daughter. The wily glint in her dark eyes concerned him. "She bears watching, Mistress Mouse. Never let down yer guard."

Bella perked like a cat about to pounce as she glanced from her father to Lorna. "Ye let him call ye Mistress Mouse?"

"I have been called worse," Lorna said while shooting him a narrow-eyed glare that he found immensely pleasing. She pulled in a deep breath and swallowed hard. "How long do we have before we must go down to the feast?" Eyes closed, she rubbed her forehead. "I would like a lie-down, if that is possible."

"Plenty of time," Bella said before he could answer. "And I shall make sure we all behave whilst ye rest. Ebby's already come back up with some clothes for ye. She can mend on them while ye have a wee nod." She hopped in place, making her braids dance across her shoulders. "Frances and Hesther are already asleep. I can watch them, if ye like. Although I dinna think they will be any trouble. I have a book from Da's library I can look at. It even has pictures."

Lorna held up both hands in surrender. "It appears Bella has everything well in hand." She appeared to start a curtsy, then grabbed her head. "Bloody hell. That's out." She took hold of his hand and shook it. "I shall see ye at dinner, aye?"

He held his breath to keep from laughing. 'Twould be rude indeed to glean pleasure from her misery. "Aye, Mistress Mouse. I look forward to seeing ye again." And he did. A great deal more than he should.

After a warning shake of his finger at his canny daughter, he left them. Bella concerned him. The wee minx missed nothing, and it would not bode well if the wily lass chose to make trouble.

"God help me," he muttered, meaning the quick prayer with every ounce of his being.

CHAPTER SIX

L ORNA FOLLOWED BELLA through the solar, the adjacent study
room, then halted in the middle of the small sitting room she
recognized as the one connected to her bedchamber. "Bella?"

"Aye?" The child paused with her hand on the bedroom door.

"I passed through scores of rooms before I found all of ye
earlier." Or had she? Lorna rubbed her pounding temples.
Perhaps the ill effects of the whisky had scrambled her mind.

Before Bella could answer, Ebby opened the bedchamber
door. "There ye be, mistress!" She eased forward with her head
bowed, cowering like a pup guilty of peeing on the floor.
"Forgive me for leaving ye earlier. I didna wish to do anything
wrong."

Still trying to hold her splitting head together, Lorna shooed
the maid's apologies aside. "Dinna fash yerself." She turned back
to Bella. "How many rooms on this floor?"

"Ye passed the long way through, I think. Prolly went
through some rooms more than once. There's not that many, but
all connect in a windy-bout sort of way. Da wanted the place for
his bairns to be like a puzzle. Keeps us safe, ye ken?" The lass's
dark eyes filled with concern as she slightly tipped her head to
one side. "Are ye ailing? Ye dinna seem well at all."

"She needs a lie-down, some willow bark tea, and a nibble of fried bread to settle her stomach," Ebby said. She ducked closer and whispered, "Mrs. Thistlewick told me about yer visit to the library. I have everything waiting in yer room."

"Did Da give ye too much whisky?" Bella asked. "If'n he did, I can have a word with him."

Lorna held up a hand to silence their chatter. All she needed was quiet and a dark room. "I just need a lie-down, aye?"

"The whisky," Bella informed Ebby with a knowing wrinkle of her nose. "I snuck a sip once. Wicked stuff. Burns like fire."

"Miss Bella!" Ebby appeared suitably shocked.

"Can the two of ye discuss my drinking habits somewhere else? If I stand here much longer, I'll be heaving out the window again." Lorna pushed past them into the bedchamber, sagged onto the bed, and curled into a ball.

Belatedly, what Bella had said hit her.

"Bella!" she called out, then grabbed her head. Have mercy. Speaking loudly goaded the beast jackhammering inside her skull.

"Aye?"

"Dinna be drinking yer da's whisky, ye ken? It'll stunt yer growth and make ye grow a beard." Lorna cracked an eye to see if the child believed her. "I had a friend once who drank whisky when she was yer age, and she ended up having to shave the hair off her face three times a day forever."

Bella's dubious expression revealed she was not that easily fooled. "No offense, Mistress Lorna, but I think ye vomited out yer good sense along with all that whisky ye tossed up."

Lorna draped an arm over her eyes. "Just dinna drink it, aye? Do ye want to feel like I look?"

"I think not," the wee lass said. "Can we talk whilst ye lie there?"

"She needs quiet," Ebby interrupted, then bumped into the bed.

"Bloody hell," Lorna groaned, and curled into a tighter ball. A fresh wave of nausea churned harder, as if her hangover had gotten a second wind.

"I have the willow bark tea, mistress, and Mrs. Thistlewick's remedy for the wobblies."

Lorna risked uncovering an eye to discover both the maid and the child standing beside the bed staring down at her. "Ye two are like buzzards waiting for me to die."

Both frowned but didn't go away.

"I give up." Lorna pushed up on an elbow. "Remedies first, and then conversation." She scooted back against the headboard, hoping their chat was short and the remedies not too revolting.

Their frowns shifted to triumphant smiles. Ebby offered a cup in each hand. Both were steaming. She lifted the one on the left. "Best drink this one first. It's the thickest, but when ye drink the willow bark after it, that should thin it out and make it easier to swallow."

Lorna tried not to gag at that prospect. She accepted the small cup half-filled with a steaming substance that resembled the tar she had seen highway workers using to patch a road.

A hesitant sniff made her feel somewhat better. It didn't smell nearly as bad as it looked. In fact, it had a cloyingly sweet, berrylike fragrance. The first sip was a syrupy rendition of elderberry wine. The acrid tartness of the willow bark brew remedied the icky-sweet aftertaste. But a subtle alcoholic burn lingered after both. Mrs. Thistlewick's magical cure more likely ran along the lines of *the hair of the dog that bit ye.*

"And here is the bread. Fried to a crisp, sure to settle yer wame and help keep everything down." Ebby offered a sympathetic smile as she took away the cups, trading them for a small plate of toasted bread that was a half-second away from being charcoal.

"Thank ye." Lorna forced a bite. While chomping through the toast's bitterness, she turned to Bella. "Yer turn, and I would be more than a little grateful if we could keep it simple, aye? My head is pounding."

"Simple is nay a problem," Bella said with a solemn nod. "I

need yer help to get that cow out of this keep afore she marries my da."

"Ye dinna like Lady Murdina?"

"Do ye?" The child's tone revealed a maturity much older than nine years.

"No." Lorna refused to insult the lass by patronizing her, and she had never been one for diplomacy. "But do ye understand why yer da is dead set on marrying her?"

"Aye." The young girl sat on the edge of the bed, her brow creased in a studious furrow. "I ken it is because he loved Mama and stepmama Corinna and was really sad when they died." She twitched a frustrated shrug. "I loved them too, but that doesna mean I want a mean old crone for my next stepmother."

"He is afraid to love again because of the heartache, Bella." Lorna wished she could explain the complicated subject to the youngling. "He doesna wish to relive the pain of losing someone he cares about."

"Well, that makes no sense at all," Bella said. "Is he going to stop caring about everyone just so he willna be sad if they go to heaven afore he does?"

Lorna closed her eyes and rubbed her forehead even though the nauseating pound of earlier appeared to be letting up. Apparently, Mrs. Thistlewick's remedies bordered on the miraculous.

She eyed the frustrated child, trying to come up with the words to help her understand. "Ye canna fight emotions with logic, my fine wee lass. When someone is trapped in the clutches of their emotions, those fears and feelings are all that make sense to them. The irrational becomes rational. I know this from experience."

The child snorted her disagreement. "But will ye help me get rid of her?"

"Aye, but remember it's the dead of winter and the ground is frozen, so it will be harder to bury the body."

Ebby gasped, but Bella looked hopeful.

"A joke, Ebby," Lorna hurried to explain. "It was a joke."

"A joke?"

Lorna silently cursed whatever force had brought her back to the past without a seventeenth-century dictionary or thesaurus. "A jest. It was a jest."

Ebby relaxed, but Bella seemed disappointed.

Deciding it prudent to steer the child away from the option of murder, Lorna shooed her off the bed. "Away wi' ye now. While I rest, go be thinking about what it would take to convince yer da to boot Lady Murdina and her weasel of a brother out of the keep—without killing them, ye ken?"

Bella's eyes narrowed, and she bobbed her head. "I will think on it." She lunged forward and wrapped Lorna in a tight hug. "Frances and Hesther were right. Ye are the kindest of the kind." Then she skipped out the door, humming under her breath.

"Would it be all right if I sit in the window to let out yer skirts?" Ebby asked. "The light in here is so much better than in my room."

Lorna slid back down in the bed, curled over onto her side, and hugged the pillow. "What skirts? I dinna have any."

"Oh, aye, ye do." Ebby opened both doors of the wardrobe. "Just look at all ye have. Himself gave orders for the trunks to be brought out and the clothes altered to fit ye." She beamed proudly as she ran a hand across the neatly folded items and those hanging on the pegs. "I dinna think it will take much work at all to make all these yer own."

An uneasiness took hold as Lorna's suspicions grew. Even though she didn't want to hear the truth, she had to know. "Ye said he ordered the trunks brought out?"

Ebby nodded as she bit a thread, then plucked it out of the hem of the deep blue material bunched in her lap.

"So, I assume that means they had been in storage some-where?"

"Aye. In the tunnels and eaves off of himself's rooms." Ebby angled the material closer to the window and pulled at more threads.

There was no other thing to do but just say it. "Which wife did they belong to?" Lorna asked, inwardly cringing as she waited for the answer.

Ebby looked up from her work and smiled. "Both, actually. And fortune smiled upon ye, mistress. Both Lady Mariella and Lady Corinna, God rest their souls"—she crossed herself—"were tall, regal ladies. Much like yerself."

"Aye, fortune smiled on me, all right." Lorna covered her eyes again and stifled a groan. In theory, she understood nothing could be allowed to go to waste, but she did not want to wear the clothes of Gunn's dead wives. That was just…wrong. "Are ye certain that willna bother…himself?"

"Why no. The chieftain is the one who ordered them fitted for ye." Ebby fluffed out the material and smoothed a hand across it. "He wasna ready until now to see them put to good use again." She smiled. "'Tis a good sign, mistress. Our poor chief has struggled for many a year with all that he has lost."

"I am sure he has." Lorna rolled to her other side and curled into a tighter ball. Whether it was Mrs. Thistlewick's concoction, the burned bread, or the willow bark tea that had tamed her pounding head and churning stomach, she didn't know. But she felt loads better than she had. Except now, she was more aware of the worrisome knot in the center of her chest.

Life had gone so horribly wrong. Yet if it hadn't, she never would have met Gunn. At first sight, his handsomeness had struck her, but it wasn't his raw alpha maleness that held her attention. No. It was the uncanny ease of talking to him. Even though they had just met, it seemed like she had known him all her life. Like a long-lost friend she hadn't seen in ages who couldn't wait to catch up on all they had missed. How the devil could that be?

"Will ye wish to wash yer face and hands before ye change for the feast?" Ebby shook out the skirt and draped it across the back of the chair.

"Aye." Lorna pushed herself back to a sitting position. "I also need a visit to the toi—uhm…chamber pot. Is it here under the bed?" That was where it was usually stored in the history books she had read.

"Oh no, mistress. Here in the wash cupboard. See?" With her mending basket tucked under her arm, the maid opened a narrow door Lorna hadn't noticed in the corner on the other side of the wardrobe. "I already lit the candle for ye and put fresh water in the pitcher. More is warming in the kettle on the fire." She pointed at several covered crocks on the stand with the basin. "Mrs. Thistlewick's daughter makes the best soaps and herbals to keep yer lady bits and oxters fresh." Then she pointed at a chest squatting in the corner. "Top drawer has everything ye need to clean off after the chamber pot, and I stocked the bottom two drawers with rags for yer courses." Ebby beamed with pride. "Mrs. Thistlewick checked and said I didna forget a single thing, but if ye need anything else, ye will tell me, aye?"

"Aye," Lorna agreed softly, somewhat overcome by the seventeenth-century lady's room and all it entailed. The challenges of personal hygiene and her monthlies hadn't crossed her mind until now. Never had she missed her favorite deodorant and tampons so much in her life. And a toothbrush and toothpaste. Her mouth tasted like someone had shite in it.

"Is something wrong, mistress?" Ebby peered at her, her pale brown brows drawn together over her worried eyes. "Did I forget something?"

"No. Nothing wrong." Lorna shook free of the shocking realizations and motioned toward the short cabinet. "I am just not certain how to find the chamber pot. That sort of cabinet is new to me."

"It is a fine thing, is it not?" The maid hurried to it, lifted the top, and folded it over to the side. Then she pulled open one door and revealed a seat with a hole in it. "There ye be." She tapped on the door below it. "Down here's the chamber pot. Either Janie or Alice cleans it out four times a day. There's a garderobe on this floor as well. That way, if the need arises, ye dinna have to come all the way back to yer wash cupboard here. Is it not grand?"

"Grand, indeed." Lorna tried to sound impressed and grateful to have such a convenience built into her room. "Thank ye, Ebby. I think I'll strip down and have a good wash, since my last shower was yesterday morning."

"Yer last what?"

"Uhm…shower. That's what I call it when…I splash. A lot." Damning herself for using modern terminology again, Lorna backed into the water cupboard and tried to close the door.

Ebby stopped the door from shutting. "But do ye not need help with yer buttons and laces?"

"I am fine. Really." Lorna wrinkled her nose and tried to play off as being secretive. "I got lazy today and didna wear my stays." She offered a sly wink. "Dinna tell anyone, aye?"

"No stays?" The maid's mouth dropped open. "Ye must wear stays. A proper lass like yerself has to."

Lorna closed her eyes and leaned her head against the door. "I promise to wear them to the feast. While I wash, how about ye pick me out something to wear, aye? I trust yer judgment."

Ebby brightened like a sunrise. "I will, mistress. All will be ready when ye finish." She allowed the door to shut, leaving Lorna in the small, windowless room.

"Give me strength," Lorna said under her breath as she hiked up her skirts, shimmied her panties down around her knees, and sat on the wooden toilet. All the intricate realities of surviving in this era threatened to suffocate her. No toilet paper. No feminine hygiene products and dubious options to keep her armpits and other bits from getting ripe. She smacked her lips and ran her tongue across her teeth. And no feckin' toothbrush or toothpaste. Or coffee or tea. Had those even been discovered yet?

"One hurdle at a time," she told herself. "Just pee."

It took a minute or two to convince herself to release the stream. Once she did, she blew out a relieved breath, then twisted to open the drawer that supposedly contained the equivalent of toilet tissue. She found fluffy clumps of wool and bits of linen torn into small squares. One of those sufficed for what she needed, but then she wasn't sure what to do with it. Did everything go into the chamber pot, or was she supposed to put it somewhere else so it could be cleaned and reused?

"Oh, bloody hell." She opted for dropping the cloth down beside the chamber pot, hoping that would be all right until she confirmed otherwise.

A light tap on the door halted her in the middle of unlacing her stomacher. "What is it?"

"Once ye remove yer things, hand them out here so ye will have more room for yer washing."

"Okay."

"Okay?"

"*Bloody hell!*" She silently cursed herself for using that word again. "I will hand them out to ye straight away."

"Good, then," Ebby said, sounding a bit bewildered. "I shall wait right here."

"Thank ye, Ebby." Lorna huffed as she finished unlacing her jacket and slipped it off. She opened the door a crack and held it out. "Jacket and stomacher. Soon the rest."

"Merciful heavens," Ebby said from the other side of the door. "How did the seamstress manage such fine stitching?"

Lorna went still in the middle of unbuttoning the waistband of her skirt. She had never been one to lie, and explaining herself in this time was straining her creativity. "I dinna ken how she did it. Wondrous, is it not?"

"Aye, it is. I wish I could train with her."

"I wish we could both train with her," Lorna muttered. "Then we would be back in my time."

"What was that?"

"Nothing. Almost done. Do ye have a fresh shift for me too?" She had to keep the girl busy while she figured out a place to hide her bra and panties. If she stashed them in any of the drawers, Ebby or one of the other maids would surely find them. She couldn't keep them on. Not with the maid expecting to stuff her into stays and help her dress.

The walls were whitewashed stone and the rafters too high for her to reach even if she stood on the commode—although she wondered if they called them that yet. She vaguely remembered Mrs. Crowley having a book entitled *The History of Toilets* that said that they did not coin the term until the seventeen hundreds.

"Oh, who gives a shite," she said as she dropped to her knees and peered up under the table that held the water pitcher and basin. Her heart lifted as soon as spotted the reinforcement wedges in the corners. If she wadded up her underthings in the smallest ball possible, she could stuff them up between the wooden wedges and the underside of the tabletop. Tonight, once everyone had retired, she could rinse them out and hang them by the fire to dry. After that, she didn't have a clue what to do with them if Ebby insisted on helping her dress each day.

She filled the basin with water, wet a rag, and wiped her face. A pat on her hair confirmed it to be a ratty mess in dire need of brushing. Maybe Ebby could help with that. She opened the pair of crocks and sniffed them. The one with the waxy white paste had the faint scent of roses, and the other held what looked like olive oil but gave off a pleasing aroma of fresh lavender. She assumed the paste was the soap but didn't have a clue what to do with the oil. Moisturizer? Then she remembered Ebby's promise that one of the two would keep her lady bits and oxters fresh. Oxters? She hadn't heard that term for armpits in ages.

Desperate for something to make her mouth feel cleaner, she rubbed her teeth with the wet linen and wiped off her tongue. She had read somewhere that castle kitchens had herb gardens. Maybe they had some mint she could use.

"Any chance to get some mint?" she called out while testing the white paste on the back of her hand.

"Shall I fetch it now?" Ebby asked. "Cook is sure to have some."

"Later will be fine." Lorna wasn't comfortable about asking

the girl to *fetch* anything. "If I could have some before bed, that would be lovely." When she wet the white paste she'd smeared on her hand, it went all sudsy. She lathered the rag with the soap and washed and rinsed the major bits that threatened to become malodorous. Once she dried, she eyed the oil, cringing at the thought of rubbing the greasiness into her armpits. It just didn't seem as if it would be comfortable at all. "Ebby?"

"Aye?"

"This oil. The lavender-smelling pot."

"Has it gone rancid, mistress? I checked before I brought it up, but perhaps I missed it had turned."

"No, no. It hasna turned." Lorna caught her lip between her teeth, trying to come up with a believable way of asking about it. "I usually use powder." There. That sounded plausible.

"The powder drew damp and molded. We had to throw it out. There willna be any more for a while yet, what with this winter's dampness." The maid sounded as if she was pacing back and forth outside the door. "I like the powder better too. Sometimes the oil keeps yer oxters all slickery for most of the day."

Left with no choice, Lorna dabbed, rubbed it in the best she could, and prayed it worked. Of course, if Lady Murdina and her brother still reeked, no one would notice if she stank a bit. That thought consoled her. "I am ready to dress now. If ye will hand in the shift, I'll slip it on and then come out for the rest."

"I can help ye slip it on." Ebby opened the door and waved for Lorna to come out. "Do ye feel refreshed now?"

It would be rude to describe the way she felt, so Lorna just smiled and nodded while trying to cover her personal bits with her hands and arms. Stiff-legged and burning with self-consciousness, she stepped out and allowed Ebby to slip the shift on over her head.

"Now the stays, bum roll, and petticoat," she said.

"Not so tight." Lorna squirmed and sucked in a deeper breath before the maid collapsed her lungs completely with the bony stays.

"But the laces must be tight to hold yer lovely shape properly."

"I am more worried about holding the air I need." Lorna tried to expand her ribcage to keep Ebby from yanking the ties any tighter.

"As ye wish." Disappointment filled the lass's tone as she tied on the pockets and bum roll. "Up with yer arms and bend forward." She held an embroidered underskirt ready to slip over Lorna's head next. After tugging it down in place, she secured the waistband with ties. Then she added a rich burgundy wool skirt, matching jacket, and embroidered stomacher that matched the petticoat. She stepped back and smiled. "I knew that color would suit ye. Adds color to yer cheeks."

"Thank ye," Lorna replied, feeling like Ebby's favorite doll. A knock on the door gave her a surge of relief. "Come in."

"Ye are dressed, aye?" Bella called out from the other side. "Frances is with me."

"All I have left is to brush my hair." Lorna held out her hand for the brush, but Ebby cocked a brow and hugged it to her chest as though ready to defend it with her life. With a defeated huff, Lorna gave in and turned so the maid could start brushing.

The children filed in and gave her critical up-and-down stares.

When they said nothing, Lorna glared at the three. "If I dinna suit ye, keep it to yerself. 'Tis too much work to change into something else, ye ken?"

"Oh no," Frances piped up. "'Tis just that ye look so much nicer than before. Ye no longer look like a bedraggled rat pulled from the sewer."

"Frances!" Hesther bumped him aside, then offered a meek bow of her head. "He means ye dinna seem so travel-weary, mistress."

Bella covered her mouth and didn't say a word.

Lorna couldn't decide if the child was trying not to laugh or keep herself from saying the wrong thing. She cast a glance back at Ebby. "Did I really look all that bad?"

Ebby held the brush in midair, looking ready to panic. "Must I answer that, mistress?"

Lorna snorted a laugh. "I must have looked a sight, indeed. Cheers to Ebby for cleaning me up proper, aye?"

The trio of scamps breathed a collective sigh of relief and agreed with hearty nods.

After several hard tugs on her hair, Lorna held up a hand. "Easy now. My head's still a mite tender from the whisky. What are ye doing to me? It's too short to be done up into anything but a short ponytail."

The children exploded with peals of laughter, and Ebby stepped around to lock eyes with her. "A *ponytail*? Why, I have never heard of such. Why on earth would ye talk as if yer head was a horse's arse?"

The maid made a fair point. Lorna had never really thought of it that way before. "So, what exactly are ye doing with my hair?"

"Plaiting the sides, and I will pin the back into a proper bundle of curls."

Lorna rolled her eyes. "Carry on, but easier, aye? It feels like ye are about to pull me bald."

"Tender head," Ebby muttered.

"What was that?" Lorna waited to see if the lass would repeat it.

"Nothing, mistress." The hair taming continued, but easier this time.

"Make haste, Ebby," Bella said. "We need to get to the hall before Lady Cow does."

"Bella." Lorna shook a finger at the girl. "I know ye dinna like the woman, but if ye call her that in secret, ye might make the mistake of calling her that to her face. Would that make yer da proud?"

Bella adopted an appropriately crestfallen appearance. "He prolly wouldna like it." Her apologetic expression disappeared.

"But I dinna like her one bit."

"I understand, but ye have to be sly with the enemy, aye? Play along so they dinna suspect ye are about to best them." Lorna figured that angle might sit better with the youngling.

"Aye," Frances piped up. "Cruel she is, but she is nay a dullard. We will have to take care with whatever we do."

"All done," Ebby announced as she stepped around and pulled a small hand mirror from her apron pocket. "Does it suit ye, mistress?"

Lorna eyed her reflection and smiled. Ebby had indeed tamed her shoulder-length hair. "I love it, Ebby. Thank ye for making me more respectable." Now she most definitely looked the part of a seventeenth-century lass. She handed back the mirror and turned to the three fidgeting bairns. "Lead the way, my fine ones. Let us ready ourselves for this meeting with the enemy."

Bella grabbed one of her hands, Frances caught hold of the other, and Hesther brought up the rear.

"Now remember," Lorna said, deciding a warning was necessary. "We are to be polite to throw her off guard, ye ken?"

"But only till she attacks first, aye?" Bella asked.

"Aye," Lorna agreed. "We willna start the battle, but we will finish it." If Lady Murdina picked on any of the bairns, all bets were off and she had dibs on the mean woman.

CHAPTER SEVEN

"Y E KEN MRS. Thistlewick assigned Forsy to yer betrothed?" Jasper said.

"Lady Murdina and I are not officially betrothed." Gunn gave a nod. "And aye, I am aware of Mrs. Thistlewick's doings."

Jasper chuckled. "Not a more stoic nor obstinate maid exists. Forsy the Fierce may undo all the work the solicitor and I did to arrange this match."

"Yer work may be undone by any number of failures in the next thirty days. If we canna achieve an amiable enough balance, the union will not happen." Already, whenever Gunn thought of Lady Murdina, which was rarely, he felt himself recoil. Not a good reaction to a woman with which he hoped to sire a son.

"I would hate to see that happen," Jasper said, then lowered his voice and moved closer. "For when she leaves, she is sure to take her son's nursemaid with her."

Jasper's insinuations pricked like a thorn and stung like nettles. Gunn maintained a blank expression and kept his gaze leveled on the guests trickling into the hall. "It was my understanding that ye clashed with the nursemaid."

"Aye, we did at that. But there is a thin line betwixt love and hate." Jasper jutted his chin higher and smiled. "She called me an arse. I consider that high praise from that lady and admire her fire for saying it."

Gunn clenched his teeth so hard his jaws ached. A dangerously possessive stirring that should not exist took root in his chest. "What happened to yer interest in Esther Oliphant?"

"Esther Oliphant is still a prudent choice for a wife, considering the lands that would come with her." Jasper clasped his hands behind his back and rocked from heel to toe. "But a man can have more than one interest, ye ken?"

"Not in this keep." Gunn sidled a hard glare at his war chief. "I willna have the unrest of a wife and a mistress under the same roof."

Jasper tipped his head as though considering the warning, then stood taller and squared his shoulders. "Perhaps Mistress Lorna would be the better choice even without the dowry. Look at her."

Gunn followed Jasper's line of sight, then swallowed hard. He had already found the wee mouse quite fetching with her mussed hair and drab clothing. But now the comely lass had turned into a beguiling beauty. The deep burgundy dress not only brought out her eyes but also revealed the trimness of her waist and an expanse of tempting décolletage.

He stifled a groan, remembering her warm softness as she had slept against his chest. "The children hover around her like bees to a hive."

"I would be more than willing to hover around her too," Jasper said. "Seat her at the head table with us, aye? Next to me."

Gunn stanched the urge to backhand his war chief. "She sits with the children."

"As ye wish." Jasper shot a sly look his way. "Perhaps I shall sit with the children as well. To prove that I can be trusted to protect them as she does."

"Yer place is at the head table on the other side of our guests. Ye ken that well enough." Gunn glared at Jasper, daring him to challenge the unspoken order.

"What the devil's got into ye, man?" The war chief cast an incredulous scowl back at him.

Before Gunn could answer, a chill raced down the back of his neck, making every hair stand on end. He turned and discovered why.

Lady Murdina stood framed in the archway with a ridiculous feather sticking out of her auburn curls. He toyed with the idea of ignoring her, but it was too late for that. They had already made eye contact. Yet the infernal woman stood there, waiting for him to come to her.

She best learn early on that their relationship would never take that path.

He made a polite bow and ushered her forward with a wave of his hand. "Welcome to the feast in yer honor, Lady Murdina."

The hint of a scowl puckered her brow as she paused a half-second longer, then swept into the room with a grand flourish of her full skirts. "Good evening, m'lord. Everything looks delightful." She extended her hand and coyly tipped her head, waiting for him to take it.

"It is either Gunn or my chieftain. Remember, m'lady?" He took her hand and briefly bowed over it without leaving a kiss behind.

She withdrew it and pressed it to her chest beneath a locket dangling above the twin swells of her ample breasts. "Forgive me. I shall endeavor to do better, *my chieftain.*"

"Nothing to forgive, m'lady. I was merely reminding ye." He offered his arm and turned her toward Jasper before the man escaped. "Ye remember Sir Jasper?"

She curtsied low, as if trying to ensure they both had a clear view down into her low-cut neckline. "Indeed I do, and 'tis reassuring to know he fights at my future husband's side to protect him."

"Welcome, m'lady." Jasper offered her a curt nod then slid his gaze back to Lorna and the children. "I must speak with Edmond. Excuse me."

"Who is Edmond?" Lady Murdina asked, but Jasper had already slipped away.

Gunn glared at the war chieftain's back, silently damning him. "Edmond is second-in-command to Jasper. He is also Mrs. Thistlewick's grandson. He saw to the bringing in of yer trunks."

"Ah yes. I remember. The large, shaggy lad." She resettled her hand in the crook of his elbow and lightly swished her entirely too elaborate skirts from side to side. With a smile that he could tell was strained, she pointedly scanned the large room, and those already gathered. "I had thought there would be more present to meet yer future wife."

"It is the dead of winter, m'lady," he said, tugging her forward. Maybe if they walked, he would find their conversation easier to bear. "Not everyone possesses the means of traveling such as yerself and yer brother. By the way, is he not coming down?"

She made a disgruntled hissing sound. "He is still abed, nursing that infernal ague with Mrs. Thistlewick's brew. Each time he awakens, he downs more of the stuff, then goes back to sleep."

"Aye, her brew has that effect. 'Tis the amount of whisky she mixes with the honey and berries."

"At least it quiets him. I am grateful for that."

He maneuvered them toward the children's table, determined to interrupt Jasper's conversation with Lorna. "Would ye care to see to yer son and how he is settling in?"

She curled her upper lip as though smelling rot, then recovered and assumed another strained smile. "Of course. I would hope he is settling in as well as I am. I shall see to him." She fluttered a hand at the children. "Frances!"

The lad didn't even look her way. He was too involved in a conversation between Bella and Hesther.

"Perhaps he nay heard ye," Gunn said. The bustling of servants and the arrival of more clansmen coming in from their chores had increased the noise level of the hall.

"Frances!" she called more sharply.

The child snapped his head around and immediately paled. Lorna broke off her conversation with Jasper, rounded the table, and placed herself between the lad and his mother. "Good evening, Lady Murdina."

Gunn noticed the uncontrollable tic in Lady Murdina's left eye had returned. "Are ye unwell, m'lady?"

"No." She released his arm and swept closer to Lorna. "Where did ye come by those clothes? I willna have a thief in my employ."

Before Gunn could object, Lorna stepped forward, closing the distance between herself and Lady Murdina. "Ye should consider yerself a verra fortunate woman, m'lady, to have achieved a union with such a charitable man. Chieftain Sinclair discovered I had gone wanting and ordered that I would never go wanting again."

Gunn nearly groaned at the lovely Lorna's choice of words.

The corner of Lady Murdina's eye twitched harder. "Indeed," she replied with a low growl. "Step aside so I might see how my son is faring."

Lorna offered the woman an insulting bow and swept to one side.

"What is that sorry chit doing at this table?" Lady Murdina pointed at Hesther.

"Hesther is only eleven years old," Lorna said, her tone daring the woman to challenge her. "Much too young to be a proper lady's maid. She belongs with Bella and Frances."

"She belongs in the kitchens scrubbing floors or in the stables shoveling manure." The snarling matron swept forward until she stood toe-to-toe with Lorna. "Ye are naught but a servant yerself. How dare ye attempt to control those I own."

"Mistress Lorna does not control anyone," Gunn said. Every person present went still as his thunderous tone carried throughout the room. It was all he could do not to bare his teeth and growl. "This is my keep, and all that happens within it is by my command. Is that clear, m'lady?"

Lady Murdina bowed her head. "Aye, my chieftain."

"Besides," he continued, "Mrs. Thistlewick provided ye with a more experienced lady's maid. Did she not?"

The lady lifted her head but kept her gaze submissively lowered. "Aye, my chieftain. She did at that." She folded her hands in front of her waist and meekly returned to his side. "It appears we have gotten off on poor footing." She tipped her head again, almost fawning. "I blame my ill temper and beg yer forgiveness. I also beg that ye give me another chance. Travel has frayed my nerves. As have worries about my future." Lady Murdina offered a hesitant smile that was almost convincing. "Allow me to prove myself. To prove I am not the screeching harpy I have portrayed myself to be."

Gunn studied her, weighing her apparent remorse. Perhaps he had not given her a fair chance. His own behavior regarding her had been somewhat unfair as well.

A sense of shame filled him as he shifted his gaze to Lorna. He had not treated Lady Murdina properly because he had allowed himself to be distracted by something that could never be. He needed a woman he would never be in danger of loving. With all his being, he knew he would never love Lady Murdina. The mysterious connection that created an unexplainable, loving bond just wasn't there.

"Please, my chieftain," she prompted softly. "Gunn?"

"We will start anew." He took her hand and brushed a kiss across it, forcing himself not to recoil. "Come, m'lady. Let us take our places at the table, aye?"

"Indeed." She slid her arm through his, pressing close enough to rub the curve of her breast against his arm. "The hall is verra fine and toasty warm." As they walked, she wriggled against him like a stable cat vying to be petted.

He assumed she meant to be seductive, but all she really did was remind him of a drunk whore who had yet to be picked for the last tumble of the evening. Desperation reeked from her like rancid oil.

He pulled in a deep breath and eased it out. Such a mindset would not do. It was more than likely his fault she behaved the way she did. He had not kept to his word to give her a fair chance. Now was the time to do better.

He disentangled himself from her cloying grasp and pulled out her chair. "M'lady."

As she seated herself and arranged her voluminous skirts, he couldn't keep his gaze from straying back to the children's table. Renewed irritation surged through him at the sight of Jasper towering over Lorna as she sat with the younglings. That she kept a hand resting across her neckline in a demure attempt at modesty eased his frustrations somewhat. At least she was not whoring for the war chief's attention.

"Gunn?" Lady Murdina asked.

"Aye?" He turned back to her, damning himself for not paying attention.

"I asked if the dark-haired lass is yer daughter?" Her smile was strained, attempting to belie the indignation flashing in her eyes. The woman was not a fool. She knew his focus had strayed yet again.

"Aye. That is my precious Bella, my greatest treasure." Pride and so much more swelled in his chest as he watched his wee lass laughing and chattering with the other children and Lorna. "My heart overflows with joy at seeing her so happy."

"I fear I may have made a poor impression on her," Lady Murdina said. "Because of my outburst. Is that why ye chose not to introduce us?"

Actually, introductions had slipped his mind, but he wasn't about to admit it. He waved a maid forward to fill their goblets. "Knowing my Bella, I think it is better that we allow her to come to ye in her own good time." He gave himself more time to come up with a suitable tale by sipping his wine. "After all, if all goes as planned, ye will be the third woman to assume the role of her mother. She could be leery of becoming attached, then losing ye as she did her mother and first stepmother."

Lady Murdina appeared to swallow the lie as easily as she emptied her glass. When she noticed his amazement at her draining the goblet, she fanned herself while holding it up for more. "Forgive me. I am not a drunkard, I assure ye. My thirst is wretched from the trip."

"No doubt." Gunn motioned for the maid and took the wine pitcher from her. "We will keep this one here, aye?"

"Aye, my chieftain." The smiling young lass bobbed a curtsy then scurried away.

"All yer servants appear so…happy," Lady Murdina said, sounding thoroughly befuddled. She filled her goblet to the rim and took another long, deep drink. "How do ye manage it?"

"I treat them with the respect they deserve. They are not possessions. They are members of my clan. Family, in fact." He stopped her when she tried to refill his glass. "No, thank ye. I still have plenty."

She winked and set the pitcher down. "It is good to know ye are not one to drown in yer cups." Her eyes narrowed as her attention slid back to the children's table. "Yer war chief appears to fancy my son's nursemaid. Should he not be seated here at the head table with us?"

"I feel sure he will join us when the meal is brought to the table." Gunn glared at the war chief. Jasper had a tendency to push boundaries, but he had never been unwise enough to challenge an order. Gunn then forced himself to focus fully on Lady Murdina. "How is it ye came to find Mistress Lorna to look after yer son?"

The lady set down her goblet and refilled it again. "She came highly recommended by a friend of mine," she said without looking him in the eye. As she stared at the children's area once again, her eyes narrowed to slits. "Highly recommended indeed."

"I see." Gunn allowed himself a smug chuckle at the poor lie. "Did ye not think it odd when she came to ye with naught but the clothes on her back?"

"An eccentricity." Lady Murdina flipped a hand as though

shooing a fly. "My friend warned me the girl was odd."

"And that nay bothered ye?"

"Oh no," she said while taking another drink. Her voice echoed inside her nearly empty goblet. "When I saw how Frances immediately took to her, I didna give another thought to her strange ways."

"Interesting." Gunn leaned back in his chair and drummed his fingers on the arm. How could the woman be so foolish as to lie about something so easily disproven? Of course, he knew she would say Lorna was the one who lied. Yet Jasper had reported that Hesther and Frances relayed the same details that Lorna had.

He glared at Jasper, willing the man to meet his gaze. When the war chief did, Gunn gave a nod, then pointedly looked at Jasper's empty chair.

Jasper grinned and nodded back, remaining rooted to the spot beside Lorna. But he showed the good sense to hold up a hand as if begging for time to finish the conversation.

Gunn agreed with another slow nod.

"Is it not fortuitous that we each retain the same solicitor?" Lady Murdina caught the base of her goblet under the pewter plate set at her place. Wine sloshed over her hand and onto the table. "Oh dear, I have made a mess." She flipped her hand, slinging droplets everywhere.

"Dinna fash yerself." Gunn caught hold of her wrist and stopped her from making it worse while he signaled for a maid.

Lady Murdina leaned his way and smiled. "Ye are s-so forgiving." Her slurring set him more on edge, causing the hairs on the back of his neck to stand on end.

"Nothing to forgive." He released her wrist as a maid appeared. The lass dried the lady's hand, then tended to the table. After all that, he realized what the woman had said before the mishap. "Yer clan's solicitor is Liam MacGibbon?"

"Aye." The rosy-cheeked matron topped off her glass, took a deep drink, then topped it off again. "He is a fine man. Do ye not agree?"

"That remains to be seen. This is the first task he has done for us." The young man had not impressed Gunn, but their former solicitor, Gerald Macray, would be difficult for anyone to replace. The fact that MacGibbon handled both parties in this delicate matter of a marriage contract also raised his suspicions. How could MacGibbon honor the best interests of both sides?

Lady Murdina lurched closer. With a teasing smile, she plucked at his sleeve, then walked her fingers down his arm. "I think yer war chief is trying to get Frances's nursemaid into his bed."

"That would be unwise." Gunn tightened his fists, willing the man to come to the head table and sit.

"Now, now," she said in a lusty whisper, then slid her hand down to his thigh and squeezed. "'Tis a cold night. A bed is much warmer with two."

He took her hand and placed it firmly back on the table. "There are hearths in every room and more blankets than can be counted." He pushed back his chair and stood, glaring at Jasper, who offered an irritating tip of his head and held up his hand again.

It was all Gunn could do to keep from marching over there and dragging the rutting bastard back to his seat. That would not do. Instead, he went to the long cabinet against the back wall, fetched a bottle of port, then returned and plopped it down in front of Lady Murdina. With any luck, the stronger wine would silence the woman and send her to her dreams with the greatest of haste.

CHAPTER EIGHT

"NO, THANK YE. I am fine with just water." Lorna covered her cup for the third time. Her stomach had finally found an even keel, and she wasn't about to set it rolling again with any form of alcohol. The kindly serving lad seemed surprised, but moved on to fill the other tankards.

"I think ye will find the wine quite good, mistress," Jasper said. His earlier grumpy self appeared to have vacated the keep and left in its place an attentive man she might even call charming. "Or I can have port or whisky fetched for ye. After all, this is a celebration."

"No, thank ye. The water is fine." She cast a glance at the children. "Besides, I have to stay alert to watch after these three and anything they might get into." As if they would. She had never met three better-behaved bairns in her life.

"Aye, Miss Bella can be a sly one at that." He tugged on the wee lass's braid, then lowered his voice as though about to tell a ghost story. "She is Mrs. Thistlewick's ablest spy."

Bella sat taller, beaming proudly. "Mrs. Thistlewick and I keep the clan safe the only way we know how. Dinna ye worry about our ways, Jasper."

"Ye need to spy on Lady Murdina and her brother," Frances

said. "Never trust them." He turned to Hesther. "Aye, Hesther?"

The timid maid agreed with a hesitant dip of her chin. "Aye."

Lorna found it strange that Frances addressed his mother as though he worked for her. The only time she had ever heard him call the woman *mother* was in the carriage, and that was at Lady Murdina's insistence.

Before she could ask why, Bella thumped her knuckles on the table. "Ye best take care, Jasper. Da is giving ye one of his fearsome looks."

Lorna looked across the way at Gunn and almost laughed. "Oh my. I hope ye dinna burst into flames from that glare. Ye best see what he wants."

"I ken well enough what he wants." Jasper offered a respectful nod in the chieftain's direction.

Poor Gunn. He looked so miserable there at the head table with Lady Murdina. Lorna felt sorry for his predicament. Well. Somewhat so. After all, he had brought it on himself.

A wee bit of jealousy nipped at her too. If she sat up there with him, she felt sure their conversations would be grand. He was so…

Leave it, she warned herself, tensing against the thought. Surviving in this time was the priority—not wanting something out of reach. The man had clearly said he wanted nothing to do with anyone he might ever care about. Besides, after the mess with Patrick, it wouldn't hurt to be alone for a while.

Bloody hell, she wished she could find a way back to her friends and the shop. She did not belong here, and burned with the intense feeling that she had fallen from the proverbial frying pan into the fire.

"What does the chieftain want?" Frances asked, pulling her from her thoughts.

Jasper leaned closer and gave the lad a conspiratorial wink. "Someday, I will explain it to ye. But for now, I best be taking my seat at the head table." He scooped up Lorna's hand and bowed over it. "I look forward to speaking more with ye, mistress."

"Thank ye, sir." Lorna gave his calloused hand a squeeze, unsure what else to do. "Maybe ye are not such an arse after all."

He rumbled out a laugh that made his cheeks even ruddier than his reddish-blond beard. "Aye, I am. But I have a good side too. Reserved for those I choose to share it with." He glanced back at the head table again, then shook his head. "But now I must go. I shall seek ye out later, aye? After the meal. Once the music starts."

"That will be nice," she said, for lack of a better answer. As he walked away, she turned to Bella. "How long do these things usually last?" She had hoped to see the bairns settled as soon as the meal ended, so she could sneak back to her room and collapse—emotionally as well as physically. She deserved a proper breakdown after everything that had happened.

Bella shrugged. "Depends on Da. From that scowl he is wearing, I am surprised he hasna sent everyone out of the hall already. He isna happy at all." Then she brightened. "Course, if he stays all growly, that will make our plan to get rid of *her* easier."

Lorna wasn't so sure about that. The way Gunn had spoken earlier in the library clearly conveyed he was determined to marry a woman he couldn't stand. And he obviously did not like Lady Murdina.

She studied the pair while picking at a crusty roll Bella handed her. Lady Murdina wanted Gunn. Badly. Several times, she rubbed on his arm and leaned close, fawning like a cat in heat.

A bit of guilt flittered through Lorna at the pleasure she got from Gunn, subtly yet firmly, setting the woman's hands aside. Once he actually leaned away, dodging her when she tried to rest her head on his shoulder.

Lorna set the bread on the edge of her plate, picked up a slippery bit of boiled carrot, and popped it into her mouth. Savory and sweet. Quite nice, actually. She nodded at the head table, then gave Bella a dubious look. "We may have our work cut out for us," she said. "He seems pretty dead set on marrying someone he canna tolerate. He's miserable, yet he sits there."

"Aye, but he gave himself a month to get out of it, remember?" Frances said while pushing his carrots away as though they were poison.

"Yes, but there's his manly pride and all that." Lorna ate another carrot, then reached across and edged Frances's vegetables back in front of him. "I dinna think Gunn will oust her no matter how miserable she makes him. It is almost as if he thinks he deserves her hellishness. Like punishment or something."

"Gunn?" Bella repeated in a teasing singsong.

"He told me I could call him that." Lorna wrinkled her nose. "But I should not have done it in front of so many." She leaned over and bumped shoulders with the child. "Help me remember not to do that anymore, aye?"

"Lady Murdina would burst her seams were she to hear it," Hesther said.

Lorna winked at the lass. "Then we should reserve that weapon for the perfect time."

"Ye ken that Jasper fancies ye?" Bella said while slipping a morsel of meat to a hound under the table. "But we canna let him know our plans. 'Twas him and the new solicitor that found her." She leaned to one side, stretching to feed another dog that had joined the first. "Do ye fancy him?"

"I dinna fancy anyone." Lorna tried not to be obvious in her staring at Gunn. Bella was a sharp lass. She would surely notice. "I am a nursemaid. Not a husband hunter."

"A husband hunter," Frances repeated with a snorting giggle. "That's what Lady Murdina is, and she's been on the hunt for a while."

"See how red she is?" Bella said. "Wonder what could be ailing her?"

"Too much wine," Lorna said. "Fair-skinned as she is, the drink makes her color run high."

The woman also laughed louder, talked louder, and pounded on the table when entertained by whatever she had just said. Gunn eyed her as if unable to believe the sight.

Jasper sat back in his chair with his head bowed and a hand over his eyes. Lorna felt sorry for the war chief turned matchmaker. As a ruddy ginger, his skin always seemed a little red, but at the moment he could pass for a boiled lobster. "Will Gunn…er, I mean, the chieftain punish Jasper for picking her for the arranged marriage?"

"Jasper is kin, so I dinna think Da will kill him," Bella replied. "But they have been known to spar a bit to settle their differences."

"Spar with each other?"

"Aye." The child held up her fists. "Fight it out, ye ken?"

"Maybe we should go over and coax Lady Murdina to retire to her chambers?" Lorna suggested. She leaned over and looked at Hesther. "Ye know her best. Reckon Bella and I would be able to get her to go?"

Hesther's pale blue eyes flared wide with fear, and the young lass seemed to shrink into herself. "I dinna ken. Sometimes the drink makes her even more filled with hate."

"Lovely." Lorna rose from the bench. "We need to try. For the chieftain's sake, aye?"

"She was his idea," Bella said.

"I know. But I hate to see him suffering." Lorna tugged on the girl's sleeve. "Come on. A good daughter always saves her da."

"Did ye always save yer da?" Bella stayed close as they wove their way through servants and tables to get to the head of the room.

Lorna swallowed hard and forced a smile. "I would have if I had ever known him."

"Did he die in battle?"

"Aye." No harm in the lie, and better that Bella not hear the ugly truth. Lorna paused a few feet from the head table and leaned down to level her gaze with the child's. "I am going to introduce ye to Lady Murdina, and then we need to figure a way to get her to her rooms."

"I could tell her she looks like the devil from all that wine."

"Tempting. But we better not. Remember what Hesther said about her becoming a mean drunk?"

Bella shrugged. "What then?"

"I dinna ken." Lorna straightened and took her hand. "I will think of something. Just go along with whatever I come up with, aye?"

The lass cast a sly glance at their objective and nodded. "Aye."

Lady Murdina didn't notice their approach. She had one eye shut, and her upper torso slightly swayed from side to side as she concentrated on hitting her glass with more wine.

Gunn rose from his seat and met them before they reached the table. His tense expression displayed a mixture of relief, embarrassment, and grave anxiety.

"Bella wanted to get the introductions over with, and then I thought we might help Lady Murdina to her rooms." Lorna offered him a sympathetic look and lowered her voice. "We didna think ye would mind if we stole her away."

"Dangle a keg of wine in front of her," he said through clenched teeth. "She would follow that straight through the gates of hell."

Lorna couldn't resist getting in a jibe. "Just remember—ye are the one who invited her."

Bella bobbed her head in agreement. "And dinna be blaming Jasper. He just did as ye bade him."

"Arabella." Gunn's tone indicated he was not in the mood for taunting. "Not tonight."

"Out of the way, so we can save the day." Lorna cast a glance toward the shadowy alcove beneath the gallery. "Over there would probably be safest."

"I cannot. Not in good conscience. I willna leave ye to deal with"—his gaze returned to his wife-to-be—"that."

Lorna pushed around him while motioning for Bella to fol-low. "Lady Murdina, I have someone here who would like to meet ye."

The woman thunked down her goblet, stretched her eyes open wide, then blinked twice. "The lovely Bella, is it?" She smiled and held out both hands. Her fiery cheeks reddened even more with the effort. "Come to me, child. Let me get a good look at ye."

Bella cast a leery glance up at Lorna.

She understood exactly how Bella felt, but they needed to do this. "I am right here," she said for Bella's ears alone.

The hesitant girl edged closer, then offered an impressive curtsy. "Welcome to Thursa, m'lady."

"Such a polite young miss." Lady Murdina caught hold of Bella's hands and pulled her closer still. "I am so happy to meet ye and become yer mama."

"It is good ye are here," Bella answered stiffly.

Lady Murdina peeled out a happy squeal and scooped the girl up into a tight hug. "Such a lovely child!"

Bella wriggled and twisted, fighting the bulging breasts about to swallow her face. She tried to push away, but the matron didn't seem to notice—she only squeezed the child tighter.

Lorna couldn't stand it any longer. She rushed in and pried Bella free of the lady's embrace. "We thought we would walk with ye to yer rooms, m'lady. The hour grows late."

Lady Murdina frowned, then jerked around and peered at the candelabrum on the table. "Does it? The first set of the feasting candles has only burned halfway down."

"But that is the third set, m'lady," Bella said. She backed up another step, pressing into Lorna's skirt and holding tight to her hand. "Mistress Lorna is right. The hour grows late, and we are weary."

Lady Murdina squinted at the lass, then lifted her gaze to Lorna. Puzzlement wrinkled her brow. "The third set, ye say?"

Lorna nodded even though she had no idea what feasting candles were or what they meant. "Aye, m'lady. The third set."

The red-faced woman stole bobbing glances all around the

room. "Where is my husband-to-be? I must bid him good evening." Then a sly, calculating smile twisted her mouth. "Perhaps he would like to escort me to my rooms."

"Forsy shall escort ye," Gunn said from so close behind Lorna that it startled her. "As is proper."

"Come, mistress," said the burliest woman Lorna had ever met.

Lady Murdina puckered an unhappy pout as she tried to rise from her chair. She teetered to one side, then tumbled to the floor.

"Oh dear." Lorna hurried to help her up, but it was as though the woman had gone boneless. "Help me out here, m'lady." A grunt escaped her as she tried to lift the matron by hooking her arms under hers and pulling. "I canna carry ye."

The inebriated lady responded with a howling wail. "No. I am staying here until I die, because he will never marry me now." She cast a pitiful glance up at Lorna. "I dinna always drink like this. 'Tis nerves that have undone me. I am so afraid he willna like me." More guttural sobbing made her flounder even more. "And I was right. H-he hates meee."

"Oh bloody hell. Just what we need. A crying drunk." Lorna turned to Bella. "If they have eaten their fill, can ye take Hesther and Frances up to yer floor? This is not going to be pretty."

"I want to stay and watch." Bella's eyes flashed with mischief.

"Arabella." Gunn bent to his daughter's level. "Do as Mistress Lorna bade ye."

"Aye, Da." Crestfallen, the wee one turned to go, then paused and looked back. "Mistress Lorna?"

Still trying to drag Lady Murdina up from the floor, Lorna paused and twisted to peer over her shoulder at the child. "Aye?"

"Ye will come by and tuck us all in?"

Lorna's heart swelled with a warmth she hadn't felt in a long while. "Aye, my wee one. I promise."

Satisfied, Bella skipped away.

Lady Murdina blubbered louder. "She likes ye better than

me!"

"I have had more time with her," Lorna said while renewing her efforts to get the woman upright. "Come on now. Ye are making a scene."

"Nobody likes me," Lady Murdina wailed.

"Forsy!" Gunn barked. "I dinna care if ye have to drag her out by her heels. Take her from here. Now."

The maid lumbered forward, pulled Lady Murdina up with ease, and looped the woman's arm across her shoulders. "Come now, m'lady. Off to yer bed."

Gunn's future wife wailed even louder as Forsy half dragged, half carried her away.

"Wow," Lorna said as she watched her go.

"Everyone out!" Gunn bellowed. The command rumbled to the rafters. "This feast is over."

Lorna kept her gaze lowered as she turned and tiptoed away.

"Stay, Mistress Lorna," he growled, then cleared his throat. "Please," he added in a much softer tone.

She clasped her hands in front of her, waiting and a little confused. Why did he want her to stay? She glanced around, watching while everyone else scurried in all directions. The great hall cleared with amazing speed. Soon, every person in attendance, servants included, had vacated the room, leaving the tables littered with half-eaten food and even a few overturned glasses. The trio of hounds Bella had slipped nibbles to jumped up onto the benches and helped themselves to the scraps. Those three would sleep well tonight with their bellies filled to bursting.

"My chieftain." Jasper re-entered from the stairwell that Lady Murdina and Forsy had used to make their exit.

"I said I wanted everyone out." Gunn angled a hard glare at the man, then bared his teeth. "That includes ye."

Jasper bowed his head, his hair glinting like shining copper in the torchlight. He held out a hand toward Lorna. "If ye would allow me to escort ye to yer floor, I would be honored, Mistress Lorna."

"She stays," Gunn said before she could answer. "Now leave."

The war chief's eyes narrowed to slits and his jaw hardened, but he acceded with a slow nod. "As ye wish, my chieftain." Then he turned with the stiff formality of a marching soldier and strode away.

"It really isna his fault," Lorna said softly. Poor Jasper. As Bella had said, the man was just following orders. "She probably fooled him into thinking she was good marriage material."

"I want her gone at dawn's first light." Gunn stormed back to the head table and glared downward. He worked his jaw as though gritting his teeth. "Her, her brother, and all who came with her. Packed and gone."

"Well, that's a bit insulting." Lorna rounded the table and forced him to face her. "What the devil did I do to give ye the red arse?"

He flinched as if she had slapped him. "I didna mean ye had to leave. Of course *ye* may stay."

"And so ye intend to doom poor wee Frances and Hesther to Lady Murdina's wrath when she is told to hit the door?"

"I canna force the woman to leave her son and maid behind."

Frustrated, she pointed at him, the tip of her finger coming within an inch of his nose. "If ye make those helpless bairns leave, I go with them." Before he could speak, she continued, "Besides, ye said the woman had thirty days to see if she fit this imaginary mold ye have in yer head. Did it ever occur to ye her drunkenness could be because of nerves? Did ye not hear what she said about fearing ye would never marry her?" Lorna had to buy Lady Murdina extra time. It was the only way she could save Frances and Hesther.

He stared at her with a heartbreaking expression of defeat. So much pain shone in his eyes. So much loneliness and suffering. Lady Murdina didn't deserve the right to cause him even more misery. He deserved happiness and love.

Her heart hitched with a dangerous twitching.

Without thinking, she reached out and touched his cheek, cupping his face in her hand. His close-cropped beard was softer than she had imagined it would be. "Dinna decide anything tonight. Too much has happened. Ye need the calming freshness of a new day to look at the situation with clear and logical thinking."

He covered her hand with his and pressed it tighter to his cheek. Then he reached out and slid his hand along her jaw, hooked it around the back of her neck, and pulled her so close that a thread couldn't slide between them.

"I know what I need," he rasped, holding her captive in his gaze.

She struggled to breathe and hold herself back. She so wanted to pull him into the kiss they both needed so badly. But she couldn't. Not again. "I will never be the *other* woman," she whispered. "Nor will I be with anyone unwilling to commit themselves to me the way I deserve." She slowly shook her head. "I will never be taken for granted ever again. Not by anyone."

The pain in his eyes made the aching within her almost un-bearable. He pressed his forehead to hers. "Ye deserve all that and so much more, my wee mouse. I wish I was the man to give it to ye."

She framed his face with her hands and made him look at her. "Ye dinna have to suffer a marriage made for breeding purposes only. Why do ye insist on keeping to this miserable path ye have set?"

The weariness of years of pain aged him before her eyes. "Because I didna die when the fever swept through the clan, but my dear Mariella did. And I survived Corinna and my son—both died because I dared to love a second time. Ye have no idea how much I fear that Bella will soon share in the curse that takes away everyone I care about."

"That makes no sense," she said. "If Lady Murdina bears ye a son, will ye not love him as much as ye love Bella and yer wives who have gone before ye?"

His expression hardened. "No. I will keep myself distant from him. For his own protection."

"Ye care about everyone in this clan." How could he not see the insanity of what he said? "I have seen the way ye are with everyone from the lowliest servant all the way up to Jasper. They dinna appear cursed. What ye fear is not reasonable."

"Ye dinna understand." He stepped away from her, went to his chair, and collapsed into it. "My dying mother placed this curse upon my head. This fear of mine is not imagined."

Sensing he needed to share this deeper glimpse into his plight, she moved to the chair beside him and sat. "Why would a mother do such a terrible thing to her own son?"

He stared off into space, seeing nothing. "Toward the end of her life, she reverted to the old ways. Dangerous ways."

"I dinna understand."

"By the time I became a man"—he drew in a deep breath and blew it out—"she had become troubled. Her mind was not right." He slowly shook his head. "She walked the halls at night, never sleeping, and began calling herself an oracle. A practitioner of the ancient ways." He shifted and locked eyes with her. "She dabbled in the darkest mysteries of the spirit world. Curses. Sacrifices. When people died, the clan demanded that my father and I end it."

Lorna rested a hand on his arm. His tense muscles rippled with the pain of his story. "If ye dinna want to go on, ye dinna have to," she said quietly.

He scooped up her hand, pressed a kiss to it, then rubbed it against the soft springiness of his short beard. "No. I need to speak of it."

She squeezed his hand and waited for him to continue, dreading what he was about to say.

"Before we lit the fires for her burning..." He paused, frowning as though trying to remember the horrible day. "She uttered words I had never heard before. Babbling that made no sense." He paused for a drink of wine, then stared down into the cup. "As the flames rose around her, she laughed and proclaimed that whoever I loved would die before I did." After another drink, he slid the cup back to the table. "She cursed me to outlive every love I would ever know and die alone in a bed cold as stone."

The terrible tale both astounded and terrified her. His mother's insanity mistaken for witchcraft? And then they put the poor woman to death? How could they bring themselves to do that?

She struggled to think of something to say. He and his father had apparently done what they felt they had to do, but it was so hard to comprehend. It also reinforced that she needed to watch what she did and said. Her life depended on it.

But her heart went out to him. This era's lack of knowledge about mental illness had not only cost him his mother, but also any peace he might know for the rest of his life.

"Words only have power if ye believe in them," she said. She squeezed his arm, wishing she could help him overcome the ugliness of his past. "A curse canna touch ye if ye dinna give it that power."

"It has already touched me thrice, my brave mouse." He pushed up from the chair, walked behind it, then leaned against its ornately carved back. "I have learned my lesson." He bounced a fist atop the wood and gave her a smile that held no happiness. "Thank ye for calming my rage. Lady Murdina may stay the remainder of her thirty days." He huffed a bitter snort. "Besides, knowing Jasper and the solicitor, if I pass on her, the next one will be even worse."

The hopeless despair in his voice made her want to cry, and she prided herself on never giving in to tears. Blinking against their threat, she went to his side. "Bad things happen to good people. Not because of curses, but because the world just sometimes…sucks." She knew that terminology wasn't good, but what else could she say? "We live in a broken place, and all we can do is grab every minute of joy that comes along. It hurts like the devil when it leaves us. But at least we can enjoy it for a little while, ye ken?" She took hold of his shoulders and ridiculously tried to shake the miserable man. "Dinna fear the joy. Ye have to hold tight to it and squeeze every bit of wondrousness out of it that ye can."

With a sad smile, he cupped her face in his hand again. "Go to yer rooms, wee mouse, before ye make me care about ye even more and risk yer life."

"Ye are a fool," she whispered, wanting so badly for him to open his eyes and see.

"Maybe so." His hand dropped away, and he walked off, leaving her there, watching him make his way out of the room with a determined stride.

A frustrated huff escaped her, and she shook her head. "Why will he not see?"

"What is it ye wish him to see, Mistress Lorna?"

With a squeaking gasp, she whirled around. Jasper stood within an arm's length of her. "Bloody hell, Jasper! Are ye trying to scare me to death?"

He chuckled. "Nay, mistress. I merely returned to ensure ye were unharmed."

"The chieftain would never hurt me."

The war chief grew serious. "The man has been under a great strain the past several years." He resettled his footing and glanced around, as though uncomfortable with what he was about to say. "He is a good man, mistress. But then, his mother was once a good woman."

"Just because she lost her mind doesna mean he will." Lorna refused to dance around the subject. "And I dinna think it verra nice or loyal for ye to be speaking about him in such a way."

Jasper glared at her, clearly perturbed. "Dinna question my loyalty to my chief. Not ever. I will serve the man until my dying day."

"Good." She didn't care that she had irritated him. It wasn't the first time and, more than likely, would not be the last. "If ye dinna mind, I shall bid ye goodnight. It has been a verra long day, and my bed is calling."

The corner of his mouth twitched as he offered his arm. "Allow me to escort ye, mistress. As atonement for rubbing yer fur the wrong way."

The teasing glint in his hazel eyes made her laugh. She accepted his offer, then fell in step beside him. "We are flint and steel, my friend. We clash and the sparks fly."

"Sparks often cause flames, mistress."

His suggestive tone rippled across her like a hesitant caress. He was testing the waters. She managed a noncommittal smile. "Verra true." She didn't want to encourage him yet didn't want to put him off entirely either. No connection sparked between them, but he seemed nice enough. However, tonight was not the night to make that decision. The whirlwind of the day's events still had her head spinning. "We shall have to take care with our flint and steel, aye?"

"Or not," he said softly as they came to a halt on Miss Bella's floor. He ever so gently tipped her face up to his and leaned in closer. "What say ye, Mistress Lorna?"

Before she could come up with a way to avoid the kiss without offending him permanently, the nearest door burst open. Frances exploded into the hall, waving both arms. "A fearsome spider has Bella trapped! Hurry! Ye must come and help!"

Thank heaven for spiders. Lorna shooed the boy onward. "Show me!" She didn't risk a backward glance at Jasper but prayed he wouldn't follow.

"This way, mistress!" The lad led her through the solar, across the library, and to the closed door of Bella's bedchamber. "Dinna be thinking I was in there, Mistress Lorna," he hurried to explain. "I heard her scream from my room."

"I wasna thinking anything ill of ye," she said. "Ye are a true gentleman for looking after the lasses."

"I shall run and tell Sir Jasper that Bella needs ye to console her." He scooted around her and took off like a shot.

Suspicions rising, Lorna turned and watched the lad disappear. "I smell a sneaky wee rat." She rapped on the door, then eased it open. "Bella?"

Bella stood at the foot of her bed already changed into a fresh shift. "Thank ye for coming to tuck me in," she said with a not-so-innocent smile.

"Where is the spider?"

The youngling's eyes rounded even wider. "What spider?"

Lorna held up a finger. "Hold that thought." She stepped back to the door and cracked it open. "Frances? Could ye come in here, please?"

With more color in his cheeks than she had ever seen, the lad reappeared. "Aye?"

She waved him inside and pointed for him to stand beside Bella. "Who came up with it?"

"With what?" Bella asked.

Arms folded across her chest, Lorna waited. Instinct told her that if she gave them enough rope, one of them would hang themselves.

"It was Bella's idea," Frances confessed. He lowered his gaze and stubbed the toe of his shoe into the carpet. "But I didna think it a bad one."

"Is something wrong with Jasper that I should know about?" She appreciated the interruption but wasn't so sure the children needed to know that.

"Da said Jasper plans to marry Esther Oliphant come spring." Bella stamped her plump little foot. "If'n he is to marry another woman, he should not be kissing ye."

"Ye are absolutely right." Lorna moved to the large bed and patted it. "In wi' ye, miss." She shifted her gaze to Frances. "Ye are not in trouble. Stop holding yer breath and go to bed. I will be in to tuck ye in proper in a bit, aye?"

The lad exhaled with a loud whoosh, then scurried out of the room.

She helped Bella settle under the covers, then sat on the edge of the bed. "Thank ye for the information about Jasper."

The child smiled as she snuggled deeper into her pillows. "I am glad ye understand."

"I do."

Bella reached over and patted her hand. "Are ye sad about it, though?"

"No." And she wasn't. She hadn't felt drawn to Jasper as she had to… Well, that didn't matter. Gunn was a lost cause. "I am verra tired. It has been the longest day of my life."

"Tomorrow will be better," the young lass promised. "Mama always told me that."

Lorna leaned forward and kissed the child on the forehead. "Yer Mama was verra wise. Goodnight, Bella."

With the suddenness of a cat's pounce, the little girl wrapped her arms around Lorna's neck and hugged her tight. "I have a plan, Mistress Lorna. Dinna ye worry about anything, ye ken?"

Lorna hugged her back, almost choking on the rush of emotions filling her. "I am glad. That will help me sleep better." As she made her way to Frances's room, she wondered what the wily nine-year-old had in mind.

CHAPTER NINE

"THERE WILLNA BE any festivities or parties of any sort until Yule?" Lady Murdina eyed him as though he was the foulest beast that ever walked the earth. "None?"

"It has been a lean year, m'lady. Be thankful we decided to celebrate the twelve days of Yule at all." Gunn glanced her way, noting she pouted like an overindulged child.

"But I thought ye one of the most prosperous clans in all of Scotland?"

"Clan Sinclair is strong and prosperous because we handle our assets wisely and dinna burn through them with carelessness." If they married, and that became a larger *if* with each passing day, he needed to ensure the marriage contract inhibited Lady Murdina's use of all clan accounts.

"I feel the need to visit my daughter. Would ye care to join me and look in on yer son?" he asked, hoping Lady Murdina declined. While her behavior and temperament had drastically improved since the first day, they simply had little left to say to one another. She had no interest in books, music, or news and was obviously bored with winter life at the keep. If she had said it once, she said it a thousand times—she missed the excitement of Edinburgh and its entertainment.

Lady Murdina tapped her chin as if giving the invitation careful thought, then smiled and shook her head. "I think not. I promised Reginald some time today. He wishes to review the contract and ensure I understand all the clauses."

"Did Mr. MacGibbon not go over it thoroughly with the both of ye?"

She batted her eyes as if stricken with motes of dust, then a nervous laugh escaped her. "Of course—but that was several months ago, and details may have been forgotten."

"Details," he repeated, an ominous sense of doom weighing heavier in his gut.

"Aye, details." She offered a smile that appeared anything but innocent, then lightly patted his chest. "Tell the lovely Bella I asked after her. She is such a precious child."

"I will." With a formal nod, he turned and headed for the stairs, feeling as though he had just lost a very important battle.

How the hell had he ever thought this was a good plan to get an heir? Better to guide Bella into an advantageous marriage and pass the chieftainship to her husband. But it was too late now. The damnable contract and, more importantly, his word bound him to Lady Murdina for at least thirty days—or more precisely, three and twenty days, since a sennight had passed since her arrival. He prayed the clear skies held so Edmond could make haste in retrieving the apparently less-than-honorable Mr. MacGibbon. The new solicitor needed to explain why he had concealed that he also represented Lady Murdina's interests.

As Gunn neared his daughter's floor, piercing screams split the air. He vaulted up the remaining steps, burst into the hall, then skidded to a stop. The screams turned into shrieks of laughter that melted into shouts and squeals.

"What the devil?" He eased open the door to the solar connected to Bella's personal library and music room. The area was empty except for the trio of hounds that worshiped his daughter as if she were a goddess. The three lay stretched in front of the crackling fire, sound asleep despite the noise coming from the next room. He shook his head at the dogs. "Fine guards, the lot of ye. Full bellies and a warm fire turns ye harmless."

The oldest mongrel with the whitest muzzle lifted his head and acknowledged Gunn's presence with a yawn and a slow thump of his tail against the floor.

"Back to sleep, old man. From the sound of it, she is quite safe."

The dog readily complied.

Gunn continued on to the library, eased open the door, and peeked inside.

"Whoever reaches the window seat first wins!" Lorna called out. "But remember, if ye touch the floor, ye burn alive, then turn into an evil ghostie. Dinna let the boiling-hot lava get ye!" She stood on a small upholstered stool, clutching her skirts high enough to reveal a mouth-watering length of leg that reached above her knees.

Gunn swallowed hard and pulled in a deep breath. The shape of her long, slender calves made him ache to untie her stockings and slide them off while trailing kisses on what he knew would be her silky skin.

Nimble as a deer, she leaped to the nearest chair and crouched to keep her balance while laughing. "Ye better hurry! I am going to beat the lot of ye."

"Oh no, ye are not!" Bella shouted as she hopped from her chair to another strategically placed footstool. She turned and waved for Frances and Hesther to follow. "This way! Hurry!"

"No, this way!" Hesther giggled as she leaped from a wooden chair to a pillow on the floor. "The pillows are easier!"

"Aye, watch this." Frances hopped like a wee frog from cushion to cushion, almost reaching the windowsill first.

Ebby stood in the doorway of one of the bedchambers, her arms filled with linens. "Here, Mistress Lorna! More stones for ye to step on!" She tossed several cloths, and they landed on the floor close to Lorna.

Lorna jumped to one of them but stepped wrong and tumbled to the floor, laughing. "Oh no! I am melting!" She rolled back and forth, laughing as she kicked her feet like a dying bug.

"We win again!" Bella shouted with an impressive leap from her perch to the window seat.

Unable to hold back from the joyous time any longer, Gunn pushed the door open wide. "And what is all this noise about?"

"Careful, Da!" Bella called out. "The floor is lava!"

"I see that." He stretched and stepped from the threshold onto a pillow, then gave a sad shake of his head at Lorna on the floor pretending to be dead. "Alas, we have lost our beloved Mistress Mouse."

Lorna cracked open an eye. "This game is not for the faint of heart," she warned with feigned raspiness, then grabbed her throat and kicked her feet in one last death throe.

"Hurry, Da, and get here with us before she comes back as a ghostie and drags ye into the lava!" Bella and the other two hopped on the window seat, waving for him to hurry.

"Well, I canna have that, now can I?" With his longest stride, he stepped from pillow, to cushion, and then to cloth. But just as he stretched to step to another pillow, Lorna shrieked like a banshee, grabbed his ankle, and tripped him.

"I have ye now!" she wailed in a ghostly voice, as he slipped and dropped to the floor.

Unable to resist, he flipped her to her back and pinned her shoulders to the floor. "I willna go without a fight, wicked ghostie," he roared.

The children squealed and cheered, but he didn't hear them. His sole focus was locked on the smiling woman beneath him, her chest heaving with the laughter and exertion of the game.

"God help me," he whispered. "Ye are so verra lovely."

Her smile faltered the slightest bit, and her breathing slowed. "Are ye strong enough to banish old ghosts and overcome the evil they spread?"

He knew in his heart she didn't mean the game. "I dinna ken," he replied just as softly.

"Return to me when ye do ken," she whispered. The movements of her supple lips hypnotized him. Then she shrieked and grabbed his hair. "Ye canna best this ghostie!"

He understood the need to return to the game with the children looking on, but ached to do nothing more than sink into her embrace and lose himself in her touch. But for the sake of the wee ones, he bellowed, "Aye, foul fiend! I can best ye with my holy *sgian-dubh*." He pulled the dagger from the sheath strapped to his calf and held it like a cross in front of her face. "By all that is holy, begone!"

With one last dwindling wail, Lorna went limp. "I am done for," she rasped as her head rolled to one side.

"Da overcame the ghostie and saved us all!" Bella jumped down from the window seat and danced around them, cheering and clapping. Frances and Hesther joined in.

"And so ends this round of the floor is like lava," Lorna said. She winked up at him. "Ye may let me up now, Sir Ghostie Killer."

He refrained from groaning as he rolled back on his heels and helped her stand. "Quite the rousing game, mistress."

"Lorna. Remember?" An unspoken invitation, an invitation he wished he could pursue, sparkled in her lovely eyes.

"Aye, Lorna."

"Children?" Mrs. Thistlewick called from the adjoining room. "Cook sent up bread, fresh from the oven, covered in butter and jam."

The trio stampeded from the room to enjoy their treat.

Lorna brushed off her skirts. She glanced back at one of the bedchamber doors and frowned.

"What is it, lass?" He followed her line of sight but found nothing amiss.

"Ebby was just there. I was going to offer her some of the bread Cook sent up. There's always more than the children and I can eat."

"Ye think of everyone. Do ye not?" Kindness shone from her.

And in the few days since her arrival, all in the keep had taken to her. Including him.

"I try." Her earlier levity faded, and she gave him a quizzical look. "Did ye need something?"

He daren't answer that question honestly. Not when she had made it quite clear what she would say as long as Lady Murdina remained a possibility as the next lady of Thursa Castle. "I came to visit with Bella, since I had not seen her today."

She wrinkled her nose. "Can Frances and Hesther finish their treat first? Then I'll take them for a walk or something so ye can have alone time with Bella."

Alarm filled him that she thought he meant to roust her and the other children from the nursery. "Nay, lass. I would never have ye do such." With a sweep of his hand, he encompassed the delightful disorderliness of the room. "'Tis obvious she loves their company as well as yers. That was quite the rousing game I interrupted. What did ye call it again?"

"The floor is lava." She fidgeted in place, seeming suddenly uncomfortable. "Children love it."

"Indeed." He studied her, wondering what was so terrible in her past that made her uneasy about sharing the truth of something as simple as a child's game. Jasper had reported that not a soul in Thurso had ever heard of Lorna Merriweather. Nor was there any shop or trade that came remotely close to resembling such a thing as a used bookstore, as she had mentioned to the driver of the coach. "How did ye come to know about such a game?"

She shrugged. "I thought it up while we were looking over the book of maps ye gave Bella. The child loves studying the names of all the places." She started picking up the scattered linens, pillows, and cushions. "She is a brilliant lass. Ye should be quite proud."

"I am quite proud, indeed." He hurried to help push the chairs and stools back where they belonged.

Lorna opened a bedchamber door. "Ebby?"

"Aye, mistress?" The maid popped her head out another door farther down. Her eyes widened, and she bobbed a clumsy curtsy in Gunn's direction. "My chieftain."

"Yer mistress wants ye to share in the bread and jam if ye wish," he said.

Ebby shook her head, stole a glance at Lorna, then bobbed another curtsy at him. "Oh no. I must not. It wouldna be proper."

"It is more proper that ye share in the treat than it is for food to be wasted." Gunn sternly tipped his head her way. "Ye ken how I feel about wastefulness, and Mistress Lorna says Cook always sends up a generous tray."

"Ye dinna wish to get Cook in trouble, do ye?" Lorna said.

Gunn picked up on the slyness in her tone but refrained from smiling.

"Never, mistress! Cook and Mrs. Thistlewick are always kinder than kind to me." Ebby glanced back and forth between the two of them. "Ye are certain it would be all right?"

"Aye," he and Lorna said in unison.

Ebby giggled, then covered her mouth, embarrassment tempering the mirth dancing in her eyes. "The two of ye sound perfect together. In that case, I might enjoy a wee taste." She hurried across to the solar and quietly closed the door behind her.

"She is always so afraid of doing something wrong." Lorna smiled at the door as if able to see the maid through it. "Ye have a true and loyal person right there."

"Mrs. Thistlewick has tried to tell her if she wouldna try so hard, she wouldna bumble so much." He moved to the window seat and sat, hoping Lorna would choose his company over that of jam and bread. He patted the cushion beside him. "Tell me, mouse. What do ye think of Thursa now that ye have had several days to judge it?"

Her expression told him the seemingly innocent question did not fool her. Rather than sit beside him on the window bench, she chose the chair next to it. "Are ye asking me about those within in the castle, the structure itself, or"—she shot a shrewd look his way—"the one who tries his best to rule it all?"

"I dinna rule," he said quietly. "I lead."

The smile she gave him warmed his heart. Dangerously so.

"A humble man," she said. "Ye are a rare beastie, Gunn Sinclair."

"Perhaps. So, tell me, mouse. What think ye of what could verra well become yer new home?"

She stared downward, worrying a fold in her skirt. "In all honesty, I canna imagine living anywhere else right now."

"Right now?"

"Aye." She lifted her head, the careful smile she often adopted firmly in place. "Much has changed since the last time I was in Thurso. I dinna think I can ever return to what I once knew."

"Ye speak in circles, lass. Obscure as an unsolved riddle." He studied her. Instinct told him everything she said was true, but that was just it. When she spoke about herself, she did it yet managed to reveal nothing.

She rose from the chair, meandered over to the hearth, and stared down at the flames. "Maybe ye will just have to accept that about me, ye ken?" She turned and pinned him with a fierce gaze. "As I have accepted yer choices about yerself."

"Well played, mouse." As he stood, he decided to test her further. "Lady Murdina's behavior has improved. Mellowed, even. Do ye not agree?"

Lorna arched a dubious brow. "I agree snakes hypnotize their prey before striking the killing blow."

"Were ye not the one who informed me I should give the woman a second chance?"

"Because I did not wish ye tossing poor Frances and Hesther from the frying pan into the fire." She bit her lip. "Or griddle. Or whatever Cook fries with."

He couldn't resist laughing. "I take it ye dinna cook?"

"Only if ye like yer food with a healthy char on it." An endearing grin pulled at the corners of her mouth. "But getting back to the subject, if ye wish to boot Lady Murdina and her brother from the keep and let the young ones stay, I have no problem with that plan of action."

"I fear it is not as easy as that because of the wording of the contract." He joined her at the hearth, noting she kept a respectable distance between them. Admiration at her tenacity to stick to her word both impressed and frustrated him. "Even though I threatened to oust her at the time, one simple night of showing her arse in front of the clan would not be serious enough to dissolve the contract before it has run the thirty days."

"So, what would it take?"

He leaned closer and lowered his voice to a mysterious whisper. "Why do ye ask?"

"Because I want to know." She shot an irritated glare at him and tossed in a curt shrug. "Why else do ye ask something?"

"Why, indeed." He squinted as he tried to remember the contract's wording. "Deception." He turned to her and made a face. "Grave deception, mind ye. Not a harmless lie of vanity."

Lorna nodded. "Anything else?"

Unable to not tease her, he smiled. "What would ye suggest?"

"What I would suggest is immaterial, since the contract is already in force," she snapped.

Delighting in her mild show of temper, he offered an apologetic nod. "Verra true. But let us suppose ye could add any terminology ye wished. What would immediately dissolve the agreement?"

Eyes narrowing, she counted off on her fingers. "Cruelty to children or animals. Rude and or demeaning to servants. Lying. Cheating. Stealing. Acting like a complete cow."

Laughter rumbled from him. He couldn't help it. "Acting like a complete cow, ye say? And how would Lady Murdina manage that?"

Lorna eyed him like he was an utter fool. "Ask yer daughter. Bella would be happy to enlighten ye."

"I am sure she would." Still chuckling, he smiled while staring at the floor. "I dinna wish to give the wee youngling any false hope, though, so I dinna believe I will ask her." He risked a glance her way. "I ken ye feel the same."

Her smile had turned sad. "I dinna want ye making a mistake that will make ye miserable the rest of yer days."

"Ye know my reasons."

She rolled her eyes. "I know yer foolish reasons well and am sick to death of hearing of them. When ye constantly walk backward rather than forward, eventually ye step in yer own shite, ye ken?"

"Bear ye no sympathy for a poor man wishing to protect his heart from more pain?"

"I bear no sympathy for a man who willna let others help him overcome the pain of his past. Instead, he wallows in it, constantly throwing it in his own face." She caught hold of his arm and shook it. "I may not be a trained counselor, but I have dealt with them enough to know that ye must be willing to do the work. Ye have to battle yer inner demons and the evil that keeps dredging up the pain. Fight them. Whenever they rear their ugly heads, beat them back with all that is good and joyful in yer life. Cast them back into the shadows and drown them with happy memories."

Unable to help himself, he pulled her into his arms and crushed her to his chest. "Happy memories," he whispered, then took her mouth with his.

Instead of pushing away, she melted into him, kissing him back with a delicious intensity that shook him to his core. She tasted of honey wine and a fierce need that rivaled his own. Then she pinched the tender flesh under his arm, twisting it until it stung like a burning brand.

He released her with a jerk. "What the devil did ye do that for?"

Chest heaving and her lips swollen and red from the kiss, she shook a finger at him. Fire flashed in her eyes. "Daren't ye ever do that again! Understand? Not ever!"

"But ye kissed me back!"

With a flustered jerk of her hand, she said, "That is not the point. Ye grabbed me up and kissed me without my permission. Never again, ye ken? Ye belong to another woman, and I have already told ye I will never play second fiddle. Never."

"But if I did not belong to another woman?"

"Aye, but ye do." She wiped her mouth on her sleeve and put even more distance between them.

"But if I did n—"

"Stop saying that!" she interrupted. "Because ye do, and there's naught to be done about it until ye either find yer spine or grow some bollocks and kick her to the curb."

He glared at her, battling with the urge to scoop her up and carry her to his bedchamber or turn her over his knee and redden her arse for her. Or both. "Ye dare speak to yer chieftain in such a rude manner?"

"I dare to speak the truth to my chieftain." She angled her chin defiantly and stared him down.

"What are ye shouting about?" Bella asked from the doorway.

"We are not shouting," Gunn said. "We are merely having a heated discussion."

The child rolled her eyes. "Ye always say that when I catch ye arguing with someone." She shook a small finger at him, just as Lorna had done earlier. "Be nice to Mistress Lorna, ye ken?"

Before he could answer, Lorna swept past him, beaming a smile at the wee lass. "He is always nice to me, Bella. I have a temper and get loud when I feel passionate about a subject. He got loud to ensure I heard him over my own stormy emotions."

Bella eyed Lorna and then him as if weighing the explanation for a kernel of truth. "What were ye fighting about?"

Lorna gave him a wily tip of her head. "Go ahead. Ye have my permission to tell her."

Cunning minx. She knew good and well he would not wish to tell Bella the truth.

He blew out a frustrated snort and resettled his stance. Sparring with this woman required more intricate parries and thrusts than any battle. Then his gaze settled on Bella's cittern. "She suggested I bring in one of the stringed instruments from abroad, a fiddle, for ye to learn, since ye play the cittern with such ease." He paused, struggling to come up with a harmless lie. "But I would rather ye concentrate more on yer stitchery and yer Latin."

His daughter did not look convinced. Instead, she folded her arms across her chest and fixed him with a squinty glare. "Ye usually make up better stories than that when ye dinna want me to know what ye really said."

"Go eat yer jam and bread, aye?" He shooed the child away. "And dinna overfeed the hounds. Ye have already rendered them useless as protection for ye."

Bella turned to Lorna. "Will ye tell me?"

Lorna smiled and shook her head. "Not today, my fine wee one. Sometimes things must be left to the adults. Ye will understand once ye are grown."

With a frustrated huff and another roll of her eyes, Bella went back into the solar and closed the door behind her.

"Thank ye," he said. "I appreciate ye not turning my daughter against me."

"I would never do that. No matter what we might agree or disagree on, I would never do anything to harm the relationship between ye and Bella. It is a precious thing that I consider sacred." Lorna's smile turned sad. "I never experienced that as a child. I am glad the two of ye have such a close relationship."

"I am sorry." He lowered his head. "Both for the fact that ye never knew yer father and also for the way I behaved earlier. I should not have taken advantage of ye in such a brutish manner. It is my hope ye can forgive me."

"On one condition." The way she eyed him made him brace himself.

"And that is?"

"Think about what I said. All of it." She shook a finger at him. "Not just the part about kissing me without my permission, but the other stuff. About fighting those inner demons." True caring and concern shone in her eyes.

"Why?" he asked softly.

"Because I like ye." She moved past him and rested her hand on the door latch. "Now come on wi' ye. Have some jam and bread with yer daughter."

"What if there is not enough?"

She arched a brow and grinned. "Then ye can go to the kitchens and fetch more."

CHAPTER TEN

"**I** LIKE THE patchwork one the best." Frances picked up the multicolored kitten that looked like God had splattered it with every color of the palette. He snuggled it into the crook of his neck, smiling as it purred louder than the others. "He is a braw wee beastie."

"He is probably a she." Lorna angled her head to the side and caught a peek beneath its tiny tail. "Aye, ye have yerself a wee lassie there. Most calicos are." She scooped up its littermate, a mewing orange tabby. "We should name this one Jasper. They have the same color hair."

Bella and Hesther giggled, but Frances was too engrossed in cuddling his favorite kitten. Three more littermates of varying colors rooted and pounced through the loose straw while their mother looked on from her perch atop the gatepost of the stall.

Lorna gathered her cloak tighter around her and leaned back against the boards. The stable was by no means warm, but it was bearable, and they all needed some fresh air. It had been two weeks, or at least she thought it had, since her tumble back through time. She missed Gracie. Lonnie and Cybil. And her shop. And every convenience she had ever taken for granted. As she scratched behind the ginger cat's ears, she wondered what her friends were doing and what they thought about her disappear-ance.

"She has gone all sad again," Hesther whispered to Bella, but her hushed tone carried through the stall.

"I am not sad," Lorna said. Well, she *was* sad, but she wouldn't burden the children with it. "Sometimes when I am deep in thought, it makes me seem like I'm sad." A pitiful lie, but hopefully they believed it.

"Were ye thinking about our plan?" Bella asked after glancing around to be sure no one else was near. "That woman sure has been acting nice since she made a fool of herself at the feast."

"It willna last," Frances said. "She is a sly one. I am a warnin' ye."

"She has thirty days," Lorna reminded them.

Bella shook her head. "Six and ten now. She has been here a fortnight."

Lorna granted the child a proud nod. "Well done on yer mathematics." That also confirmed she had been in the past for two solid weeks. Between sidestepping Jasper's advances and trying to ignore her growing attraction to Gunn, the days had somewhat muddled together. "Did Freyda teach ye, or does yer da bring in a tutor?"

"Mama taught me a little reading. After she went to heaven, Mrs. Thistlewick helped me learn more reading and how to do sums." Bella dangled a piece of straw in front of a kitten, then giggled when it pounced. "All Freyda knew to teach me was stitching and how to mix dyes for threads."

"What about the cittern? Who taught ye to play so well?" Every evening, Bella played lively tunes on the instrument that looked like a pear-shaped guitar. Lorna hadn't known the name of the instrument until Gunn told her.

The wee lass shrugged without taking her gaze from the playful kitten. "I just play what sounds nice to me, and everyone seems to like it."

A natural-born musician. Lorna rose and brushed bits of straw from her skirts. "Well, ye play beautifully. Maybe ye could teach me how."

"Teach ye what?" Jasper said from behind her.

"Will ye stop sneaking up behind me?" Lorna shot him an irritated glare. "It is just plain rude."

The war chief cocked his head to the side and looked even prouder. "I nay sneaked. Ye merely failed to hear me."

She ignored that and turned back to the children. "Are ye ready to go in by the fire?"

All three shook their heads. "We are not cold," Frances said, holding his sleepy little calico closer. "'Tis warm here in the straw with the kitties."

"They have the good sense to come inside if they get cold," Jasper said. He slipped his hand into hers and turned her toward him. "Would ye care to go for a ride?"

"A ride?"

"Aye, a ride." He flashed a bright smile. "I know the day is brisk, but the horses need a good jaunt, and I thought ye might enjoy it."

"I canna ride." There was no getting around it. She had hoped the subject wouldn't come up until spring, but now it had.

"What do ye mean ye canna ride?"

"I dinna ken how to ride a horse." How much plainer could she put it?

"Then ye can ride with me," he said, his tone filled with innuendo. "We shall stay even warmer."

"Da said the messenger brought a missive from Esther Oliphant," Bella said with a sly grin. "Did ye get it, Jasper?"

The war chief's mouth tightened, making his ruddy beard twitch. "Aye, Mistress Bella, thank ye."

Lorna seized the opportunity Bella had so artfully provided. "Who is Esther Oliphant?"

He cleared his throat and shuffled in place. "Daughter to the chief of Clan Oliphant." He avoided her gaze, squinting at something on the other side of the stable.

"Jasper means to marry her come spring," Bella said as if on cue.

"I had considered it," the war chief said through clenched teeth. Then he offered Lorna a nod that begged her understanding. "But now, I am none too certain. My interests could verra well lie elsewhere."

"Yer interests should remain with Esther Oliphant," Lorna gently advised. "A chieftain's daughter is a fine match. One that shouldna be rashly tossed aside." She kept her gaze firmly locked with his, willing him to get the message and accept it. Jasper was a nice enough man, but theirs would never be anything more than friendship. She simply was not attracted to him.

He pulled in a deep breath, slowly released it, then nodded. "I see."

"Ye are a good man, Jasper." She softened the blow with a smile. "But I am not the woman for ye."

The tension seemed to leave him as quickly as it came. He gave her another teasing look and chuckled. "Ye dinna ken what ye are missing, lass."

"It is a loss I will strive to overcome." She patted his arm. "On wi' yer horse riding, aye? I willna keep ye."

"Nah, 'tis too cold after all."

A snorting laugh escaped her. "Ye are a true rascal."

He winked. "Ye have no idea." He peered over the side of the stall at the children. "Mistress Bella, yer da has locked himself in the library again. Been there all day, and none will interrupt him. The maids need in there to clean, and the lads have more wood ready for his fire that is surely burning low by now. Mrs. Thistlewick would rather ye be the one to interrupt him." A wider grin split his beard. "She says if he barks at her again for opening that door, she will box his ears for him."

"If ye had not brought that woman here, he wouldna keep hiding in there." The child placed her kitten back down in the straw and stood.

"The man is canny enough to find a reason to reject her anytime he wishes. He chose the wording of the contract. All he must do is use it." Jasper shot a side-eyed look at Lorna. "But it was brought to my attention that a certain someone informed him he should grant the lady the full thirty days."

Bella fixed an impressively accusing glare on Lorna. "Is that true?"

"If Lady Murdina leaves, then Frances, Hesther, and I have to leave with her." Lorna waited to see if that would soften the child's scowl. It did. In fact, wisdom far beyond the years of most nine-year-olds shone in her eyes.

"Could Da not keep the three of ye here and just send away the lady and her brother?"

"Yer father said he couldna come between a woman and her son." Lorna cast a smile at Hesther. "He might be able to keep Hesther here, but not Frances. Ye wouldna wish to doom the lad to that, would ye?"

"What have ye been plotting, Mistress Bella?" Jasper waved the child forward with a soft gruffness in his tone.

"Never ye mind," the youngling said. As she stepped out of the stall, she caught hold of Lorna's hand. "Ye need to come with me, since it seems he listens to at least part of what ye say."

"Hesther, Frances? Will the two of ye be staying out here with the kittens or coming inside?" Lorna hated leaving the two alone. They always seemed so vulnerable.

"We will stay a bit longer, mistress," Frances said without looking up. "Me and Hesther are used to the cold."

"Dinna stay out here too long," Lorna said, troubled by the child's response. Why were he and Hesther *used to the cold*? She turned to Jasper. "Are ye coming?"

He shook his head. "Our fine chief and I have already sparred enough for one day. I shall be busy tending to other duties unless I am summoned."

"Lovely." She squared her shoulders and gave Bella a warning look as they made their way across the packed snow of the bailey. "Yer da is sure to be in a mood if he has been in there all day. I wonder what happened?"

"Maybe Lady Cow showed her true self."

"Bella." While Lorna completely agreed with the moniker the child had chosen for the woman, she didn't feel right about condoning it. Somebody had to be the adult and take the high road.

The child rolled her eyes. "Sorry."

Lorna squeezed the wee one's hand. "I know it's hard to be kind to those who dinna seem to deserve it, but they are the ones who need it most." With a conspiratorial wink, she added, "At least until the woman does something so terrible that we must declare all-out war on her."

"She will." Bella bounced a self-assured nod. "Frances and Hesther willna speak about her much. Too afraid she will find out. But from what little they have said, the lady canna be *nice* long. 'Tis not in her nature."

"Well, let us hang up our cloaks and see if we can brighten yer da's mood." Lorna swept her cloak off, hung it on a peg just inside the kitchen door, then hung Bella's beside it.

"We could bring Da a treat." The child tipped her nose higher and sniffed. "Cook's bannocks smell near done, and Da loves them fresh from the ovens. 'Specially with butter and honey."

"A fine idea." The toasty warmth of the kitchen wrapped around them like a welcoming hug, making Lorna want to curl up in the corner and bask in it. The rich aroma of baking bread started her mouth watering. They wove their way through multiple baskets of root vegetables, a pair of maids churning butter, and the worktables where two more lasses rolled and kneaded dough.

Cook, the name she insisted everyone call her, stood in front of the large stone ovens, feeding sticks of wood into the center fire chamber. She was a large, elderly woman, and years of bending over pots had stooped her back. When she turned and noticed them, her bright red cheeks plumped with her cheery smile. "Good day to ye, lassies! I wondered why my wee mistress had not turned up for a bannock fresh off the fire."

Bella ran and gave her a hug, making the matron's eyes crinkle even tighter. "We were playing with Mosie's kittens in the stable!"

"Were ye now?" Cook gave a solemn nod. "Good mouser, that Mosie is. Glad to know she has some wee ones to train up to follow in her footsteps. If ye wish, ye can take her a nice saucer of cream later. I will have the girls set it aside while they are drawing the butter."

"Mosie will like that." Bella hugged her again.

"We thought we would take himself a nice tray of warm bannocks," Lorna said. "Sir Jasper informed us he's been in the library all day and is sure to be hungry."

Cook shared a dubious look then cocked a sparse brow. "Locked himself in there again, eh?" She shook her head and clucked like a nesting hen. Moving with a slow, hitching waddle, she motioned for them to follow her to the long stone bench beside the ovens. "Alice! Fetch some of the freshest butter and himself's favorite honey. And a pitcher of ale. The tray is over there. Hie wi' ye now whilst we pick out the best of the bannocks to brighten our chief's day."

"Yes'm." One of the lasses churning cream handed off the chore to the other girl working with her at the tall wooden casks. The remaining maid stepped between the churns and continued sloshing both plungers up and down to coax the liquid into releasing its solids.

"Shall I have one of the lassies bring it?" Cook asked as she finished filling the tray with Gunn's favorites.

"I can get the tray," Lorna said. "And Bella can carry the pitcher."

Cook approved with a smile, then lumbered back to the ovens. She cast a knowing wink their way before bending to check the fire again. "God be with ye for interrupting him."

"God be with us indeed," Lorna repeated as she led the way down the narrow corridor. Just as they turned into the hall that ended at the chieftain's sanctuary, Lady Murdina emerged from their target, closed the door behind her, then paused to straighten her clothing and hair.

An unjust pang of jealousy hit Lorna, then quickly shifted to an ominous spark of suspicion. It was Lady Murdina's smug expression. The woman appeared too well pleased with herself. As if she had just gotten away with murder. The lady's evil smile became even more menacing when she lifted her head and spotted them.

"My, my. What have we here?" The she-devil sashayed closer, her swishing skirts reminding Lorna of the sound of a guillotine blade cutting through the air. The conniving matron feigned delight, fluttering both hands while examining the contents of the tray. Without asking, she plucked the plumpest of the bannocks off the plate, ripped a steaming chunk from it, and popped it into her mouth.

"These are for my da," Bella said. She pushed between the tray and Lady Murdina. "And *only* my da."

"Now, Bella." Lorna tried to defuse the situation by turning aside and holding the tray out of Lady Murdina's reach. "He willna miss the one, and if he does, we will fetch him more."

Lady Murdina smiled down at the little girl, then bristled with a chortle that resembled a warning growl. "That is right, child. Listen to yer nursemaid. After all, before too much longer, whatever belongs to yer father becomes mine as well."

Lorna glared at the vile woman. Those words were a call to battle if she'd ever heard one. She shoved past and rudely bumped the woman aside so Bella could lead the way to the library unhindered. "Excuse us, Lady Murdina. The chieftain likes his bannocks hot from the oven."

"Oh, they will be long cold by the time he awakens," the lady called out in a chilling tone. "But by all means"—she saucily tipped her head toward the library—"continue on." Then she turned and sashayed down the hallway, humming loudly and out of tune.

"She has done something," Bella said.

"I agree." Panic rising, Lorna nodded at the door. "Hurry and open it so we can make sure yer da is all right."

"Da?" Bella called out as she swung the door open wide and waited at the threshold. No answer came. Not a sound filled the library other than the quietly crackling fire in the hearth.

"Bella, I want ye to stay right here, ye ken?" A suffocating sense that something was very wrong closed in on Lorna. What had that vile woman left behind for them to find?

"No, I want to see about Da!"

Lorna blocked the way, then bent and looked the child in the eyes. "Not until I check the room. Something is amiss here. I feel it. Please, Bella. Yer da would want ye to wait until I call ye in."

The lass's bottom lip trembled, and her dark eyes filled with tears. "If she has hurt him…"

"If she has hurt him, she will pay." Lorna caught the child up in a hug, then stepped back and looked her in the eyes again. "I swear it."

"I will wait here till ye call. Because Da would want it." The youngling resettled her footing and tipped a determined nod. "But hurry."

Lorna nodded as she slid the tray onto a nearby table. "Gunn? Bella and I have some fresh bannocks for ye. Still hot enough to melt some of Cook's freshest butter."

Silence. Then a low, ominous moan.

She rushed toward the sound, across the room to the seating area facing the hearth. When she rounded the center couch, she jerked to a halt. Gunn lay sprawled across it, his kilt shoved up around his waist and his impressive man parts exposed. Mouth ajar. His eyes partially open but almost glazed. Arms and legs as limp as a child's rag doll. Another guttural, wheezing sound came from him.

Lorna moved to his side and yanked his kilt back down where it belonged, offering him what dignity she could. "Gunn?"

He gurgled without moving his partially open mouth.

"Dear God in heaven. Is it a stroke?" She checked his pulse, then tried to heft him and prop pillows under his head and back before he choked. As she tried to look into his eyes, her toe bumped something and knocked it farther under the couch. "Bella! Fetch Jasper! Hurry! Yer da needs him." She didn't look to see if the child listened or not, knowing Bella would do what was best for her father.

"What did that hag do to ye?" she whispered. She pulled his eyelids open wider. His enlarged pupils gave her pause. Both were extraordinarily dilated, but matched in size.

He yanked away, working his jaw as though shouting, but no sound came out. He twitched and flailed, knocking her aside. She watched his movements, noting that while they were erratic, there appeared to be no paralysis.

During a lull in his battle with what only he could see, she jumped in close and smelled his breath. Perhaps a hint of wine, but there was another scent she couldn't quite place. Sort of sickly sweet, with a hint of anise.

Old Mrs. Crowley from the bookshop had held a fascination for poisons and the macabre. The eccentric old woman had loved studying medieval deaths by poisoning. Lorna had always been more interested in the plants that provided the lethal effects.

She dropped to her knees and searched under the couch, hoping it was Gunn's wineglass she had kicked.

"No!" he shouted.

She sprang out of the way just as he rolled off onto the floor, swinging his arms and kicking. He had to be drugged.

Fighting panic and afraid he was about to die, Lorna leaped over him and recovered the wineglass from under the couch.

"If ye die, I will never forgive ye!" She sniffed the glass and came up with the same sickly-sweet anise aroma. After piling pillows and cushions all around him, she ran to the cabinet covered in decanters and took a whiff of each one. None of them matched the scent of the glass that he must have dropped, since its dredges matched the odor on his breath.

"Help!" she screamed into the hall. "The chieftain has been poisoned!"

She returned to Gunn, dropped to the floor, and tried to prop him upright against her. She supported him with her legs clenched around him and held his head back against her chest. "Gunn!" she shouted. "Fight it! Fight it with all that is in ye!"

Jasper charged into the room, followed by Edmond and Mrs. Thistlewick.

Mrs. Thistlewick crossed herself and stood to one side. Jasper and Edmond knelt beside their chieftain.

"That wretched woman poisoned him." Lorna fought to keep Gunn leaning back against her and as upright as she could. She hadn't a clue what else might help. Then it hit her. "He needs to either vomit or drink liquid charcoal. Or both. I dinna ken how, but we have to either dilute or get rid of whatever she gave him."

"How do ye know it was her?" Edmond asked, cringing as Gunn shouted an unintelligible stream of gibberish.

"Bella and I met her in the hall, coming out of this room. Would a normal person sashay out of here and leave him in this condition?" Lorna hugged his head back against her and wrestled her legs over his flailing arms. He seemed to be weakening into another lull. "There is a glass in my pocket. It was beside him when I came in. As though he dropped it."

"Let me check it. I ken my apothecaries well enough." Mrs. Thistlewick dodged his twitching legs and recovered the glass. She ran a finger down inside it, then touched it to the tip of her tongue. "Heaven help him. 'Tis deadly nightshade, and a fearsome amount. It numbed the tip of my tongue."

"Where is Bella?" Lorna asked. "She does not need to see this."

"I want that woman hanged for this," Bella said from the other side of the couch. Pale as fresh cream and tears streaming down her face, she pointed at Jasper. "As daughter of the chief, I order her hanged from the tower! Now!"

Gunn bucked and thrashed, knocking Lorna backward, but

she held tight, determined to keep him from doing himself harm. If Lady Murdina had given him a tincture of belladonna in his wine, hallucinations could make him out of his mind for as long as three days. Or so she had read. Of course, that was if he survived.

"We dinna need to kill her right off," she said to Bella. The child should not be saddled with a decision that would follow her all her days. "Lock her up until yer da heals so he can mete out her punishment. Vengeance is his right, ye ken?"

"What if he doesna heal, Mistress Lorna?" Bella moved closer, her tears streaming faster. "What if he dies just like Mama?"

"We must not think that way, ye ken? But if the worst happens, I will stay with ye till ye run me off with a stick." Lorna knew the child would recognize a lie and was mature enough to deserve the truth. As Gunn's throes went into a lull, she nodded at Jasper. "Jasper is here, and Mrs. Thistlewick too. Together, we will all see justice done and we will all be here for ye."

"He has gone still. Is he dead?" Bella hiccupped a quiet sob and came closer still.

Still hugging him back against her chest, his head resting on her collarbone, Lorna smoothed Gunn's hair out of his face, then took Bella's hand and pressed it to his throat. "There. Feel his heartbeat? 'Tis fast and a bit erratic, but it pounds strong. Feel it?"

"What about what ye said we should do for him?" Jasper asked. He kept his gaze locked on the rise and fall of his chieftain's chest.

"I dinna ken how." Lorna wished she possessed more medical knowledge. "I am afraid if we try to pour anything down his throat or gag him so he will vomit, he might choke." With one arm still locked around him and her legs clamping his arms to his sides, she leaned back against the couch. "I dinna ken what to do other than pray."

Bella snuggled down next to her and rested her head on her shoulder. "I am afeared, Mistress Lorna."

"I am too, my wee one."

"That witch should be cast into the dungeon," Mrs. Thistlewick said as she wiped her eyes with the corner of her apron. "And her brother with her."

Lorna shook her head. "No. Not yet. We need to figure out her angle before we confront her."

"Her angle?" Jasper repeated.

"Aye." Lorna idly combed her fingers through Gunn's hair, trying to put it in order. "Why would she kill him? How would that benefit her? They are not man and wife yet." She frowned at the war chief. "Or is there something in the contract about what happens if Gunn dies before the thirty days are up?"

"Nay. If the man dies, she gets nothing but a noose." Jasper scratched his chin as he studied the temporarily relaxed chieftain. "Was this how ye found him? In the floor out of his mind?"

"She told us that soon everything that was Da's would be hers," Bella said. "When we met her in the hall bringing Da bannocks."

"Was this how ye found him?" Jasper repeated, locking eyes with Lorna.

"No." She subtly tipped her head toward Bella.

Mrs. Thistlewick picked up on the unspoken message. "Mistress Bella, come with me. We shall see if Cook knows of a remedy." She held out her hand. "Hurry, lass."

Bella's expression hardened. "No. I want to know how Mistress Lorna found my da."

Lorna pulled in a deep breath and slowly let it out. "Yer da would not wish ye to know, Bella. Someday. When ye are older and I have his permission, then I will tell ye. Not before. It would not honor him for me to do otherwise, ye ken?"

"Ye wouldna wish yer father dishonored?" Mrs. Thistlewick said. "Now would ye?"

The child's mouth tightened into an angry line, but she agreed with a curt dip of her chin. "I never want my da dishonored." She took the housekeeper's hand but then paused and gazed at her father. "Dinna let him die," she whispered to Lorna.

"Please?"

Lorna blinked back tears and lifted her chin. "I will do everything in my power to keep him alive. I swear it."

As soon as the door clicked shut behind them, Jasper pinned her with a fierce glare. "How did ye find him?"

"Sprawled on the couch with his kilt shoved up around his waist as though he had just been ridden hard."

"She means to make him think she carries his child," Jasper said, then added a low-throated growl. "Crafty bitch. I wish I had never laid eyes on her in that pub."

"In this condition, I doubt he could perform." But then she remembered his semi-erection. As though he had just finished.

"I can tell by yer face his pestle looked as though he had just ground the corn." Jasper shook his head. "Damn her straight to hell and back."

"Even if she was able so to seduce him, that doesna mean she is pregnant." Of course, if the woman kept track of her personal timeline, it could increase her odds. "No wonder she drugged him. I dinna think he would risk fathering a child with her until after they married."

"He wouldna risk fathering a child with her at all," Jasper said. "Planned on ousting her once her time ran out." The war chief scrubbed a hand across his face. "And here I thought he had finally come to his senses."

"If he made the mistake of telling her…" Lorna left the rest unsaid as Gunn came to life again, fighting as though beset upon by demons. "Hold his legs! I canna keep a hold on him if he starts bucking."

Edmond sat on one of the chieftain's legs, and Jasper held down the other. Gunn roared like a captured beast.

"How long will he be like this?" Edmond asked.

"Could be as long as three days," Lorna said, straining to hold him tight without cutting off his air.

"Be thankful," Jasper growled as he repositioned and pinned down Gunn's lower half. "It means yer chieftain fights to live."

CHAPTER ELEVEN

I T TOOK GUNN a moment to realize that he leaned back against a person rather than cushions or pillows. Not exactly in their lap, because they had their legs wrapped around him and their feet resting on top of his thighs. Their slow, steady breathing somehow eased him, made him feel warm and comforted.

He blinked hard several times to force his eyes to focus. Every blink made the sharp pain in his head pound harder. No light beat back the darkness of the room except the glow from the hearth. Praise God for that. Even the gentle brightness of the shimmering coals split his skull with the force of a war hammer. Arms and legs heavy as lead, he lay there with his eyes squeezed shut, trying to remember where the hell he was, how he got here, and what woman slept with their arms and legs around him.

He worked his jaws, raking his tongue against the roof of his mouth. A strange numbness afflicted it, as though he had drunk something scalding hot. His gut clenched and rolled, warning all was not well in his belly either. Perhaps if he lay still, the beast clawing at his innards would calm.

Eyes still closed tight, he hazarded a feel of the slender arms and legs around him. What woman would do this? Aching skull or not, he forced his eyes back open. Squinting against the light, he twisted around to identify her.

Lorna sprang to life and clutched him tighter. "Shh...it's all right, Gunn. It's all right. I am here." Her voice crackled with hoarse weariness. "I have ye. Ye are safe now, *mo ghràidh*. Go back to sleep."

He swallowed hard and relaxed back into her comforting embrace. She had called him *my dear one*. What ailment had she pulled him through by clinging to him in the darkness? "Lorna?" he said. Or tried to. His voice broke, shattering into bits of unintelligible air. He forced a cough that stirred the pain in his skull and tried again. "Lorna?"

"Gunn?" She didn't loosen her hold, but excitement and joy swelled in her tone. "Have ye come back to us?"

"Aye," he managed to say loud enough to be heard.

"Praise God Almighty!" She started sobbing, hugging him tight and rocking back and forth. "We were so afraid ye had left us for good."

"Dinna rock." He found the strength to pat her arms. "Guts. Head. Pain. Please...stop."

"So sorry." She went still but rained kisses down the side of his face while her hand stayed pressed across his forehead, holding him close. When she hugged her cheek to his, the wetness of her tears made his heart leap.

She cared about him. Enough to weep for joy that he had returned from whatever hell had tried to take him.

"Do ye remember anything?" she asked.

He started to shake his head, then groaned and clutched it. "Hell's fire. Demons pound inside my skull."

"That's because ye are coming out from the deadly nightshade's effects. Mistress Thistlewick said if ye survived, ye would be miserable afterward. At least for a little while."

The more aware he became, the more he found sweet relief in her cradling him. But what she said made no sense. He had not eaten any poisonous berries or drank any potions. "Nightshade?"

"Aye. We think she slipped the tincture of belladonna into yer wine. But of course, she would never admit it." A heavy sigh shifted her behind him as she hugged her cheek to him again. "Thank heavens ye lived through it. Bella will be beside herself when she sees ye are all right."

"I canna remember a bloody thing." And the harder he thought about it, the more his head ached. "Who is *she*? Who did this to me?" Although he only knew of one female potentially capable of such a thing.

"Murdina." Lorna tenderly stroked his forehead. "I will no longer address her as *Lady* because she is not one. Would ye like to try a sip of water? Mrs. Thistlewick had a chamber pot chair brought down for when yer stomach rebels. And a pair of buckets for the heaving if it comes. All are right here close if the water triggers anything."

"Brought *down*?" he repeated, feeling like a helpless fool. "Where is *here*?" The room was so dark. All he could see through the narrow slits of his squinting eyes was the fire.

"The library. It is where Bella and I found ye."

"I canna remember a feckin' thing, can barely see, and dinna ken if I can even crawl to a chamber pot." He wanted to rage, lash out, charge through the keep, find Murdina, and wring her bloody neck. "I am weak as a mewling kitten."

"Well, that's because we have been here in the floor for almost two days now. When I wasna wrestling to keep ye from hurting yerself, Jasper was." She shook against him with a weak laugh as she patted his chest. "Thank heavens ye fought him harder than ye fought me. I dinna ken how I wouldha held ye otherwise. But ye are alive. That is all that matters. And I will help with whatever ye need. Dinna ye worry about that."

"Instead of nursemaid to my daughter, ye have become nursemaid to me." A small part of him found comfort in her caring, but the greater part of him hated it. He should protect her, protect all in this keep. Not the other way around.

"I am not yer nursemaid," she corrected him quietly. "I am yer friend."

He covered her hand where it rested on his chest and squeezed it. "I dinna want ye to be my friend, Lorna. Not when ye have made my heart need ye to be so much more." A tense knot loosened in his chest as though relieved he had finally accepted the truth and said the words aloud.

She pressed a kiss close to his ear. "Heal first. We will discuss everything else later. Yer healing is all that matters right now. Understand?"

"As long as ye stay here with me." He held her hand tighter. He would not make the mistake of pushing her away again.

"I will. Swear it on my own headstone." She gently pushed on his shoulders and helped him sit up higher. "Now, let's get ye up on that couch, aye? By bum's gone numb again from sitting on the floor so long."

That made him smile, and he couldn't resist asking, "Shall I rub it for ye to help bring back the feeling?"

She laughed. "Now I know ye will be fine. Come on now. Concentrate on turning to yer knees and climbing up onto this couch. We can talk of bum rubbing when ye are stronger."

"My arms and legs are heavy as iron and clumsier than a newborn colt."

"It's the drug. Weakens muscles something terrible." She slipped out from behind Gunn but stayed on her knees beside him with an arm wrapped around his waist to hold him steady. "Just move slow. Ye have not used those muscles for anything other than fighting through yer seizures."

By the time he collapsed onto the couch, he was sweating as if he had climbed the highest mountain in Scotland. As Lorna slid another pillow behind him, he caught hold of her hand. "For a woman who swore she would be second to none, ye cared for me as if I was yer own."

She sat on the edge of the cushion beside him. Avoiding his gaze, she stared at their hands as if searching for the right words. After a deep breath, she offered a bewildered shrug. "I care about ye and couldna leave pulling ye through this hell to someone else." A smile teased her lovely mouth into a bow. "Yer daughter ordered Murdina hanged from the tower." With a somber tip of her head, she leveled her gaze with his. "Ye already have yer heir, Gunn. Brilliant as she already is, she will make a fine chieftain someday."

"'Tis a rare thing for a woman to lead a clan. And would be more difficult for her because she is a lass." He started to shake his head, then thought better of it because of the pounding. "I dinna wish her to have to battle for respect every day of her life."

"Women do that regardless of any title they bear." She patted his chest. "Let me fetch ye some water, aye?"

"Not yet." He held tight to her hand, needing to hear her confirmation she felt as much tenderness for him as he did for her. "Ye know there will be no more Lady Murdina, aye? Whether by Bella's order to hang her or mine to have her packed up and sent away."

She didn't speak. Just turned and gazed at the fire, staring at the flames.

"Lorna?"

"There is something else ye should know." She released a heavy sigh. "The woman swears she could be carrying yer child because of yer coupling with her two days ago."

"What coupling?" he demanded so loud it made him wince and grab his head.

"The day Bella and I brought ye fresh bannocks to coax ye into coming out, Murdina exited the library, straightening her hair and clothes." Her scowl hardened, deepening the shadows created by the firelight on her profile. "She was smug that day. Proud as a cat that had just lapped up all the cream." She turned back to him. "I made Bella wait in the hall because I sensed something wasna right." She squeezed his hand. "And that is when I found ye sprawled on this couch with yer kilt shoved up around yer waist as if…"

"As if she had just ridden me hard," he finished for her.

She nodded.

He raked a hand across his face, then covered his eyes. "I swear I dinna remember any of it. Not even her being in here."

"She must have given ye one hell of a dose. 'Tis a miracle ye lived through it."

Still rubbing his pounding forehead, he gritted his teeth. "I had planned to tell her that the marriage would not go through. Perhaps I did. I dinna ken for sure."

"That is what Jasper figured." She rose to her feet, pressed both hands to her lower back, and stretched. "I am going to fetch that water. Ye will try a sip, aye?"

He caught hold of her skirts and stopped her before she stepped away. "Ye know I would never bed that woman? Not willingly?"

She gave him a weary smile. "I know. But I also know that if she turns out to be pregnant, ye canna let her leave here until she bears the child and ye take it from her to raise here. No innocent should be exposed to a person willing to do what she did out of pure greed."

"Ye forgive me, then?"

"There is nothing to forgive." She twitched her skirt free of his hold. "Now let me get yer water."

He watched her go, hoping she truly meant that she bore him no ill will. Since he had finally found the courage to risk his heart once again, he feared he had waited too long and she wouldn't believe him. "Ye said Bella ordered the woman hanged?"

"Aye." Lorna took the pitcher off the table at the other end of the couch and filled a glass. "Jasper and I convinced her that ye should have the opportunity to deal with the she-devil." She paused and slowly placed the pitcher back on the table. "The only way Bella would agree was that we promised if ye died, we would carry out her order." She knelt beside him and slid an arm under his shoulders. "Raise up a bit so ye dinna choke."

"A kiss would keep me from choking," he said, turning his face to hers.

"I am not above bribery," she replied. "But drink first. A few sips. Then ye shall have yer kiss, aye?"

The water went down well enough. He managed almost half the cup to ensure he received his reward. As she eased him back down to the pillow, his gut let out a deep, grumbling gurgle.

She arched a brow and eyed his middle. "That did not sound good at all. Do ye need a basin?"

"Nay, my precious mouse. I need my kiss."

With a hesitance that endeared her to him even more, she touched his cheek and looked into his eyes. "It isna fair the way ye have made me care about ye," she whispered, a sheen of tears making her eyes glisten.

He slid his fingers along the curve of her jaw and up into her messy curls. "I fear ye have that wrong, my own. 'Tis yerself who unlocked my heart." Cupping her face in his palm, he teased his thumb back and forth across the velvet of her cheek. "Ye hold the key, dearest mouse. Now and forevermore."

"Aye, *mo ghràidh*. Just as ye hold the key to mine." She nibbled the gentlest of kisses across his mouth, then lifted her head and smiled.

"More," he said, stretching upward.

She pressed the center of his chest. "Later. When we are both better rested, aye?"

His stomach clenched and growled again like a caged beast about to break free. Ominous cramping hit low in his gut, making him hug an arm around his middle. "This willna bode well," he groaned as a cold sweat peppered his brow. "Pull the commode closer, then leave, ye ken?"

She dragged the chair closer, then turned to help him rise. "I willna leave with ye weak as ye are."

"I will not have ye here while my innards turn themselves inside out." Head swimming, he tried to focus on getting to the chair without passing out. "Please, Lorna, I beg ye. Leave me with a shred of dignity, aye?" He had already been shamed enough for allowing himself to be duped by that witch.

"Fine, then. I will wait in the hall. Just outside the door."

Concern filled her face as she set the buckets closer to the chamber pot chair. "But if I hear a loud thud, I am coming back in."

He waved her away, no longer able to speak while maintaining a hold on the demon about to rip from his bowels.

>>>><<<<

LORNA WEARILY LEANED back against the door, wincing at the sounds coming from inside the library. Between bouts of retching, Gunn groaned and shouted in Gaelic that his arse was on fire. Maybe. It had been a long time since he had used that language for anything other than words of endearment.

She understood his need for privacy but felt guilty about standing in the hall when she could help him with cool, damp cloths and sympathy. Each time he went quiet for a short time, she eased open the door only to have him bellow, "Out!"

"Well, his hearing is fine." She wondered if it was the squeak of the door hinges or the floorboards that gave her away. But at least he was alive. That was all that mattered. She hugged herself. No, that was not all that mattered. Not only did he live, but had also decided to risk caring for someone again. And that someone was her.

"Dear God in heaven," Jasper said as he rounded into the hall. "Is he…?"

"He is all right." She waved him forward. "Remember what Mrs. Thistlewick said about the aftereffects of the belladonna?"

Renewed retching, loud and rumbling, came from the other side of the door.

Jasper made a face. "Shitting fire too? Like she said?"

Lorna nodded. "From what I can remember of my Gaelic, he either said his arse is on fire or he is shitting fire. I am a little rusty."

"Either way." Jasper shrugged. "I should alert Mrs. Thistlewick. She might have a tisane to help settle his guts."

"Before ye go, please go in there and check on him. He refused to let me stay in there while he…" She left it at that.

Jasper squinted at the door as though it were a fire-breathing dragon. "I dinna ken so much about my going in there." Leeriness shouted from the war chief. "The man doesna handle ailing well. 'Tis usually best to leave the beast to himself."

"Coward."

Both of Jasper's brows hiked to his hairline as he jabbed a finger at the door. "Ye are damn right I am when it comes to that."

"Please?" She mustered the most pitiful expression possible. "I am worried about him, and he probably needs both the buckets and chamber pot emptied by now."

"I damn sure willna be doing that." He threw up a hand and spun about to leave. "I shall fetch a couple of lads to take care of that wee delicacy and get Mrs. Thistlewick to brew a tisane." Partway down the hall, he paused. "What about Bella? Should we wake her and let her know?"

Another loud growl rumbled from within the library, making Lorna shake her head. "Let the child sleep. Hopefully, the worst of it will have passed by morning and he will be fit to see her."

Jasper nodded and continued down the hall, leaving her standing there helpless outside the door.

Exhausted but determined to stay at her post, she leaned against the wall and slid down to the floor. Arms propped on her knees, she rested her head atop them. After what felt like only the blink of an eye, the sound of footsteps jarred her back to her feet.

Mrs. Thistlewick, with a steaming teakettle in one hand, a hefty mug in the other, and her apron pockets bulging, led the way. A trio of lads followed. One carried an armload of linens. The next toted more steaming kettles, and the third toted a pair of empty buckets. Jasper brought up the rear, his expression darker than a storm.

"Ye should go to yer bed, lass," Mrs. Thistlewick said after a hard up-and-down scowl of her.

"No. I promised him I wouldna leave." Lorna opened the door for the parade but stopped Jasper from entering after the others. She closed the door, glanced down the hall behind him, then kept her voice low. "What is it? Ye have a face like thunder."

"I spoke with Forsy about Lady Murdina." His jaws flexed as though he fought not to spit after saying the woman's name. "She said the woman was ill yesterday morning."

"That is ridiculous. It canna be because she is pregnant. Not this soon." Lorna struggled to keep her voice to a whisper. "She only had sex with him two days ago. Jumping the gun a bit on the theatrics, is she not?"

"Jumping the gun?" he repeated slowly.

"An old saying I will explain later." She was too feckin' tired to filter her words and translate them into seventeenth-century vernacular. "Did ye tell Forsy to watch the she-devil close and report everything?"

"Of course," he said, giving her a disgruntled cut of his eyes.

"What about that brother of hers? Laird Leckness?" The man had only made a rare appearance or two outside their rooms ever since they arrived. "Is he still sick?"

"He may have died by now, for all I know." Jasper snorted his disgust. "According to the maids, the lazy bastard only rises from his bed to foul the chamber pot. He's nay allowed them to change his bed linens since he and Lady Murdina arrived."

"Odd behavior for a laird." Lorna wished she could remember some sort of history about Clan Auchinleck, but for the life of her, she couldn't. "If ye were him, would ye not be concerned about getting back to yer clan no matter how small it was?"

"I fear our new solicitor didna check them as closely as he claimed." Jasper bared his teeth as though about to growl. "'Tis a man I sought on the recommendation of our old solicitor's brother."

"What happened to the old solicitor?"

"Dead."

"Ye dinna think they paid yer new solicitor off, do ye?" Under the circumstances, and from what Jasper said, Lorna didn't trust any of them.

"If I find out they did…" The war chief left it at that. His deadly tone and fierce expression left no doubt about his intentions.

She leaned back against the wall, closed her eyes, and massaged her temples. So much deception—or at least ways of possible deceit. She'd always thought the past was simpler. How wrong she was.

"Mrs. Thistlewick was right," Jasper said, interrupting her muddled thoughts. "Ye should go to yer bed."

"I promised him I would stay." She lifted her head and pulled in a deep breath. "Once he is more comfortable, I will go to bed." Squaring her shoulders, she forced herself to stand taller. "The guards know Murdina is not allowed out of her rooms, aye?"

"Of course." Jasper snorted. "The entire clan is aware she attempted to kill our chief." Then he grinned. "Murdina? Are ye that familiar with the witch?"

"The only title she deserves is Rat Queen. Not *lady*."

The library door swung open, and a smiling Mrs. Thistlewick ushered the lads with the buckets out and waved Lorna inside. "He is asking for ye, lass." She arched a brow at Jasper and gave a leery shake of her head. "He wishes to speak with ye as well. Tread carefully, war chief."

Lorna patted him on the arm and winked. "Dinna worry. I will protect ye."

He rolled his eyes. "I thank ye, mistress." With a bow, he held the door for them. "After ye, dear ladies."

The housekeeper shook her head. "I am off to brew another tisane. The one I got down him willna grant him much relief because most of it came back up." Beaming a proud smile, she added, "But he is already finding some ease from what little stayed in him." With her clacking heels marking her steps, she headed down the hall at an impressive pace.

"Are ye coming in here or no'?" Gunn bellowed.

Lorna rounded the end of the couch. "Ye nearly scared me away. I thought it was a sore-tailed bear that had gotten in here and started growling."

"I am a feckin' sore-tailed bear." He raked a hand down his face, then irritably plucked at the blankets covering him. "And that old woman is trying to bake me alive. She had the lads stoke the fire, then piled every cloth in the keep on top of me."

Lorna couldn't help but laugh. Gunn apparently didn't handle ailing well and had recovered enough to complain. A good sign indeed. "How about if I remove all the blankets but one, aye? I am sure Mrs. Thistlewick is just trying to sweat the last of the poison out of ye."

"And that is another thing." With eyes red-rimmed and bloodshot, he shoved himself higher up in the pillows and glowered at Jasper. "Tell me again where ye found that woman."

The war chief swiped a hand across his brow. "It *is* a mite warm in here." He frowned at the fire roaring in the hearth. "Shall I tame the blaze a bit before it reaches the soot and shoots flames out the chimney?"

"If I were not so weak, I would rise from here and thrash yer arse for ye, man. Answer the question. Ye told me Clan Auchinleck's solicitor contacted ye when we made it known I wished to marry again and had offered a contract with terms. That woman told me their solicitor is also *our* solicitor. Were ye aware of that?"

Lorna pulled up a footstool beside the couch, lowered herself to it, and rested a hand on Gunn's chest. His heart pounded strong but fast. He needed to settle down. "Ye need to breathe and calm yerself. This does not all have to be resolved this verra second. It is not even dawn yet."

"I canna rest until I know the answers to all the questions I should have asked before I allowed that foul woman into my keep." His jaw hardened and his mouth flexed into a taut, frustrated line. "I was a fool to trust so blindly. I willna be such a fool again."

Jasper's shoulders slumped, and he hung his head as if sentenced to the gallows. "I take full responsibility, my chieftain." He released a heavy sigh as he lifted his head. "However, in my defense, this would never have happened had Old Gerald still been alive to handle our affairs. And no, I didna ken that wee bastard MacGibbon was their solicitor as well. He conveniently failed to mention that."

"Jasper is loyal to ye, and ye know it," Lorna gently reminded Gunn. "Ye both are strong, honorable men that happened to fall prey to the sort of lowlifes who only care about themselves." She understood exactly how they felt. "But the last thing ye need to do is become divided over it." Leaning closer, she forced Gunn to look at her. "Dinna let them best ye that way. Reunite yer forces and overcome them."

He reached out and cupped her cheek in his calloused palm. "Ye are a wise woman, my precious mouse. Thank God Almighty ye are here." His gaze slid back to Jasper. "And thank God Almighty that the marriage contract is the only document Liam MacGibbon touched for us, aye?"

"Aye." Jasper widened his stance, appearing ready to charge into battle. "With yer permission, I shall send Edmond to round up the man and bring him here. I dinna wish to leave yer side whilst ye are still weak from the poison."

"This time of year it will take the lad a month or longer to get to Inverness and back."

Lorna interrupted them with a jaw-cracking yawn. "Sorry." She rubbed her gritty eyes. "Personally, I dinna think we should do anything other than keep Murdina locked in her rooms until we have all had some decent sleep and are fully rested. Weariness makes for rash decisions that could be fatal." She rolled her shoulders and stretched her aching neck by tilting her head from side to side. "Besides, I feel sure the woman will fake being pregnant. Although I am not quite sure how she thinks that will help her when her time has run its course." Then a terrible thought hit her and she groaned.

"What?" Gunn tried to sit upright, then fell back into his pillows. "Lorna?"

She closed her eyes and rubbed her throbbing temples. "What if she was already pregnant when she got here?"

CHAPTER TWELVE

G UNN PACED BACK and forth in front of his desk. Three full
days lost while healing enough to deal with this feckin'
mess. But thank the Almighty for Lorna. She'd kept him sane.

The depths of her patience and understanding amazed him.
He had already told the priest there would be a wedding before
Hogmanay. Now to convince Lorna to agree—no matter if Lady
Murdina turned out to be with child or not. After all, as his
precious mouse had said, the father of the child did not matter.
The wee bairn needed rescuing from its mother's clutches as soon
as it was born. With any hope, today would lend a bit of clarity so
they might better plan their future.

The door hinges creaked, announcing Lorna had arrived with
Hesther and Frances. Gunn assumed a kindly, non-threatening
air. Or at least he hoped it was. As skittish as those two were, they
would never speak their minds if they became more afraid than
usual. At least they looked more braw and healthier than they had
when they first arrived at Thursa. A fine rosiness now pinked
their cheeks, and neither resembled a frail, bony waif any longer.
Their improvement made him smile.

"Here we are," Lorna said, gently steering them by their
shoulders. "And remember what I said—ye can say absolutely

anything, and no one will ever know but myself and the chieftain." She bent and brought her face closer to theirs. "Ye can trust us, aye? Ye understand that?"

Frances frowned and shifted in place. The boy looked ready to run. Hesther clutched her hands together so tightly, her knuckles turned white.

"Hesther," Gunn said. "Yer former mistress is locked in her rooms because of her treacherous behavior. She can harm ye no longer."

The meek girl, tiny and delicate as a cobweb, looked much younger than her eleven years. She offered a timid shrug, but kept her gaze fixed on the floor. "Aye, my chieftain. I ken it well enough. But she always seems to know everything. Sometimes even afore we speak it." She inched back a step, taking refuge in the folds of Lorna's skirts. "I am sorry, mighty chieftain. Please dinna turn me out."

Lorna gave him a pleading look.

"I would never turn ye out, Hesther. Nor will we send ye away when we finally rid ourselves of yer vile mistress." He resumed his pacing but kept it to a slow, meandering walk rather than the frustrated stride he needed. Perhaps that would make him appear less frightening to the children. He turned and settled his focus on Frances. "We dinna wish to be rid of ye either, Frances. Ye understand that, aye?"

The lad started rocking back and forth from one foot to the other. His face grew redder by the moment. Just as he seemed ready to speak, he turned and pinned an imploring expression on Hesther. She jerked her head with a hard shake. A clear and emphatic *no*.

"What is it, lad? Ye are safe here." Gunn crouched in front of the boy and gently took hold of his hand. "Thursa is yer home now." He tipped his head toward the girl. "Hesther's too. And ye should know by now that my Bella would fight to the death to protect the both of ye. Ye are like the brother and sister she always wanted."

Lorna eased around the children and took her place beside him. "We need yer help verra badly. That woman nearly killed this fine man to manipulate him for money, land, and title. The more ye tell us about her, the better we can decide what should be done with her. Ye dinna wish us to let her loose on the unsuspecting world just to be rid of her, do ye?"

Frances eased closer. Hesther grabbed his hand and tried to pull him back. "Nay, Frances. Nay," she said in a frantic whisper.

"I willna be the coward she turned me into. Not anymore." The boy yanked his arm free and jabbed a finger in her face. "And ye should tell them everything too, Hesther. She treated ye even worser than she treated me."

"Tell us, Frances. Tell us everything ye can," Gunn said.

"My name wasna always Frances," the child said. "It used to be Murray. When Lady Murdina lured me and my sister off the streets of Edinburgh…" He paused and glanced back at the trembling girl. "She told me whenever someone called me Frances, I better answer to it or it would be a hard lashing and nothing but water for a week every time I forgot." He flinched, then shrugged it off with a pitiful shiver. "I got better at remembering I was Frances after the first whipping."

"So ye are not her son?" Lorna said, her eyes narrowing.

The boy shook his head. "No. She told me I had to act like her son or she would see me sent to the worst poorhouse she could find. Put us both there and tell them not to feed us nothing but scraps not fit for dogs."

"Nay, brother," Hesther said. Her voice became louder than it had ever been before. "She meant to send ye to the poorhouse, but she said she would sell me outright to Darley's Place rather than just the three nights a week she rented me to them."

"Darley's Place?" Gunn asked.

Hesther stared at the floor, and her breathy whispering returned. "Aye, my chieftain. A whorehouse that likes their girls small like me."

"I am going to kill that woman," Lorna said through clenched teeth. "Slow and painfully."

Gunn bowed his head, feeling the same. "Neither of ye will ever live through such hellishness again." He stood and battled with the urge to charge up to Lady Murdina's room and wring her sorry neck. It took a long moment to curb the rage pounding through him. After several deep breaths, he dipped a nod at Frances. "I suppose she had ye pose as her son to lend credence to my marriage requirements, aye?"

The child nodded. "And she took up Hesther to make extra money while looking like she was fancy enough to have a lady's maid." He wrinkled his small, upturned nose. "Appears to me that her and that man didna have much when it came to coin."

"What man?" Gunn asked. "Her brother?"

"I am nay so certain he is her brother," Hesther whispered. "Even if he is, she hates him. And he hates her."

"How do ye know she hates him?" Lorna asked. "Did she say so?"

"She calls him names," Frances said. "And he calls her worser names." His small, round face wrinkled with a tighter scowl. "They might be family somehow. But I dinna think he is her real brother. One time, I heard him saying he was thankful they didna share any blood because she was such a…" He paused. "I canna remember what he called her that time. It was more than one word, and they was long ones."

"A 'devious, worthless bitch,'" Hesther said as though reciting a lesson.

"Well, that pretty much sums her up," Lorna said. She turned to Gunn. "She lied about having a son, whored poor Hesther out, tortured Frances, then tried to kill ye. I say we turn her over for the courts to decide what to do with her."

"Aye," he agreed. "But ye said we should protect the bairn if she truly carries one. Is that still what ye wish, or should I send a message to Edinburgh's constable to come fetch her and take her to the tolbooth?"

Lorna sagged into a nearby chair, appearing defeated. "No. If she is pregnant, whether the child is yers or not, we canna let her leave here with it." She fixed the children with a compassionate look. "Especially not after all we just learned."

"Is there anything else ye could tell us about her?" Gunn asked. He turned to Hesther. "Do ye ken if she was with child when she came here?" The prospect of that woman bearing his babe repulsed him more than he could ever say.

Hesther cringed and shook her head. "I am sorry, my chieftain. I dinna ken."

"The both of ye may go," he said, dismissing them with a weary nod. "And I thank ye for all that ye told us."

The two looked at Lorna as though waiting for her permission.

"It's all right." Without rising from the chair, she gently shooed them toward the door. "Go on with ye, my brave warriors. Find Bella, aye? She is probably with the kittens."

They each gave Gunn a polite bow, then ran from the room.

"How could she treat them that way?" Lorna stared at the door as it closed behind them.

"I dinna ken." Gunn knelt beside her. "I am so verra sorry for all of this. More than ye will ever know."

"I am too." She gently touched his cheek and offered a sad smile. "For a man determined to keep himself isolated and uncaring, ye are not doing a verra good job of it. Just look how many are depending on ye to care about them."

He covered her hand with his and turned a gentle kiss into her palm. "Ye made my loneliness too unbearable to continue. For the first time in a long while, I ached for it to end." He glanced back at the door and huffed a soft laugh. "And aye, I do have many more depending on me to care about them, and I am glad of it." He turned back and kissed her hand again. "I am especially thankful that ye are one of them."

A slight frown creased her brow. "Ye know even less about me than ye know about that she-devil upstairs. Do ye not fear to trust me?"

"It is my hope that someday ye will find the strength to confide in me." Still on one knee, he gently tugged her closer and held both her hands. "My heart knows I can trust ye," he said softly. "That is all that matters. It is the connection between us." He couldn't resist indulging in the sweetness of her mouth with a kiss that left him longing for more. But he forced himself to stop. More was at hand to settle between them. "But there is a thing I must ask ye, dear one. Something we must decide."

"And what might that be?" She leaned back, eyeing him as though dreading what he might say.

"Would ye be my wife, Lorna? We can marry before Hogmanay and begin the new year with more hope and light than my heart has known for years."

"*Before* Hogmanay?" Both her brows twitched higher, and she stared at him with her lips slightly parted. "This is December twenty-first."

"Aye." An uneasiness filled him. She had not said yes, but then again, she had not outright refused either. "I see no reason to wait." But the hesitation in her eyes made his heart ache for her to say the words. "Ye dinna answer, my own. Does that mean ye willna have me?"

"No! Of course I will have ye!" Her declaration enabled him to breathe again. "It's just…" She slid out of the chair and joined him on the floor.

"It is just what?" He dreaded to hear what came next.

She bit her lip, cringing as though about to confess some grave sin. "We have only known each other a short while. And then there is the Rat Queen left to deal with. Some here consider her yer wife already, since ye gave a feast in her honor and sat her at yer side. It doesna take much to become man and wife in Scotland, ye ken?"

"She is not now nor ever will be my wife. I will make that clear to everyone." He went from kneeling to sitting then pulled her into his lap and propped them both against the wall. "And I dinna wish for us to wait for however many months it takes to resolve the issue of Lady Murdina."

Lorna snuggled to his chest, tucking her head under his chin as if trying to hide. A sigh escaped her, then she whispered, "And I am afraid."

He pressed his cheek to her hair. "Of what, my own? Tell me what ye fear, so I might chase it away."

"I love ye," she said so softly he almost didn't hear.

He swallowed hard, praying she had truly spoken those precious words, and they weren't his own wishful imaginings. Ever so slowly, he eased her out from her tucked cowering and lifted her face to his. Smoothing wisps of her silky hair out of her face, he offered a teasing smile. "Why does loving me make ye afraid, my brave mouse? Were ye not the one who once challenged me to find my own courage?"

"Aye, but there is so much…" Her gaze searched his. She seemed unable to find the words to suit her. "So much…"

"So much what?"

Worry creased the smoothness of her brow. "So much ye dinna ken about me." She barely shook her head. "I am not what I seem, and I have no way to explain it." A small laugh escaped her along with a desolate shrug. "I still dinna understand it myself."

Her worries perplexed him. Not only because he yearned to know all her secrets but also because whatever fretted her had built a wall between them. "I will tell ye all that ye seem to me. When I am done, tell me what I failed to name, aye? Every last bit of it." He swept his fingers through her hair, tugging it free of its pins. "Trust me to understand, precious mouse. Without full trust between us, we canna build a life together."

She stared at him, unblinking, as though weighing her choices. "Before we start this dangerous truth-telling," she said, "I beg one promise from ye."

"Anything, my own. Name it."

"I ask for the same promise ye gave Hesther and Frances." Her rueful look cut him to the core. "Swear ye willna put me out.

Because I have nowhere else to go."

Rather than argue the ridiculousness of what she suggested, he unsheathed his dagger and held it up like a cross. "I swear I will never put ye out, m'love. Not for any reason." Then he set the blade aside and cupped her face between his hands. "And now I will tell ye about the woman I see before me." He stroked his thumb across the softness of her cheek. "She is beautiful to gaze upon, and the generosity of her soul and the kindness of her heart increase her beauty tenfold. She walks with the ferocity of a protective lioness, caring for the weak and downtrodden." After a slow, tender kiss that made him need her even more, he continued. "This woman of mine tastes of honey wine and an unfathomable love that both thrills and frightens me." He slid his hands across her shoulders, down her arms, and took hold of her hands. "Now tell me what it is about ye that I have failed to name."

She lowered her gaze to their hands. "I have never lied to ye, but I know ye often wondered what I was leaving unsaid." She twitched a nervous shrug without looking up. "I had to leave a lot unsaid, though. Because if I spoke half the things I could have, ye would either think my mind had left me or that I was a witch and should be put to death to protect yer clan."

Her words shocked him. He opened his mouth to deny their truth, but she stopped him with a quick shake of her head. "No. It is my turn now. Remember?"

She was right. "Aye, my precious one. Forgive me and please continue." He prayed that this unloading of her soul would grant him the rights to her heart and their marriage before Hogmanay. Surely nothing she was about to say could be so dire.

She wet her lips, pulled in a deep breath, and eased it out with a decisive nod. "I told ye all that had happened the night before I found myself alone and wandering in the snowstorm, aye?"

"Aye. I remember." He had often thought about her strange tale, wondering what terrible thing had come upon her to make her forget how she came to be on his land.

"And how I once owned a used bookstore in Thurso? Ran it with the help of my dearest friends?" Her eyes misted over, but she blinked fiercely against the tears. "I think I told ye that, did I not?"

It might be her turn to speak, but perhaps he should also confess all he had done to untangle the truth of her tale. "There has never been such a bookstore in Thurso, dear one. And I must tell ye that when I sent Jasper to discover more about ye, no one in the town had ever heard of ye."

Her nervous smile puckered tighter, making him wonder if she was about to be ill. "That is because my bookstore and friends are still where I left them—in the year 2022."

Surely he had misheard. "Say again?"

This time her tears escaped her rapid blinking. "After I broke it off with Patrick, I was so angry that I didna pay attention to where I was going. I stepped off the cliff, and just as I fell, the brightest northern lights show I had ever seen exploded all around me." She slid her hands free of his and hugged herself as if not trusting him to do it. "It made me feel sick and all topsy-turvy with spinning. Then everything went black, and when I woke up, I was back on the cliff. In the frozen grass. First, I thought I was dead. Then I recognized the place and started walking to get back to town. Back home." A hiccupping gulp escaped her, and she bowed her head. "But I couldna find anything that was supposed to be there. No matter how hard I searched. Hook's Cafe on the edge of Thurso had disappeared—as had everything else I once knew."

"What year were ye born?" It was all he could think to say. The shock of all she had just shared had locked his ability to reason.

"1994." She pulled a square of linen from her sleeve and wiped her nose. "July twenty-eight." Mouth quivering and eyes squeezed shut, she tucked her head to one side in a pitiful shrug. "I swear I am telling the truth." More tears coursed down her cheeks. "I dinna ken how I came to be here. I just know...I am here."

Even though all she said was incomprehensible, deep in his heart and soul, he knew she spoke the truth—whether it had truly happened or she merely thought it had because of some overwhelming tragedy foisted upon her. She believed her story with every fiber of her being. And therefore, he must believe it too.

He pulled her close again, gently rocking as she collapsed against his chest, sobbing. Perhaps she grieved for those she believed she had left behind. Friends. Family. All she had ever known. Or at least thought she had ever known. He struggled to fathom how such a thing could be true, then berated himself. Why could it not be true? Many things happened in the world that no one could explain.

"I believe ye, dearest mouse," he whispered. When she didn't react, he said it louder. "Lorna. My love. I believe ye, and none of that matters. All that matters is that ye are here now, and I love ye with a fury that nothing in heaven or earth could ever set aside."

With a shuddering sniff, she pushed herself upright and stared him in the face. "Ye believe me? Really?"

"Aye, I do." A pitiful mess with her red nose, splotchy cheeks, and mussed hair, she had never looked lovelier to him. He ached for a kiss but sensed she needed more words for now. "I willna pretend to understand all that ye said or how it could be, but I do believe ye—because I love ye and my heart says it is so."

She crumpled with another keening cry and threw herself back against his chest.

Not knowing what else to do, he released a heavy sigh and gently stroked her hair. Sometimes lasses just needed to cry things out. Mrs. Thistlewick had told him that once a long time ago.

Then she mumbled something into his tunic.

"What was that, my weepy mouse? I couldna hear ye."

She sat up and wiped her nose with her bedraggled square of

linen. With the look of a child caught stealing food, she said, "I am not a virgin."

He wanted to laugh but didn't dare. However, a wee bit of teasing was impossible to resist. "I didna think ye were. Not a woman of yer age, ye ken?"

She glared at him. "Well, I am not exactly past my best-by date either."

"Nay, my love." While he wasn't certain that she meant she wasn't close to spoiling, he guessed as much. Gently but firmly, he eased her closer until the irresistible temptation of her mouth was within a hairsbreadth of his. "Ye most definitely are not past yer best-by date. Now tell me, I beg ye, will ye grant me the honor of becoming my wife before this weary old year passes?"

"Ye are certain ye still want me? Even after all I just told ye?" Worry and concern shouted from her. From the pucker of her brow to the way she chewed the corner of her lip. "I dinna want ye regretting it."

"Dinna fash yerself, m'love," he said softly, then said it again with a long, slow kiss. "Just say the words I long to hear."

Without a word, she pulled back and almost stood, wrestling with her skirts. Then she straddled him and gave a suggestive smile while settling back down onto his lap. Both nearly undid him. "I would marry ye this verra minute." She slid her hands up around his shoulders and laced her fingers in his hair. "But might we wait to fetch the priest until a little later?"

"Most definitely." He trailed his hands down her back, then up beneath her skirts, and cupped her lovely arse in both hands. "I have dreamt of this," he said in a rasping whisper before covering her mouth with his.

She moved against him with a needy purr that vibrated into him. He released her buttocks long enough to yank his kilt out of the way so their naked flesh slid together in delicious greeting.

"I plan to relish ye long and slow this first time," he said between kisses.

She didn't answer, just reached between them and settled his cock inside her hot, wet depths. "Sorry," she said with a breathless nuzzling of his neck. "We can do long and slow next time, aye?" She rocked her hips and released a tantalizing gasp. "I couldna wait any longer. I have wanted ye so verra long."

He held tight to her, helping her ride harder and faster. "Aye." The words came out in a groan. "Long and slow next time." He rolled her to her back, sprawling her beneath him and settling in with a pounding rhythm.

Arching, she met him thrust for thrust. Her breathless cries spurred him faster. She clutched him and shuddered, sending him straight to wondrous oblivion.

Arms locked, he drove deep and hard, then stayed. Gloriously agonizing spasms shook him as his seed left him.

The library door flew open so hard it banged against the wall. "Chieftain?" Jasper shouted from the threshold.

"Get out!" Gunn roared. "Now!"

The door slammed shut.

"I suppose we should have locked it." Lorna shook beneath him with a lazy giggle, mischief in her eyes.

He winked. "Now ye are my wife. We have a witness to the consummation."

Her smile faded, leaving in its wake a dangerous thoughtfulness. She barely shook her head. "This seems so impossible. Ye believe me and love me anyway."

"I believe ye *because* I love ye." He resettled his weight so as not to crush her, resting his forearms on either side of her head. His old, unrealistic fears nagged at the back of his mind. What if the same thing that brought her to him decided to steal her away? Send her back to her time? "Swear ye willna leave me, Lorna. I couldna bear it, ye ken?"

She gave him a look that made him swallow hard. "If fate decides to rip me away," she said softly, "know that I did not go willingly, aye?"

He ran his thumb along the fullness of her bottom lip. "Ye will fight like the fury ye are? To stay with me?"

With a gentle touch of his face, she gave him an encouraging smile. "I will fight with everything in me. To stay at yer side. Through this life and the next."

CHAPTER THIRTEEN

S TILL WARM AND tingly from their wonderful clearing of all misunderstandings, Lorna shook out her skirts, then checked her hair. "Bloody hell. My pins. Help me find them. Ebby gets so frustrated when I lose them."

"And how might I ask do ye lose them without me?" Gunn paused in his scanning of the floor and cast a jealous look her way.

"There are more ways to lose the silly things than what we just did." She combed her fingers through her hair, cursing the messy curls. "It's just long enough to get in the way but still too short for a decent braid. I wish I had never cut it."

He handed her three pins, then grinned and plucked two more from the laces securing her stomacher. "Why did ye cut it...and how many are we looking for?"

"Seven. Usually. Ebby thinks the number six has something to do with the devil, or some such nonsense. I dinna remember exactly what she said." She tried to tame the tresses into some semblance of order and pin them back in a simple knot before they slipped free again. What she wouldn't give for another elastic band or plastic hair clip. The simple band she had brought from the future had snapped. "Ugh! It's like a wriggling eel or something. I dinna ken how Ebby manages it. And I cut it because I needed a change. I tend to do that when I am unhappy."

"Good to know." He came up behind her and nibbled a trail of tingling kisses across her nape. "If ye ever cut it again, I will know I have not kept ye pleased."

"I dinna think that will be a problem."

And she didn't. This incredible man believed her. He had accepted her unbelievable story on her word alone. It both amazed and touched her. It also meant more to her than all the riches in the world.

She gingerly patted her hair one last time. "This is as good as it's going to get without Ebby's expertise. If ye want to see if Jasper is still in the hall and find out what he wanted, I am ready."

"Hmph." Gunn pulled her back into his arms and held her close so she could feel what he would rather be doing than speaking with the war chief. Even through her petticoat and skirt, the hard length of him tempted her to lock the library door and forget everything beyond it.

"Gunn," Jasper called out from the hall. "I fear this canna wait."

"I will kill him," Gunn promised softly.

"No. Ye know he wouldna interrupt us again unless it was urgent. He knows what we were doing." She attempted to placate him with a quick kiss. "Later, aye? We have the rest of our lives." She didn't want to wait either, but he was the chieftain, with all the responsibilities that entailed.

"Come in with ye, man." Gunn snorted like a disgruntled bull as he adjusted the folds of his kilt in a futile attempt at hiding the tenting created by his erection.

Jasper entered, his expression grim. "Lady Murdina has escaped her rooms."

Immediate fear for the children clutched Lorna. "I should find the bairns."

Gunn caught hold of her. "Wait. We need to know more first." He motioned the war chief closer. "How?"

"I am not certain." Jasper stood there, scowling, his fists clenched. The man's anguish was obvious. "Forsy said when she went to give the woman her daily tisane, Lady Murdina was gone." He slowly shook his head. "The guard at the door is a good man. Alert. Loyal. He said he neither saw nor heard anything."

"She had to have found the tunnels," Gunn said. "I shouldha ordered access to her rooms sealed." He pounded his fist into his palm. "I am a damned fool. Underestimated that deceitful wretch again."

"There is more," Jasper said. Dread and something even darker filled his tone. "Her brother is dead."

"Dead?" A sense of impending doom made Lorna's heartbeat pound hard into her throat. "I have to find the children. Now."

Gunn waved her on. "Go!" Then he caught her back and pressed his *sgian-dubh* into her hand. "Do whatever ye need do to keep yerself and the bairns safe. Understand?"

"I will." As she ran from the room, she tucked the short dagger snugly between her breasts. The annoying stays finally proved useful, holding the blade in place.

Headed for the stables, she slowed only long enough to snatch her cloak from the peg beside the kitchen's rear door. The wonderful day had suddenly gone bleak and forbidding.

If the woman was in the tunnels, she could hide like a rat in the walls for days. Desperation must have driven her to it. What could she possibly hope to accomplish by leaving her rooms? Surely Lady Murdina had enough sense to realize that she had no means of escape from Thursa. Not only could all in the clan recognize her on sight, but it was the dead of winter and bitterly cold. The snow left by the storm from weeks ago was still as thick as the day it fell.

"Children?" She tried not to sound as panicked as she felt even as she broke into a run and charged into the stable. "Children?"

"Here with the kittens," Frances called out.

Now that she knew they were safe, she could breathe. She eased around the glowing brazier that the stable master kept burning in front of the stall where the mother cat and kittens stayed. The gruff old man had mumbled something about keeping the chieftain's daughter from coming down with ague from the cold, but Lorna had caught him smiling down into the stall and watching the kittens on more than one occasion. It was more than a little clear he intended the warmth of the brazier for the wee felines as much as the bairns.

But as she cleared the iron firepit and looked into the stall, she halted, and the choking panic returned. "Where is Bella?"

Both children looked up. "She said she would be here after she used the garderobe," Frances said, then frowned. "But she shouldha been here by now. Reckon she is feeling poorly?"

"Which garderobe?" If Bella had been on her floor, she would have used the privy attached to her room. Lorna struggled to keep the panic out of her voice. "Which one, Frances?"

"The one off the kitchens," he said. "We found her with Cook after we left the library."

"I just left the kitchens," Lorna said. Her stomach churned with all the dire possibilities.

"What is wrong, mistress?" Hesther asked in a trembling whisper.

They needed to know so they could be on their guard, but Lorna loathed alarming them. "Murdina escaped through the tunnels and Leckness is dead."

Both children paled and cowered deeper into the stall.

"Come with me." She urged them toward her. "Better that we stay together."

They scrambled up out of the straw, grabbed her hands, and huddled close.

"Ye said we were safe," Hesther softly accused her, tears streaming down her face.

"And I meant it," Lorna said. "I will fight with everything in me to keep ye safe." She pulled them both into a hug, then looked them in the eyes. "But we have to make sure Bella is safe too. How long has it been since she told ye she would join ye?"

"I dinna ken." Frances shifted with a worried shrug. "We was busy playing with the kitties."

"Then we have to find her." Lorna held tightly to their hands, maneuvered around the brazier, then out of the stable. Once they cleared the obstacle, she ran as fast as she could without dragging the younglings off their feet.

As soon as they burst into the kitchen, she could tell word had spread fast. A kitchen maid startled and skittered to the side, and two others paused in their chopping of vegetables long enough to cross themselves and glance upward while mouthing silent prayers.

"Have ye seen Bella?" Lorna asked Cook as the woman ambled around a skinned carcass with a cleaver raised.

Cook resettled the kitchen weapon in her hand and pointed it at the narrow hallway beside the pantry. "Said after she visited the garderobe, she was headed for the stables to play with Mosie's kittens with the rest of the bairns." She squinted at the row of cloaks hanging on the pegs beside the kitchen's outer door. "That there wrap on the end is hers. My Bella has more sense than to venture outside without it."

"Stay here with Cook," Lorna said to Hesther and Frances. She hurried down the hall and stood in front of the closed curtain that granted a bit of privacy to the individual using the wooden plank with a hole in it. "Bella? Are ye all right, lass? Ye have been in there a good while."

No response came from the other side of the curtain.

Lorna ripped it open to find the garderobe empty. She stared at the space, panic and fury churning within her.

Heart pounding even harder, she hurried back to the kitchen. "She is not there. Ye heard nothing? No sound of scuffling or a cry?"

Cook slowly shook her head, then buried the meat cleaver into the carcass with a hard slam. "If that witch hurts our Bella..."

"I need to find Mrs. Thistlewick and see if maybe Bella got distracted and went to see her." She squeezed Hesther's and Frances's shoulders. "Can they stay here with ye? I know they will be safe here."

"Course they can." Cook wiped her hands on her stained apron and waved them over. "None dare enter my kitchen lest I welcome them. Come over here, my wee ones." When they failed to budge, the kindly soul gave them a wink and motioned for them again. "I need ye to sample the sweets for Yule to see if the recipe is just right, ye ken? 'Twould help me greatly."

The two turned and eyed Lorna.

"Stay here, my brave ones," she said. "I hope that Bella changed her mind and decided to help Mrs. Thistlewick in the apothecary."

They both nodded and edged toward Cook, their faces shining with tears.

Cook shooed her onward. "Find our Bella so that we might all breathe easier."

Lorna ran for the apothecary, but her steps slowed and her hopes fell. Mrs. Thistlewick stood in the center of the great hall, wringing her hands as she spoke with Gunn and Jasper. All three turned and stared at her as if sensing her dismay. Unable to speak, she shook her head and clutched her fists to her chest.

"What?" Gunn charged toward her, closing the distance between them in a few strides. He took hold of her shoulders and squeezed.

She felt his fears as deeply as her own. "I canna find Bella," she whispered.

He didn't speak. Didn't blink. Just stared at her as though frozen in time.

Mrs. Thistlewick and Jasper joined them. "What now?" the housekeeper asked.

"I canna find Bella." Lorna's voice broke as she announced it a second time. She swallowed hard, struggling to regain control. "Cook last saw her a short time ago. Bella told her she was going to visit the garderobe, then go out to the kittens with Hesther and Frances." Lorna shook her head. "Bella never showed up in the stable."

Gunn's hands slowly fell away from her shoulders. He turned to Jasper with his teeth bared. "Every man. Into the tunnels. Find my daughter and bring that woman to me."

Loads of crime stories, some fictional, some true, flooded back to Lorna. She caught Gunn's arm and pulled him back. "Wait. We have to think this through. If ye close in on Murdina and she feels threatened, she might hurt Bella."

"Surely ye canna expect me to stand here and do nothing?"

"Of course not. I am just saying we have to think everything through. If ye flood the tunnels with warriors, I fear for what might happen. She could hear ye coming for her and…" She couldn't bear to finish that sentence. They had to play this deadly game better than Murdina. "Did she kill her brother, or did he die of whatever was ailing him when they arrived?"

"Slit his throat," Jasper said. "But it looked as if he just lay there and let her do it."

"She probably waited until he passed out from the whisky," Mrs. Thistlewick said. "He had the maids bring fresh bottles daily."

"Why would she kill him?" Lorna turned and stared at the archway that led to their rooms. "Remember how Hesther and Frances said they didna believe him to be her brother?"

"Could be he turned on her and threatened her somehow," Gunn said. "But none of that gets my Bella safe. The woman must be mad to think she can gain anything other than a snapped neck from threatening my daughter. I understand the point ye make, dear one, but I must take action. We waste precious time standing here discussing it."

"Then only take a few. Those who know the tunnels best," Lorna said. Murdina had probably been working on this for days. Who knew how long she had tested the tunnels to see where they led?

"Mistress!" Out of breath and wild-eyed, Ebby stumbled out of the stairwell, waving a ragged parchment overhead. "Lady Murdina has Miss Bella!"

Before Lorna could make it to Ebby, Gunn outdistanced her and snatched the paper from the maid's hand. After scanning the note, he turned back to Ebby. "Where did ye find this?"

"On the floor of Miss Bella's solar."

"What does it say?" Lorna squinted at the erratic scrawl, made even more difficult to decipher by blotches of ink and smears throughout the script.

Gunn lifted his gaze from the missive and locked eyes with her. "If we send anyone other than yerself into the tunnels to fetch Bella, she will cut my daughter's throat just as she did her brother's."

The prospect of wandering among the damp, dark passages made Lorna swallow hard. She had never been good at mazes or puzzles and was none too fond of close places either.

But she had no choice. She had to save Bella.

"How extensive are they?" The more information she had, the less her imagination could run wild. "Do they run throughout the entire keep or only exist in important areas to escape a siege?"

"They run the full of the keep." Gunn scrubbed a hand across his mouth. "Where there is a wall, there is a passage. Some lead nowhere. Others connect and create routes that would make hiding for days or even weeks possible. And there are many traps throughout."

Lorna tried not to think about searching behind the walls for that long. "She canna know them as well as she thinks she does. She has only been locked in her rooms for a few days."

"Aye, but who knows how long she has been studying them?" He gave a frustrated snort. "She couldha started mapping them out the day she arrived."

Lorna wiped her sweaty palms on her skirts. "Get me a candlestick. Extra candles. Water and bread, maybe?" The keep was huge. Who knew how long it could take her to find Murdina? She gave Gunn a hopeful look. "I dinna suppose ye have them mapped out, do ye? That would save me time and keep me out of the dead ends and traps."

"I canna ask ye to do this."

The strain in his voice made her throat ache with the urge to sob that they had no choice. Instead, she managed a calm but stern tone. "Ye didna ask me, and I am doing it. Is there a map or not?"

Gunn shot a curt nod at Jasper, who took off in the general direction of the library.

"Ebby and I shall see to the lighting and supplies," Mrs. Thistlewick said. She waved for the maid to follow, and they both scurried toward the kitchen hall.

"Ye have the *sgian-dubh*?" Gunn shifted his weight from one foot to the other, as if unable to bear the fact that this task was not his to do. "A dirk is more effective but canna be so readily concealed."

Lorna patted her chest. "The dagger is tucked right here. I can get to it easily." She tried to reassure him with a confidence she did not feel. "And once upon a time, I was quite the knife thrower. The talent will come back to me should I need it." At least, she hoped it did. That particular skill had bought her many an ale in the pubs of her time. She had never been particularly good at darts, but daggers were a different story.

He scrubbed his palms together, then closed his hands into fists. "I canna let ye go alone."

"But the note said—"

"I dinna give a damn what that note said. She plans to kill ye both, then flaunt it in my face before I kill her." He took hold of her shoulders again and pulled her closer. "She has no honor but knows that we do. That is what she is counting on. I have hunted this type of evil before. Ye must not follow the limits they set. To win, ye must make yer own rules."

What he said made sense. She rested a hand on his chest, feeling his heart pound as hard as hers. "Do ye have any thoughts on where she might have made her nest?"

His expression turned calculating. "Even with the thick outer wall, the passages will still be colder than the Earl of Hell's heart. But three of the false tunnels end against hearths. The chimney wall would give off some warmth. If she has found one of those, I would lay odds that is where she stays, unless she plans to slip into empty rooms long enough to warm herself."

"That would be hard for her to do unless she bound and gagged Bella and left her somewhere."

Jasper stormed back into the hall. Lorna held out her hand for the map. He handed it over without a word. She unrolled it, and her heart lurched. Gunn hadn't lied. Passages, priest holes, and cunningly placed traps in the form of sudden drop-offs honeycombed the walls of Thursa Castle. "There is no way she could learn all this in three weeks' time."

"That is what I am counting on." Gunn tapped on three areas on the map. "These will be the warmest." Then he tapped on a fourth. "This is the entrance where she more than likely snatched Bella."

"Let me go with her," Jasper said. "I know the tunnels as well as Bella does." His fists went so tight that his knuckles popped. "And it is my fault the woman is even here. I shouldha been more cautious."

Gunn clapped a hand on the man's shoulder. "Ye had no way of knowing things would come to this. I need ye on this side of the walls. Place a man at every escape from the passages, but they are not to kill her if she emerges. That pleasure is mine alone, ye ken?"

"I understand." Jasper gave a respectful nod, then turned and charged away.

Mrs. Thistlewick and Ebby returned bearing the items Lorna had requested, except for the candlestick. Instead, Ebby held up a metal cylinder by its bale. An elongated window of sorts was cut out of the front and the metal bent outward, like small reflective shutters that successfully aimed the light outward.

"'Tis wicked hot," the maid warned as she handed it over. "Oil feeds the flame from the crock in the bottom, so be sure and dinna tip it much. With the shields the way they are, it will be hard for that wretch to see ye with the light blinding her."

"Aye," Mrs. Thistlewick agreed. "It will last longer than candles as well. We put a fresh jar of fat in the bag with yer bread and tinderbox so ye can refill it."

"Perfect." Lorna tied the laces of the cloth bag to her belt, then accepted the lantern. She lifted it, peering closely at the workmanship. "A grand design to be sure."

"Our smithy is verra talented." Gunn turned her toward the hallway that ran beside the kitchens. "We will enter at the one in the outer hallway."

"Chieftain, wait!" Ebby called out, rushing after them with a dark garment held high. "The blackness of yer overcoat will help hide yer léine should the light happen to fall upon it."

"Ye are a true gem, Ebby," Lorna told her. The dark leather would indeed help camouflage him.

"That ye are, lass," Gunn said as he hurriedly donned the coat. As Ebby had foreseen, it hid the parts of his tunic that his waistcoat didn't cover.

The maid blushed at the praise, then caught her fist to her mouth and looked ready to cry. "God watch over ye both," she whispered, then hurried away. "And God watch over our sweet Miss Bella!"

Mrs. Thistlewick crossed herself three times as they passed her. Eyes closed, she moved her thin lips in silent prayers.

"Ye would think we are off to war against an army," Gunn said for Lorna's ears alone.

"Never underestimate a woman scorned." She switched the lantern to her nondominant hand and pulled the *sgian-dubh* from between her breasts. "Wait a bit before ye come in after me, aye? In case she lurks near the opening."

"I have hunted evil before, my dearest mouse."

"Dinna be snippy," she said as he brought them to a halt.

180

"What are we stopping here for?"

"How do ye intend to use the map with it stuffed in yer belt and yer hands full?"

She stared down at the lantern in one hand and the dagger in the other. "Fair point." She shoved the knife back in place between her breasts and pulled the map free.

As she turned toward the kitchen, he stopped her again. "Nay, love. We will enter through the door just past this archway. That way, if she waits as ye suggest, we will cut her off and force her to exit at the garderobe."

"Cook has her meat cleaver ready. If Lady Murdina comes out through the kitchens, there willna be enough left of her to feed to the dogs."

"While I would hate to be robbed of my vengeance, such an end would be appropriate." He nodded at a stone block at about eye level that was noticeably smaller than the rest. "When ye push hard upon that stone, the lever system will cause this door as well as its frame to swing open."

"A fake door? Are all the entrances hidden this way?"

Gunn shook his head. "Nay. Some openings are hidden behind tapestries or paintings. Others behind furniture. The largest of all is in the library. An entire wall of stone swings out and requires a great deal of strength to activate the pulleys that set it back in place. Press the stone, and when the passage opens, ye will see it reinforced to prevent the enemy from breaking through the wood of the door itself."

After a deep breath, Lorna pushed the block. Cold, dank air hit her in the face as the entrance slowly creaked open. She lifted the lantern and guided the beam, flashing it first one way, then the other. Bloody hell, the way was narrow. It also shot straight ahead, leaving no place to hide. She forced herself not to look back and search for Gunn. Instead, she moved forward at a slow, steady pace, alert for any sign of Murdina and poor Bella.

After she had continued on for a few paces, the door resealed with a heart-stopping thud, surrounding her in darkness except for the lantern. Cold sweat dotted her upper lip and everywhere else.

I can do this. I have to do this.

She pulled in another slow, deep breath. The place held plenty of air. She was fine and needed to stop being such a coward. She could do this.

The air reeked of musty dampness and the greasy sootiness of her sputtering lantern. But there *was* air. That was all that mattered.

Her heart jumped, and she swallowed a shriek as warm breath brushed across her ear.

"It is all right, my love. I am here."

His presence strengthened her. She turned her head until her cheek brushed against the bristly softness of his beard. "I am glad ye are here," she said just as softly.

He nudged the small of her back, silently urging her onward. She lifted the lantern and moved faster as her eyes adjusted. According to the map, just up ahead was probably where Murdina had snatched Bella. When she reached the spot, she paused and gave the area a closer look to see if any clue was left behind. Other than a few faded scratches probably from the builders, nothing stood out.

With two possible directions from which to choose, Lorna decided to step up the game. "Bella!" she called out as long and as loud as she could force. "Bella, I am coming for ye! Dinna be afraid."

Then she heard it. To the right. The loud echo of taunting laughter.

The infuriating sound made her itch to find Murdina and teach her to pick on someone who could fight back rather than wee bairns and lonely men blinded by their painful pasts.

CHAPTER FOURTEEN

L ORNA SHOVED THE map back into her belt and followed the
intermittent laughter and scratching sounds coming from the
passage to the right. Anger and worry fed her pace. She moved
faster until almost running.

A hard yank on her belt knocked the wind from her. Gunn
pulled her back and whispered against her cheek, "Slow yerself.
She means to lead ye into that pit up ahead."

Teeth clenched, Lorna silently raged at herself. How could
she be so gullible and allow Murdina to manipulate her like that?
She patted his arm and nodded while holding the lantern higher.
The blackness of the floor a few strides farther revealed the trap.

Two could play that deadly game. She crouched and cast the
beam of light across the floor, searching for anything she could
use to drop into that hole and make some noise.

Gunn knelt beside her and pressed close again. "What are ye
doing?"

She placed her mouth close to his ear. "I want her to think I
fell in there. Lure her to us." In the flickering light, she made out
his nod of agreement.

The largest thing they found was a broken block discarded by
the stonemasons. Gunn moved it to the pit's edge, then nodded

back at the lantern. He was right—they had to douse the light if she meant to make Murdina think she fell.

The cold sweat of her mild claustrophobia returned, sinking its teeth deeper into her fears. She swallowed hard and shook it away. She *had* to do this. For Bella's sake.

Before she killed the flame, she got the tinderbox out of the bag and held it tight. That would keep her from fumbling to find it in the inky blackness.

She motioned for Gunn to drop the bait. He dipped his chin in agreement and threw the block into the pit; it bounced off the sides and filled the passage with the echo of its tumble. She cut loose with a loud scream, then dwindled it to nothing more than a whimper. With Gunn crouched beside her, she pinched out the lantern's flame. Now they would wait and see if Murdina took the bait.

The woman didn't make them wait long. Up ahead, deep in the darkness, a pinpoint of light flickered. Lorna eased the dagger free and slowly stood without a sound. Gunn rose beside her. His comforting heat and familiar scent gave her the courage she needed to stay sane in the suffocating blackness.

The light bobbed closer until Murdina's face appeared to float above the flame. The excitement glittering in her eyes and the cruel slant of her mouth made Lorna wonder if the she-devil teetered on the edge of madness.

She almost felt sorry for her. Almost.

As soon as Murdina reached the pit, Lorna let the dagger fly.

The wretch screamed and grabbed her shoulder. Her candlestick dropped, plunging them back into total darkness. The scrabbling of her steps and muttered cursing faded into an echo as she scuttled away like a rat seeking safety in the shadows.

"Shite!" Lorna swept her arm through the blackness, found Gunn's hand, and pressed the tinderbox into it. "I was aiming for her throat. We have to hurry and catch her. Because of me, she might hurt Bella."

He struck a spark and relit the lantern, then lifted it, flooding light across the narrow ledge to the left that led around the pit. "Dinna fash yerself, m'love. Ye did well to hit her at all in this darkness. With her injured and lacking her candle, we will catch her. Come." He caught hold of her hand and took the lead, lifting the lantern high to light their way.

An enraged scream echoed back to them, followed by a steady stream of garbled shouting that Lorna couldn't make out. "What is she saying?"

"I dinna ken, but it gives me hope. Remember, my Bella is a wily minx."

Lorna's spirits rose as well. Bella was a canny child who knew the tunnels better than any of them. She hoped the wee lass had managed to escape. But even if she had, they still needed to flush Murdina out of the walls and confirm Bella's whereabouts.

They came upon the woman, muttering and backed against the chimney wall with her hand clamped to her shoulder.

"Ye may have won this time, but ye willna win the next," she said while sidling along the wall.

"There will be no next." Gunn handed the lantern to Lorna and lunged forward. He grabbed Murdina's wrist, twisted her arm to the small of her back, and growled, "Where is my daughter?"

The woman's once beautiful face twisted with an evil grin. "Dead! I threw her in that pit ye passed."

Lorna fought the urge to run back and look. Murdina had to be lying. Had to be.

"Lift the lantern," he said. He jerked the woman's hands behind her back and bound her wrists with a strip of leather he ripped from his coat. He spun her about and clenched her face in one hand. "Where is my daughter?"

"Ye are hurting me!" she cried, trying to twist free. "And I already told ye."

He released her face, grabbed her by her disheveled mop of hair, and steered her back the way they came.

"Ye mean to throw me into that pit and make me starve to death!" The woman locked her legs and refused to walk.

Gunn shoved her forward with a hard push. "I willna have the stench of yer evil trapped within the walls of my keep. Walk, damn ye, or I will be more than happy to drag ye."

She spat at him, then turned to spit at Lorna.

Lorna lifted the lantern and shined the beam into the woman's face. "Get moving and be thankful Gunn is so merciful."

"Gunn?" Murdina screeched his name like a raven cawing to the winds. "Gunn? Ye wasted no time in worming yer way into his bed, did ye?"

"At least I didna have to drug him to do it." Lorna couldn't resist. She still had doubts that Murdina and Gunn had actually completed the act. Especially since deadly nightshade caused such severe muscle weakness. But none of that mattered now. Murdina had lost.

The harpy screeched again and lunged toward her, but Gunn yanked her back and shoved her forward down the tunnel. She twisted and writhed, then went limp and dropped to the ground. True to his word, Gunn dragged her until she cooperated and walked.

After what felt like forever, they reached the dreaded hole where Murdina swore she had cast Bella to her death.

"Shine the light into the pit," Gunn said, anguish filling his voice.

Praying that Bella was not at the bottom, Lorna aimed the beam downward. She nearly dropped to her knees with relief. The light revealed nothing other than what appeared to be a decomposing rat.

He gave a satisfied snort and forced Murdina around the pit.

Once past it, she struggled and kicked. "Ye canna kill me or ye will never find her. I misspoke when I said it was this pit." She screeched while trying to twist around, baring her teeth like a wild animal. "'Twas another trap I put her in. Where are ye taking me? What are yer intentions?"

He remained stoic, shoving her toward the exit with a hurried, determined pace.

Lorna ran to keep up. She wondered too what Gunn's intentions were but remained silent. That was his choice. Especially depending on where and when they found Bella and what her condition was.

When they reached the end of the passage, he activated a floor lever with a hard kick, then squinted as the door swung open wide. His expression turned grim as death as he dragged Murdina into the great hall. When he reached the center of the area between the rows of tables, he threw her to the floor. "Shackle her. Hands and feet. Then throw her into the cell."

Four of his men rushed forward. They grabbed her by her arms and legs and carried her away. She screeched and howled dark obscenities that even shocked Lorna's modern sensibilities.

"What is *the cell*?" Lorna asked Mrs. Thistlewick, who had rushed in to meet them.

"The lowest point in the dungeon," the housekeeper said with satisfaction. "The only time prisoners are brought up from there is when it is time for their execution."

Mrs. Thistlewick reached for the lantern, but Lorna held it back. "No. I have to go back and find Bella. Murdina refused to tell us where she was." She ached to hug that sweet lass until she squeaked to be let go.

Without waiting for Gunn or telling him where she was headed, she hurried back down the hallway and activated the secret door.

Once inside, she eyed the floor lever before glancing back at the opening. "Let's just leave the door ajar, shall we?" After all, with Murdina captured, stealth was no longer a worry. "Bella!" she shouted every few steps while striding through the darkness at a steady pace. It wasn't nearly as overwhelming, since she had been this way before.

After passing the first pit, she reached for the map in her belt and discovered it was gone. Her mouth grew dry and her heartbeat pounded in her ears until it was almost deafening. "No need to panic." She leaned back against a wall, pulling in slow, deep breaths while visualizing open fields of heather. They had followed this same stretch, then turned to the right when Murdina laughed. After they passed the pit, not that far up ahead, they found her.

Then she remembered. The current route, the only route she knew, seemed to dead-end against the hearth wall where they had captured Murdina. "Well, bloody hell. Now what without the map?"

But perhaps not all was lost. She thought back over all that had happened, studying it for the slightest clue. This was where Murdina had fled to once wounded. Had it been a mere coincidence, or was this her nest?

With painstaking care, Lorna slowly directed the beam back and forth all around the passage, scanning the floor and walls for anything that might tell her something about Bella's whereabouts.

Something reflected the light and gave her pause. She moved toward it and discovered her dagger. "Lovely." She cleaned the blade by wiping it on the sole of her shoe, then tucked it into her belt. "Bella!" she called out again, hoping to hear something. "Yer da dragged Murdina out to the great hall. They shackled her and threw her into the cell. If ye are hiding, my wee one, it is safe to come out. I swear it."

Nothing but silence answered, and there was no sign of the child. All she heard was her own breathing. Without the map, she had no idea which direction to take.

She directed the light across the floor again, trying to find anything that might tell her what to do. Whitish scrapes across the part of the floor stained dark by dampness caught her attention. Several wide, uniform arcs led her gaze to a partially opened wall. Another passage? But if this was another way out, why had Gunn gone to the trouble of dragging Murdina out the way they had entered?

If only she hadn't lost the map. Lorna stared at the scrapes, debating whether to retrace her steps and look for the map or abandon her search for the child completely.

"No. I canna give up."

She eyed the wall that was partially ajar. The opening was almost wide enough to squeeze through—but so narrow, it made her catch her breath at the thought of worming her way through it. But Bella would easily fit. This had to be what threw Murdina into an enraged fit earlier. Perhaps Bella had slipped out this way.

Shining the light on the wall, Lorna searched for a hidden lever to open it wider. If this wasn't another way out, perhaps it was a hiding place and Bella was somewhere beyond it.

Then she reasoned if the child had made the wall open this much, the switch had to be within a nine-year-old's reach. She searched lower. Her heart jumped as the beam swept across a small oblong block of stone protruding from the wall. "I am coming, Bella!" She shoved it as hard as she could. It didn't budge. Perhaps she needed to use both hands. She set the lantern on the floor, gripped the stone, and shoved again. The thing gave just a little, eking out a grinding sound.

"Well, bloody hell." She glared at the wall, tempted to give it a good, swift kick, but logic won out. Frustrated at the failure, she stuck her face in the opening and called out again, "Bella! Are ye in there? Can ye make some sort of sound?"

The faintest scratching came to her, but she couldn't decide if it was beyond the wall in front of her or behind her in the passage.

"I canna ignore that and take the chance of leaving Bella in the darkness." She could just imagine how terrified the little girl had to be, whether she knew the passages by heart or not. They were cold, dark, and filled with insects and rodents that Lorna would rather not think about.

Determined to activate the mechanism and make the wall move, she picked up the lantern, positioned her rump square on the protruding stone, and shoved with all the strength her legs possessed.

The lever stone gave, and the wall shifted, bumping her and

knocking her back into the space. Before she could right herself, the wall slammed shut again, catching her skirts and crushing her bag of supplies between the walls. "Damn it! No!" No matter how hard she pulled, the seam between the walls refused to set her free.

Caught in the wall, she sagged back against it. "I canna believe this."

The lantern revealed she was trapped in an area that was roughly the length of a bed and about three times as wide. A dank, boxy sort of room. "Or a good-sized tomb," she muttered, then smacked at something tickling across her nape. "Off me, vile beastie!" Whether a spider or her imagination, she wanted no part of it.

Her chest tightened and her heart pounded faster with every passing second. She swallowed hard and tried to regain control. "Ye have air. Mrs. Thistlewick knows ye were coming back in here, and ye left the door open. Once Gunn misses ye, he will be here in no time and activate the lever and open the wall."

Talking aloud helped. Some.

But heaven help her, she was thirsty, and the walls had crushed her water and spare lamp fuel inside the crack. "Ye will be fine. Calm yerself." She tried to fully stand, but her snagged garments wouldn't allow it. "Well, bollocks."

There had to be another release lever on this side. All she needed to do was find it. As she hitched sideways to shine the beam along the other wall, her left foot hit something sticking up out of the floor.

"There ye are, my precious key to freedom." Renewed hope chased all her phobias away as she kicked the lever just as Gunn had done at the other doorway.

Nothing happened.

"That's all right. We'll just try it again." Twisting as far as her pinched skirt would allow, she kicked it so hard that pain shot up her leg. The wall didn't move. Worse yet, the lantern flame flickered with a warning sputter.

She fell back against the wall again and pressed a hand against her chest. If the light went out and left her trapped in darkness…

She stomped on the lever again and again until breathless. "Open, ye bloody thing, open!"

Her hand brushed against the haft of the dagger in her belt. If she could cut herself free, at least she could sit on the floor until help came. "Help will come. Gunn will come." With the cloth held taut, she sliced through, cut it away, and sagged to the floor in a defeated heap. "All I have to do is stay calm." The lantern's flame sputtered lower. "Stay calm," she said louder.

Then the light went out, unleashing the beast of darkness to swallow her whole.

She closed her eyes and hugged her knees to her chest. "Gunn will come." She repeated the mantra over and over, fighting against the cold sweat and nausea overtaking her. Even with her eyes squeezed tightly shut, she could feel herself getting dizzier by the moment. "Must not panic. Gunn will come."

The longer she sat there, the louder the demons in her mind whispered she had just been buried alive. She covered her ears, squeezed her eyes tighter shut, and forced herself to think of Gracie, of Lonnie, the shop—anything to get her thoughts off being sealed inside a wall.

Without realizing it, she'd started rocking. "Ye just had to go to that cliff with that fool. None of this wouldha happened if ye had just told him to go to the devil while standing in the shop."

But then she would never have met Gunn. Or Bella. Or wee Frances and Hesther. Tears squeezed free. She loved them all. And no one had ever touched her heart as Gunn had.

"He will come," she whispered into the darkness. "He will come and everything will be all right."

She hugged her knees tighter and pressed her forehead against them. "Please let him come," she prayed. "Before it is too late."

CHAPTER FIFTEEN

"**D**A!"

Gunn's heart lurched at the voice he had feared he would never hear again. He spun about and dropped to his knees with his arms open wide. "Bella!"

She hit his chest at full force. "I got away! But hurry, we can catch her. I know where she is." She clung to him, her arms wrapped around his neck, squeezing tight as if never letting go.

And he hoped she wouldn't. Never had he ever been so afraid of losing her. "Are ye all right, my wee one? Whole and unharmed?" He peeled her away and held her out, scanning her for any sign of injury.

"I am fine, Da." The youngling squared her shoulders and beamed with a proud smile. "I used my *sgian-dubh* to cut free. The one Jasper gave me last birthday. Cut right through that old cow's ribbons that she thought would keep me trapped. Ye shouldha heard her screeching when she found me gone. Sounded like the terns when their nests are robbed."

"I heard her squawking, my braw beastie, and I knew it was ye who caused it." Relief and so much more filled him that he almost couldn't breathe. "That is how Lorna and I tracked her to her wicked hidey-hole." He curled her back into his arms, rocking from side to side as he hugged her tight. "My precious Arabella. Ye dinna ken how worried I was. Lorna was beside herself too."

Bubbling out a joyous giggle, Bella kissed his cheek, then stretched and looked all around. "Where is Lorna? I want to hug her too."

Gunn peered about, then stood and turned, scanning the entirety of the hall. "Where is Mistress Lorna?"

"Bless my soul." Mrs. Thistlewick clapped her hands to her cheeks. "She returned to the tunnels in search of Bella."

"Alone?" An ominous dread knotted in Gunn's gut. Had he gotten his precious daughter back only to lose the woman he loved? "How long has she been gone?"

"Not long," the housekeeper said. She pointed to the hallway housing the entrance they had used to access the tunnels the first time. "I am sure ye can catch up with her with no trouble at all."

He caught Bella up in another big hug, then set her back to her feet and gave her a stern but loving look. "Stay here whilst I fetch her, aye? She doesna ken the way of the passages." When he straightened, he spotted something on the floor next to the arch. "By my soul, is that the map?" He charged over and scooped it up, then stared at the open entrance to the tunnels. Fear of the worst within him grew, like a great black stain slowly spreading.

"I am coming with ye, Da." Bella appeared at his side. "I ken the tunnels better than anyone."

Tempting as it was, he wanted her safe with Mrs. Thistlewick, not wandering the passages again. "I would rather ye stay in the hall till I return." He pointed at the open door to the passage. "I feel sure if she went this way, she is retracing the steps we took earlier. I will probably find her where we captured Murdina."

Bella caught hold of his sleeve as he turned to go, but it was her pained look that stopped him. "If she goes into the priest hole and makes the wall move again, she willna be able to get back out. I fouled the lever to try to trap the witch."

"Fouled the lever? How?"

"Old Master Grogan showed me when I was a wean, in case enemies stormed the keep. All I had to do was remove one of the shims leveling the corner piece." She belatedly crossed herself and added, "God rest his soul."

"Can ye undo it?" Gunn held his breath, praying his daughter would give him the answer he so badly needed.

She shook her head. "I dinna think so. Master Grogan never said anything about putting it back."

"Fetch the smithy," Gunn bellowed. "Iron bars. Hammers. Men to man them. Now!" Master Grogan had been the overseer of building Thursa, a kind man who had lost his family to the same fever that took Bella's mother. He handled his grief by indulging every child in the clan with intricately carved toys and answers to their endless questions.

Bella caught hold of his hand again. "Let me run and see, Da. Mayhap she is merely lost and not trapped at all."

"I willna have ye go alone." It didn't matter that the child knew the way better than anyone. All he knew was he had just gotten her back after fearing her lost forever.

He strode back into the main hall and hailed Jasper. "Bella and I must go ahead. Lorna may be trapped in the priest hole behind the kitchens. I canna wait for the smithy."

"I will bring them." The war chief thumped his chest, then crossed himself. "God be with ye all."

"A light for ye, chieftain!" Ebby came running with another lantern fashioned the same as the other but larger. "This one holds more fat than the one Mistress Lorna carries." Eyes brimming with tears, she pressed a fist to her chest. "My prayers are with ye. She is the kindest soul. I dinna want to lose my mistress."

"I dinna want ye to lose yer mistress either." Gunn took the lantern and handed it to Bella. "Lead on, Arabella. Pray we find her safe and whole."

The child took the glowing cylinder, ran to the tunnel entrance, and charged inside without hesitation. Gunn kept close, thankful for once that his daughter had always disobeyed him when it came to the maze running throughout the walls. That disobedience could very well save Lorna's life.

Bella paused at the pit and dangled the light over its edge while squinting downward. "She remembered it, Da. She isna here." Without waiting for his response, she scurried onward toward the passage's offshoot that led to a solid wall and the priest hole.

Gunn wished the place was flooded with light so he might see ahead. "Lorna!" he called out, straining to pick up on the slightest response. "Give me the lantern, lass. I can hold it higher and cast the beam farther. Ye can call to her too, if ye like." He didn't add it would make him feel better for both of them to rage like banshees until Lorna answered.

"If she is in the hole," Bella said, "the wall will keep her from hearing us. Master Grogan said that was why he ordered the stone cutters to make those blocks extra thick. So enemies couldna find those hiding within."

When they reached the end of the passage, Gunn's heart fell to the pit of his stomach. Cloth protruded from a seam in the wall. He dropped to one knee and ran his fingers across it. "Her skirt," he whispered, almost choking on the words.

Bella rested a hand on the stone and bowed her head. "I am so sorry, Da. I didna mean it to hurt Mistress Lorna."

He turned and swiped the tears from her cheek. "Dinna fash yerself, my wee one. We will get her out. I swear it." He pulled his dirk from its sheath beneath his arm. "Show me where ye removed the shim."

The youngling directed him to the lever stone. "Right there. See the space?"

He shoved the blade into the crack as far as it would go, then pushed on the lever with his foot. Nothing happened.

"Master Grogan said it wouldna work that way," Bella said. "Once the balance of the shim is gone, the wall and both levers must be completely reset." She sniffed and wiped her eyes as she bowed her head again. "I am so sorry. 'Twas meant to trap that wicked cow."

"Shh, lass." He pulled her into a hug and tried to comfort her even though he felt like raging at all the powers, both the old gods and the new. They could damn well stop toying with him. He was feckin' tired of their sorry games that fractured his heart and soul. "All we can do is wait for Jasper and the men. They will bring pry bars and hammers."

With her face buried in the front of his shirt, she sobbed all the harder. Bella was not a fool. She knew the sealed-off room would not keep Lorna alive for long. The priest hole was intended for short periods of hiding only. The air would go foul after a few hours.

Clatter echoing from the mouth of the tunnel gave him hope. He patted Bella on the back. "Listen."

She lifted her head and wiped her nose on the back of her hand. Even in the shadowy light, he saw hope in her teary eyes. "Jasper! Hurry!"

Gunn rose to his feet and joined his daughter in her call. "Hie yerselves! The mistress of this keep is in peril."

Several lights bobbed into view, making a glowing line down the narrow passage. Jasper led the men, single file, all of them bearing iron rods and hammers. "We will have the Lady Lorna returned to yer arms in no time," Jasper said.

Gunn held out his hand. "Give me a prying bar."

One of the men placed a heavy rod in his palm. It was longer than he was tall and had a beveled end. He wedged it in the crack above the cloth dangling from the stone. As he leaned into it, Bella ran forward and stopped him. "No, Da. From the bottom. Master Grogan said we must always lever the swinging doors from the bottom. 'Twill loose them from their hinges carved into the wall and make them easier to move."

"I would listen to her," Jasper advised. "She was Grogan's shadow every time she slipped away from Freyda and Mrs. Thistlewick. Even though she was little more than five years old at the time, he always called her his canniest apprentice."

"Ye are certain?" Gunn asked her.

"Aye, Da. Master Grogan let me watch him balance them all and test them to see that they worked proper. Said someone needed to know how to work them for when he left for heaven and couldna help us anymore." She pointed to the corner of the wall beside the fouled lever. "Lift here with all yer might, then the others can wedge their bars into the side to keep it from closing as ye force it back."

"Good enough." Gunn nodded at Jasper and the other men. "Ye heard her." He wedged his pry bar into the bottom of the stone where Bella had instructed. With all his might, his heart, and his soul, he bore down on the rod. Dust filtered down from the ceiling, and the wall groaned with a great grinding of stone against stone.

The others rushed forward, planted their bars into the ever-widening crack, and shoved hard to keep the wall from sliding shut once more.

"'Tis working!" Bella called out. "See her clothes? They slipped down to the floor. The block is moving."

"Again!" Gunn growled, repositioning the bar and bearing down on it even harder. Sweat poured off him. Pain ripped through his straining muscles. None of it mattered. He would get his Lorna freed. Then a thunderous crash and a scream shot terror through him.

"Stop! The ceiling is caving in!"

"Lorna!" He dropped to his knees and pressed his face to the opening. It was a crack as wide as three of his fingers. "Lorna, speak to me. Are ye hurt?"

Her pale fingers appeared, wiggling as she sobbed. "I canna bear this, Gunn. I canna. Please save me."

"Are ye hurt, m'love?" He pressed a kiss to her fingertips, wishing he could pick up the damnable stone and toss it out of the way. "Breathe, love, and tell me. Are ye injured? I am right here and willna leave ye. I swear it."

"I am not hurt," she said in a pitiful whisper. "But the roof fell at one end and trapped me in a wee space almost too small for one of Bella's dogs." Her quiet sobbing tore his heart in two. "I canna bear this much longer. My heart. The pounding of it. No air. I canna breathe. Gunn, please—dinna let me die."

"Lorna! Listen to me." He had to make her focus on him. "Ye can breathe. Feel the fresh air coming into the space. Put yer nose to this crack and breathe it in. Feel it?"

An ominous grinding shifted again and more dust filtered down.

"It is going to crush me. It's slowly falling more." She wiggled her fingers while almost choking on her sobs. "I love ye, Gunn. I am so sorry I didna wait for ye to come and search for Bella with me."

"Ye will not die," he growled. "I refuse to allow it." He turned to Jasper. "Hand me an iron thick enough for her to wedge in there and keep the stone from falling more."

Jasper shot him a look of disbelief and mouthed, "We have none that strong."

"Do it," Gunn ordered him through clenched teeth.

One by one, he fed three of the shorter iron pry bars in through the crack. "Wedge them, my brave wee mousie. Ye can do it. Wedge them against the stones." He prayed she would do it and it would give her a wee bit of comfort. Even though he knew nothing would hold that block, should it decide to give. He needed her calm so he could save her. Somehow.

"This willna work." Her desolate tone made him afraid. She was giving up.

"Lorna. Listen to me." He shoved his fingers through the crack, reaching as far as he could. "Place the bars as best ye can, aye? When ye are ready, ye will take my fingers. The men will force the door the rest of the way and I will pull ye free, m'love. I swear it."

"It willna work," she said in a teary whisper. "The stone will fall before the opening is big enough."

He feared the same but refused to accept it. Twisting around, he waved Bella forward. "Think, my wee one. What would Master Grogan do?"

Her tears glistening in the lantern light, Bella slowly shook her head. "I dinna ken, Da. The roof stone should not have come down like that."

Gunn bowed his head. "I will not lose another loved one." He repositioned himself at the opening and shoved his fingers back through the crack again. "Have ye wedged the irons, dear one?"

"No."

The quietness of Lorna's answer shook him to his soul. She might as well shout her decision to give up and die. "Lorna! Do as I told ye, ye ken?"

"If I do, will ye promise me something?"

"Aye. Anything."

"Promise ye willna be afraid to find someone to love. This is not some curse. It's my stupid fate because I rushed in without thinking." The softness of her sad laugh trickled into the passage, tearing at his heart. "I have always done that, ye know? That's how I found ye, remember?"

"I remember." He curled his fingers around hers, his heart breaking. "Now do as I ask, love. Ye never know when fate might change her mind because of my sheer stubbornness."

She blew out a resigned sigh that made him smile. "Give me a minute, aye?"

"I will give ye anything ye wish, my love—except permission to die and leave me."

She sighed again but didn't comment. Instead, she scuffled around in her small space, clanking the irons and muttering curse words.

He pressed his forehead to the stone and silently prayed, *Dinna take this courageous woman from me. She is mine, ye hear? Ye have stolen enough from me to last a thousand lifetimes. Torture me no more!*

"My skirt is caught again," Lorna said, sounding despondent.

"Take it off. Strip down to yer shift," he said. "Ye will slip through the opening faster."

"Are ye going to grease me with goose fat too?"

"If not for the fact that it would take too long to fetch it, aye, I would." At least her mood had lifted a wee bit. He needed her to fight to live.

He motioned for Jasper and the other men to put their pry bars in place and wait for his signal. He arched a brow at Bella and gave a pointed look at the far side of the area, warning her to stay back. His daughter was not a fool. She knew good and well what could happen.

Bella stepped away, gave an obedient dip of her chin, then clasped her hands in prayer.

He shoved his hand as far into the space as he could, ignoring the grit of the stone biting into his flesh. Blood trickled, warm and hopeless, down his arm. "Are ye ready, my love?" he whispered.

"Know that I love ye," Lorna whispered back. "More than I ever realized I could love anyone."

"As soon as I pull ye free, we will fetch the priest to bless that vow, aye?"

She touched her fingers to his. "Aye."

Ready to claim this rare woman for all time, he gave Jasper a nod.

"Now!" the war chief bellowed, then joined the rest in shifting the stone as fast as possible.

The inner side of the structure shuddered. Lorna cried out, pawing at his fingers as though trying to dig herself free.

"More!" Gunn roared. "Faster!" As the opening widened even more, he reached in and grabbed her wrist.

"It's coming down." Lorna tried to wriggle free of his grip. "Save yer arm! I am lost!"

"More!" Gunn shouted again, wedging his arm deep into the slowly increasing space. The entire wall shuddered, dusting them with bits of stone. The passage was at risk of caving in, but he didn't care. Lorna would not die alone. The doorstone suddenly gave. Gunn yanked her to his chest and rolled to the other side of the passage just as the inner slab of the priest hole crashed to the floor.

She clung to him, screaming as more debris showered all around them.

"Shh...my love. We are safe." He pushed up to his knees and then his feet, cradling her to his chest as he stood. "'Tis just the walls grumbling. It will settle."

"Push it back in place," Bella called out. "Master Grogan said the door stones could be braces if need be."

Jasper and the men hurried to obey, and the unholy sound of stone battling stone faded.

"Bella," Gunn said. "Run, fetch the priest. Bring him to the hall so ye can have a new stepmother before another hour passes."

She took hold of a lantern and shot off like an arrow.

Jasper motioned for the men to leave, then touched his hand to his chest and tipped his head at Gunn.

Gunn responded with a grateful nod and dropped a kiss into Lorna's hair. "My love. It is all right now. Ye are safe."

She still clung to him, softly sobbing, her face buried in his tunic.

"Lorna?"

"I canna bear this darkness anymore," she said in a pitiful whisper. "I canna breathe, Gunn. Please save me."

God help him. His dear one still thought herself trapped. Holding her tighter, he traveled through the passage in long strides, following the string of lanterns that Jasper and his men left behind to light the way. "I will have ye in the light soon, m'love. Verra soon."

She kept her face buried in his chest, no longer sobbing, but instead gasping as though unable to draw in enough air.

He moved faster, cleared the last of the passage, and burst into the hallway. Jasper and his men lined the way, cheering and clapping. Servants and clans folk followed suit. Gunn didn't slow.

The great hall was the room with the largest space and the most light this late in the day.

Once he reached the center of the area between all the tables, he stopped and knelt, holding Lorna in his arms.

"I beg ye all to stay back. She is not well after the ordeal." Gunn swept the room with a look they all understood and obeyed. "Light more candles and stoke the fires. I want this room ablaze with brightness." With a touch as gentle as a whisper, he stroked her hair and rained kisses across her forehead. "Open yer eyes and breathe, m'love. See that ye are safe." When she didn't respond, he feared the tunnels had broken her mind.

He sat on the floor and held her in his lap. "Lorna," he whispered. "Come back to me. I beg ye. Ye swore never to leave me. Remember?"

Her lashes fluttered and her chest slowly rose and fell. She opened her eyes as though waking from a dream. The faintest smile tugged at the corners of her mouth. She let go of his shirt she had knotted in her fists and touched his cheek. "I knew ye would come for me."

"Always, m'love. I will always be here for ye."

She stared at him as if unable to get enough of looking at him. Her brow puckered for a brief moment, and she bit her bottom lip. Tears welled in her eyes.

"What is it, dear one?"

"I didna find Bella, and I dinna ken if I can bring myself to go back into that darkness. Forgive me." She blinked hard in a vain attempt to not cry. "I have become a coward."

"Ye are no coward." His tone came out so stern that Mrs. Thistlewick gasped from behind him. He ignored the woman. This was between himself and his lady love. "Dinna ever say that again. Do ye understand, precious mouse? Not ever."

"But I failed ye. I failed Bella."

"Ye failed no one." He supported her so she might sit taller. "Bella is safe. Gone to fetch the priest, in fact."

"She is safe?" Her glorious blue-green eyes widened and relief shone in her smile. But then her expression melted into a look of worry. "Fetching the priest? Did someone die while saving her?"

He unleashed a satisfied laugh, unable to hold it back. "Nay, m'love. She is fetching him to witness our vows. Remember?"

It was then that she seemed to notice everyone gathered around the fringes of the room. "Ye sat in the floor. In the middle of the hall? In front of everyone?"

"I did."

"And I am in yer lap. In my shift."

"Aye. Ye are."

After another shy glance all around, she leaned closer and whispered, "Why?"

"Because ye were in such a state after yer ordeal that I thought ye needed the largest and brightest room in the keep." With a grin and a shrug, he added, "'Tis a mite too cold to be taking ye outside in yer shift."

Her smile started small and timid, then grew until it sparkled in her eyes. "I love ye."

"And I love ye as well, my dear one. More than ye will ever know."

"I got him!" Bella shouted from across the room. Face red and trying to run, she yanked the elderly priest along behind her.

"Have ye the strength to stand, m'love?" Gunn tipped his head toward the pair coming their way.

"Aye."

He helped Lorna rise and stand at his side.

Mrs. Thistlewick rushed forward, wrapped a shawl around her, then gave her a quick hug. "We canna have ye marrying the man in yer shift, now can we?"

Lorna smiled up at him. "I would marry him wearing as much or as little as he wished."

Laughter rippled through the crowd, then was quickly silenced when Father Thomas *harrumphed* a stern clearing of his throat. With his prayer book tucked in his arm, he gave Bella a kindly nod. "Do ye wish to stand there beside yer new stepmother whilst the Almighty hears their vows?"

"Can Frances and Hesther stand with me too?" she asked.

"They can," Lorna answered, then turned to Gunn. "Aye?"

"Aye, m'love. They are now a part of our family as well." He hugged her to his side, unwilling to let any space exist between them. It didn't matter that her strength had fully returned. He held her for himself. "All I ask is that we get on with it. Aye, Father Thomas?"

"Get the bairns in place, my chieftain." The man waggled a bushy gray brow and patted his prayer book. "God and I are ready."

Bella took her place beside Gunn, and Frances and Hesther stood beside Lorna. "Go ahead, father," Bella sang out. "I dinna want Da to change his mind."

Laughter bubbled through the room again. Even Father Thomas smiled. "Verra well, then. I shall start by hearing the bride's words." He nodded Lorna's way. "Yer full name, child?"

"Lorna Merriweather."

He stared at her, then blinked and frowned. "That is yer *full* name?"

"Aye. 'Tis the only name I have ever had."

"Verra well, then." The holy man cleared his throat again. "Do ye, Lorna Merriweather, pledge yerself as wife to this man? Swear to love and honor him whether the two of ye live in plenty or in want? Through sickness or health? In fair times or foul? Do ye pledge to be faithful to him all of yer days, forsaking all others till death shall part ye?"

"I do," Lorna whispered.

"Say again, child? I ken well enough that the Almighty heard ye, but I be a mite deaf." Father Thomas turned an ear her way.

"I do," she repeated loud and clear.

The priest nodded. "Good enough, then." He pointed his prayer book at Gunn as though it were a weapon. "The Almighty Lord kens well enough that ye have not had an easy way of it, my son. 'Tis why he chose to bless ye with this woman and two more bairns. Do ye pledge yerself to be her husband and honor her all the rest of yer days? During times of plenty or days of want? In sickness or health? In fair times or foul? Will ye forsake all others till death shall part the two of ye?"

"I will." Gunn smiled down at her and hugged her even closer.

"Then let no man dare to put asunder what God Almighty Himself hath joined this day. These two are now one in His eyes." Father Thomas lifted both hands to bless them. "By the grace of the Almighty, the blessings of the church, and the sacred land of our bonnie Scotland, I now pronounce ye man and wife." He grinned. "Go on and kiss her, my son."

Gunn swept Lorna up into his arms and covered her mouth with his. She wound her arms around his neck and kissed him back with a fierce, sweet hunger that rivaled his own.

The hall exploded with clapping, stomping, and cheers.

"Light the Yule fires!" Jasper roared over the noise. "What better way to mark our chieftain's long-overdue happiness?"

"Cook!" Mrs. Thistlewick called out.

"Aye?" the laughing woman answered.

"We'll be needing that boar after all!" The housekeeper clapped. "Stations, my lovelies. We have a celebration to prepare."

Gunn pressed his mouth close to Lorna's ear and whispered, "Are ye up to this revelry, m'love?"

"Aye, husband." She eyed her attire, then gave him a look that flooded him with even more heat. "Although a wee lie-down before I dress would not go amiss."

"Say no more." He swept her up into his arms and headed for the stairs.

CHAPTER SIXTEEN

S HE WAS MARRIED. To Gunn. Lorna stood in the middle of his large bedchamber, hugging herself, suddenly overwhelmed with a rush of indescribable emotions. Mostly good, but a few insecure ones too. The realization that she was now a permanent resident of the seventeenth century and all that entailed hit harder now. Why it hadn't before, she had no idea. All she knew was that even though she loved this man and his people with a fury that consumed her, a tiny part of her feared this era and the events yet to come.

"Lorna?" Gunn edged closer. "What is it, dear one?"

"A month ago I never wouldha believed I could ever be this happy." She reached out to touch him, then noticed the griminess of her hands and arms, and drew them back. "I am covered in filth." For the first time since emerging from the tunnels, she saw he was too. "We must have made quite a sight while saying our vows."

He moved to the pitcher and basin on the cabinet beside the hearth, then cast a smoldering glance back at her. "What better way to start our union than by giving each other a bit of a wash, aye?"

"Indeed." She moved to his side. Crocks of soaps and oils,

almost identical to the ones in her privy closet, waited beside the basin.

As he poured the water, she noticed the raw, bloody knuckles on his right hand. She snatched up a soft linen cloth, dampened it, and gently cleaned his wounds.

"I am so sorry," she said as she wiped the dirt from his arms, then his face.

He halted her ministrations and slid a hand along her jaw line, then laced his fingers in her hair. "'Tis a small price to pay for the joy filling my heart at this verra moment." After brushing a tender kiss across her mouth, he angled her face to one side and frowned. "Ye have scrapes too, precious mouse. Rest easy while I clean them."

With a fresh cloth, he cleaned her bruised cheekbone with a gentleness that almost made her weep. She covered his hand with hers and whispered, "This is why I love ye."

"Because I tend yer wounds?" He huffed a soft laugh, then flashed that dimple that always stirred her.

"Aye," she said. "The ones on the inside as well as those on the outside."

"As ye do for me." He drew her closer and ran the damp cloth down her throat and across her collarbones while easing the neckline of her shift wider open and encouraging the garment to fall into a pile at her feet. "Such beauty."

Without taking her gaze from his, she unbuckled his belt and tossed it aside. His great kilt slipped to the floor, leaving him in nothing but his boots and léine. Heart pounding and burning with an ache to melt into him and have him melt into her, she slid her hands up under the softness of his linen shirt. The warm hardness of his rippling muscles caressed her palms as she pushed the cloth upward and off over his head. She teased her fingers through the dark blond hair dusting his chest and nibbled a trail of loving kisses in their wake.

His breathing hitched as he pulled her closer and molded his hardness against her. "I dinna think I will ever get enough of ye," he said while nuzzling his way along her throat and even lower.

"Good." She laced her fingers through his hair and tightened her hold. His searing kisses made it difficult to remain standing.

As if reading her mind, he swept her up, carried her to the bed, and eased her down into the nest of pillows. He paused long enough to kick off his boots before joining her. "We may miss the celebration." He took her mouth while pulling her closer.

She arched into him, curled a leg over the muscular leanness of his hip, and squeezed. "This is the celebration." She guided his mouth lower. He complied with a rumbling groan, licking and tasting as if she were his own personal feast.

"Sweeter than wild boar," he teased.

"And not nearly as dangerous." She shuddered and caught her lip between her teeth as he nibbled lower still.

"I wouldna say that." He tickled her thighs farther apart, lowered his head, then drove her mad with artful flicks of his tongue.

No longer able to speak, she gave herself to the sheer delight of every sensation, fisting her hands in the bedclothes. A primeval cry escaped her as the delicious ecstasy crested, then crashed through her, wave after wave, making her buck for more. Hands buried in his hair, she pulled him up to her, arching to take him in. "I need ye. Now."

"Good." His kiss claimed her with an urgency as he settled between her thighs. He teased against her opening, then drove in deep with a long, low growl. "Never get enough," he groaned, moving with a slow, pounding rhythm.

"Never," she echoed, meeting him thrust for thrust. The hardness of his flexing muscles paired with the hot smoothness of his skin sliding against hers drove her even faster to explosive oblivion. His taste. His heat. Their scents mingled into one. The sensations branded her with the searing ancientness of mates bonding for life.

Then he slowed the primeval dance, his breathing strained and slow.

Stroking his sides, she arched to kiss him, moving her hips to urge him back to driving fast and hard.

"Slow down, m'love," he rasped. "I want this to last longer."

She squeezed the meaty cheeks of his arse and moved her hips more. "We can do slow when we are old. I need ye now."

"I canna refuse ye." He drove into her even fiercer than before.

And she exploded, screaming her bliss as he roared with his. He slumped across her, shuddering as they both struggled to catch their breath, still trembling with the delicious aftershocks of sensation.

"That was a proper consummation," she said, loving the feel of him on top of her. He started to move, but she tightened her hold. "No, I like ye like this."

"Am I not crushing ye?"

"Only in a good way." She kissed his shoulder, reveling in the salty-sweet taste of him. A lazy, warm sleepiness lulled her inhibitions and made her say whatever popped into her head. "Yer bed is much nicer than mine."

His laugh rumbled a delightful vibration through her. "This is yer bed now too, my precious one. As are these rooms." He gave her a tender, lingering kiss, then lifted his head and smiled down at her. "I need ye in my bed each night and by my side every day."

She teased her finger across his dimple. "I think we were meant to be," she said softly. "Maybe that's why the northern lights brought me to ye."

"Perhaps so, my precious lady." He pressed a kiss to her forehead and lingered there for a long moment before lifting his head and smiling down at her again. "I say we toss obligations to the wind and let the clan celebrate without us. What say ye, *mo ghráidh?*"

There was a timid peck on the bedchamber door.

"I say our obligations have come a knocking, dear husband." She caught his face between her hands and gave him a quick kiss.

"We canna ignore them. It could be something to do with the bairns."

A heavy sigh escaped him as he rolled off the bed and glared at the door. "Enter!"

Lorna scrambled to cover herself. Gunn might have no qualms about greeting visitors naked, but she did.

The door opened the tiniest bit. "Sir Jasper sent me, my chieftain," Ebby said through the crack, her voice quaking. "Edmond has returned with a high constable from Edinburgh."

"A high constable from Edinburgh?" Lorna repeated. "I thought Jasper sent Edmond to Inverness to fetch the solicitor."

"He did." Gunn pulled on his boots, yanked on his léine, then belted his great kilt around his body with impressive speed. He tossed a glance at the barely opened door as he raked his hair back and secured it with a strip of leather. "Ebby, yer mistress needs help dressing." Before the maid responded, he strode back to the bed and leaned close, lowering his voice for Lorna alone. "We will receive the high constable together. In the library."

Clutching the bedsheet to her chest, she feared what the constable might want. She couldn't remember an Earl of Caithness being caught up in any political turmoil. At least not in this century. But that didn't mean things couldn't change or that she just hadn't read about it. After all, her very presence had to have altered history's timeline.

"Stay with me," she said. "Let Jasper find out what the man wants."

With a gently chiding look, he shook his head. "I am chieftain, m'love. The task is mine to bear. Not Jasper's."

"Will ye at least wait in yer solar until I am dressed so we can go down together?" She ached with the need to protect him. It might be silly, but she didn't care. She would do whatever it took to guard her new family and keep them safe. "I dinna want ye going down there alone."

He tipped his head. "Aye, *mo ghráidh*. I shall await ye in my solar."

She pulled him to her for another kiss, then whispered against his mouth, "I love ye."

"And I love ye, precious one." He playfully tugged on the tress curled against her cheek. "Make haste, aye?"

She nodded, then floundered out of the bed with the sheet wrapped around her. "Ebby, hurry!"

The maid burst into the room, dipped a stumbling curtsy at Gunn as he exited, then rushed to the wardrobe and threw the doors open wide. "I took the liberty of moving yer things in here when the chieftain went to fetch ye from the tunnels." She cast a shy smile back at Lorna. "I knew in my heart the two of ye were meant to be."

"I am glad ye were so sure." Lorna returned to the washbasin, tossed the grimy water into the bucket beside the cabinet, and refilled the wash bowl with fresh water. After wetting and soaping a rag, she moved closer to the fire to do her scrubbing. What she wouldn't give for a hot shower or a warm, sudsy bath. Instead, she had cold water and a hearth fire. But she wouldn't complain. Because now she had something she had never had before: love and a family.

"M'lady!" Ebby snatched the rag out of her hand. "The chief's wife doesna wash herself. Her lady's maid does it for her. Mrs. Thistlewick said so."

"M'lady?" Lorna relinquished the task with a sigh. "Why the sudden *m'lady?*"

"Not only are ye the lady of this keep," Ebby said while scrubbing her back, "but ye are a countess as well, since himself is the Earl of Caithness." She paused and gently angled her closer to the fire. "Ye have a wicked bruise coming on. Mrs. Thistlewick will need to fix ye a comfrey poultice for that."

Now that Ebby brought her attention to it, that side of Lorna's back was tender. "It probably happened when Gunn yanked me out of the hole before the rock fell."

"Praise God Almighty he was able to save ye." Ebby rinsed out the rag, wet another, then started wiping down Lorna's arms and legs. "We've no time for washing yer hair, but I can brush it till it shines." She cast a glance at the rumpled bed with the sheets and blankets dragged off into the floor. "And I shall tell Alice and Janie that bed needs changing. Yer water pitchers are nearly spent too." She tossed the rag into the bowl, snapped open a long fold of fresh linen, and started rubbing Lorna dry. "We will get every bit of it seen to whilst ye are gone to the library."

"I dinna wish ye to miss the feast." The concept of servants who would hop every time she said *scat* still made Lorna uncomfortable. And she didn't want to cause anyone to miss something as special as a Yuletide celebration. The mouth-watering scent of Cook's roasting boar and the buttery yeastiness of the freshly baked breads and pies had filled the keep since before dawn. "I can straighten the bed, and that pitcher on the end still has plenty of water."

Ebby's mouth dropped open and her eyes flared as wide as if Lorna had suggested they set the place on fire. "Ye will do no such thing, m'lady!" She clucked like a fussing hen while vigorously rubbing scented oils into Lorna's skin. "I can see right now that ye are going to be the death of me until ye ken how to behave like the mistress of this keep."

"The mistress of this keep cares about each one of ye as though ye are family," Lorna said. "Ye are not slaves that are supposed to jump at my every whim."

"Ye are a kind woman, m'lady, but me and all the rest of the servants need to be needed here. 'Tis good for the soul to earn yer keep. That's what Mrs. Thistlewick always says." Ebby hurried to the wardrobe and drew out an outer skirt and jacket that Lorna hadn't seen before. The deep richness of the blue was fit for royalty. The maid draped it across the end of the bed, then opened a nearby trunk and pulled out a fresh shift, embroidered underskirt, and stockings.

Lorna gave up. It was the way of things in this time and would take years to change it. "Well, let's hurry and get me fit for company, aye? I can hear Gunn pacing in the next room."

With impressive efficiency and a surprising lack of clumsiness, Ebby helped her dress in record time.

After smoothing her hands down the heavy weave of the wool skirt, Lorna hurried into the solar. Gunn stood at the window, whisky in hand, scowling as though preparing to wage war.

"Are ye ready?" she asked softly, resenting the potential drama overshadowing what had turned out to be one of the most precious days of her life.

He turned from the window, and his scowl disappeared. "Ye are loveliness itself."

"Thank ye."

With a wry grin, he lifted his glass. "I dinna suppose ye wish a wee bit of fortification first?"

She wrinkled her nose. "Better not. I dinna think it wise to loosen my tongue or vomit on the man."

With a deep chuckle, he set his glass on a table and offered his arm. "Let us go, then, and find out what brings one of Edinburgh's high constables to Thursa."

"Hopefully, Mrs. Thistlewick has oiled the man with food and drink, so he will be more pliable."

"Oiled the man?"

A frustrated huff escaped her. Just because Gunn knew her story didn't mean that she should use terminology from her time. Someone could overhear. "It's a saying I should not have used, since it sounds as though we are going to fry him. Sorry."

He patted her hand and hugged her arm closer. "I knew what ye meant, mouse. Dinna fash yerself."

As they stepped out of the stairwell, Mrs. Thistlewick met them, wringing her hands. "Edmond took the man into the library. Jasper kent ye would want to speak with him in private rather than in the main hall." She flipped a hand at the closed door at the end of the hall. "I sent in food and extra drink. Just so ye know, he is a fair-sized man. I thought his humor might improve if we filled his wame and wet his tongue with whisky."

Lorna flinched. Mrs. Thistlewick's assessment didn't sound promising. "Do ye think he will be trouble?"

The housekeeper twitched a shrug. "I dinna ken, m'lady. Part of his foulness is surely from the damp cold here at Thursa. He said more than once that his bones had never ached so much in his life."

Gunn tugged her forward. "Come, m'love. We have kept the man waiting long enough."

"Not nearly as long as I would like." But Lorna lifted her chin, squared her shoulders, and tried to summon a gracefulness she had never possessed before.

As soon as they entered the library, the large, barrel-chested man struggled to hoist himself from the depths of a cushion-filled chair beside the hearth. He huffed and puffed until almost wheezing by the time he rocked to his feet and stood. Red-faced, but bearing a polite smile, he proffered a bow to Gunn. "Constable Murchison Erskine, Lord Caithness. I beg yer forgiveness for my uninvited intrusion into yer fine home."

"No intrusion at all," Gunn said. "Although I must say, yer visit comes as a surprise. Edinburgh is quite the trip to manage at this time of year." His gaze shifted to Edmond. "And especially since our man's destination was Inverness. Not Edinburgh."

"I did go to Inverness," Edmond said.

Jasper thumped the lad's chest with the back of his hand and cut him down with a pointed glare.

"Sorry, my chieftain." The hulking Edmond backed up a step, as if trying to disappear into the shadows.

Lorna felt bad for the young man who was more like an oversized pup than a warrior. "Did ye come upon Edmond in Inverness, Constable Erskine?"

"My wife," Gunn said with an indulgent smile.

The constable bowed politely again. "I did come upon yer man in Inverness, m'lady. It turned out that my men and I were seeking Liam MacGibbon as well."

"Why so?" Gunn asked. "And did ye find him?"

Constable Erskine puffed up like a proud peacock. "Oh, that we did, m'lord. And I hope ye rest easy knowing that he is well on his way to the tolbooth in Edinburgh." He bobbed his head, making his fleshy jowls bounce. "Of course, he willna hang till spring, when the weather improves."

"The charges?" Gunn asked.

"Many, m'lord." The constable gimped closer to the fire and shifted his weight from side to side as though his feet pained him. "Murder. Practicing as a solicitor without a license. Blackmail. Coercion. Quite the list."

"Murder?" Lorna repeated.

"Aye." Erskine bobbed his head again. He rubbed his arse as he backed closer to the fire. "He helped a whore murder her husband after he drew up a will for the man and his heir—a nephew we are also seeking, as he appeared to be in on the scheme as well."

The back of Lorna's neck tingled, and an excited knowing made her heart beat faster. "The whore wouldna be Lady Murdina Sullivan? And the nephew Reginald Leckness?"

The constable's eyes bulged. He slid an awe-filled look back to Gunn. "Does yer wife have the sight, m'lord?"

"That she does." Gunn squeezed her hand. "We consider it a blessing."

Lorna took the squeeze as a subtle request to let him do the rest of the talking.

"Lady Murdina is currently in my dungeon," Gunn said. "For not only trying to poison me but also for kidnapping my daughter and trying to kill my wife." He snorted as though trying to rid himself of her stench. "I assume yer visit here is to collect her?"

"Aye, m'lord. Her and Leckness."

"She slit Leckness's throat," Gunn said. "But there is a matter ye should know of. The woman swears she is with child." He squeezed Lorna's hand again. "We dinna wish an innocent babe to suffer having such a mother. If a bairn is born to her, we would take it in and raise it as our own. Dinna send it to a place for foundlings."

"The madam at Darley's Place swore the woman was barren," the constable said. "That one was in on the blackmailing too, and offered information to escape the noose. Lady Murdina forced Lord Sullivan into marriage by not only saying she carried his child but by also threatening to make his rather…" He gave Lorna an apologetic nod. "She threatened to make his unnatural preferences at the brothel common knowledge at court and among his peers. After the will was drawn up, signed, and witnessed, she murdered him with the help of MacGibbon and Leckness. A servant witnessed the scene and escaped afore they ended her as well." He cleared his throat. "'Tis my understanding that MacGibbon and Lady Murdina are rather familiar with one another."

"If they inherited the man's wealth, why did they bother trying the same scheme on Chieftain Sinclair?" Lorna couldn't remain silent any longer. She offered Gunn an apologetic wiggle of her nose, then turned back to Erskine. "She tried to force him into marriage before he married me." With a pointed look to make sure the constable understood, she added, "Of course, my husband does not possess unsavory tendencies that she could use for blackmail along with claiming pregnancy."

The constable shook his head. "Another Sullivan nephew stepped in and contested not only the will but the marriage. Stopped the estate and all the coin from going to anyone."

"Ye might also wish to check into the affairs of Mr. Moray Macray in Inverness," Jasper offered to the constable as he refilled all their glasses. "'Twas him who recommended Mr. MacGibbon's services to us."

Erskine replied with a wink and a smirk. "That man will share a cell with Mr. MacGibbon. The tolbooth became his new residence before my men and I left for Inverness."

"Such a bloody mess," Lorna said without thinking. She clapped her hand over her mouth as soon as the words slipped out.

"Indeed." The constable chuckled.

"Ye and yer men will surely stay for our Yule feast and the celebration of my marriage to this fine woman, aye?" Gunn hugged her to his side. "After all, Lady Murdina is quite comfortable in the dungeon, and Leckness is already dead. Buried at sea, as a matter of fact. Frozen ground doesna yield to the shovel, and I refuse to keep grave fires burning to thaw it. I willna waste good wood on that bastard."

The constable beamed a broad smile that plumped his full cheeks even more. "I would consider it an honor, m'lord." He bowed several times, chuckling all the while. "Thank ye for such generous hospitality, m'lord." He bobbed his head at Lorna. "And ye as well, m'lady. May God bless ye both with many happy years and a keep full of healthy bairns."

"Thank ye, Constable Erskine." Lorna smiled at the man, then noticed for the first time since they had entered the library that the muscles of Gunn's arm no longer flexed hard and tense beneath her fingers as though warming up for battle. It made her breathe easier. Now that all the pieces had fallen into their proper places, they could relax and get on with enjoying their lives. "If ye will excuse me now, I need to check on the bairns."

Erskine bowed, then swept his glass up from the table and held it for Edmond to refill.

"I feel the need to see my daughter as well," Gunn said. "I nearly lost her today."

"I understand completely, m'lord." Erskine gave a solemn nod. "I've three wee daughters of my own. Precious blessings, they are."

"That they are," Gunn echoed.

After a dismissive tip of his head, he accompanied Lorna out into the hall. As soon as he closed the library door behind them, he took her into his arms and kissed her. Hard and thorough.

When he lifted his mouth from hers, a breathless laugh escaped her. "What was that for, *mo ghráidh?*"

"We are free to live our lives now. Nothing hanging over our heads." With a tenderness that made her heart swell, he brushed his thumb across her cheek as he laced his fingers deeper into her hair. In a seductive whisper, he added, "We should go upstairs and see if we can lose yer hairpins so Ebby can fuss."

She molded herself against him, aching to melt into him again. "They are changing the bedclothes and filling the water pitchers," she whispered back. "I dinna ken if they are done or not."

"They are done because I will order them out." He kissed her again, then gently framed her face between his hands. "No one will ever keep me from ye, my precious one."

"Good." She smoothed her hands up his chest. "Because I need a great deal of loving."

"And ye shall have it, my sweet mouse. Ye shall always have it."

EPILOGUE

Meanwhile, back in the 21st century
December 31, 2022
Thurso, Scotland

GRACIE HELD UP the wreath of red roses interspersed with holly and white silk ribbons. "Roses were her favorite. The darkest red ones. Never seen her so happy when I got her some on her birthday." She cast a teary-eyed smile at Lonnie and his wife Cybil. "Thank ye for coming here with me today. I know it's bitter cold."

Lonnie sniffed, then swiped the back of his hand across his nose. "We loved her too, Gracie."

"Aye," Cybil quietly agreed.

"I still canna believe that bastard got away with pleading mental." Gracie clenched her teeth as she fluffed the wreath's ribbons into fuller bows.

"Leastways he got life at that facility," Lonnie said. "And he did sound awful barmy at that hearing." He nodded down at the white-capping waves crashing into the rocks at the base of the cliff. "'Twas kind of a nice lie he told, though. 'Bout Lorna diving off into the arms of the mirrie dancers that night. Ye ken how she loved her northern lights."

"And they never found her," Cybil added. She crossed herself while peering down at the rocky spires stretching their razor-sharp fingers up through the sea's froth. Then she lifted her gaze to the wispy white clouds skittering across the pale blue sky. "Mayhap she did fly away into their magic." She offered Gracie a sad smile. "She wouldha loved doing that. Ye know she would."

"Aye." Gracie swallowed hard. "That she wouldha." She unfastened her favorite pin, a bright red enamel poppy, from her lapel and secured it to the center of the main bow on the wreath. "When she finds this, she will know we still love her and miss her something fierce."

"And that we will never forget her," Lonnie said, swiping at tears. He pulled a small golden cross from his pocket and wired it to the wreath. "May God watch over her wherever she may be."

"Aye," Gracie said. "God bless her and keep her." Then she closed her eyes and threw the wreath out over the sea. The wind caught it before it hit the water and carried it out of sight.

"Angels are taking it to her," Cybil whispered.

"I hope so," Gracie said. She turned and plodded back to the car, aching for the best friend she had ever known.

January 2, 1623
The Mirrie Dancer Cliffs near Thursa Castle

"THIS IS WHERE I woke up…so to speak." Lorna snuggled deeper into the furry hood of her cloak, squinting against the brightness of the wintry sun glinting off the snow. She crunched through the icy crust of the drifts as she made her way to the top of the cliff. "'Tis beautiful, aye? The best spot to watch the northern lights." As they neared the top, a flash of red and green at the crag's edge caught her eye. "What is that?"

"I dinna ken." Gunn held fast to her arm. "Wait here while I see."

"Yes, dear husband."

He gave her a good-natured glare. "Dinna use that tone with me, my precious mouse. 'Tis my duty to protect ye."

That made her smile. A warm sense of contentment filled her. She was happier than she ever thought possible. As he reached whatever it was lying in the snow, he leaned over and frowned down at it before picking it up.

"What is it?" She hurried to his side, unable to stand it any longer. As she laid eyes on the lovely wreath of her favorite roses, she lost the ability to breathe. Without a word, she took it from him, touching the blooms with sad reverence. Tears blurred the image of the enamel poppy pin she had bought for Gracie so long ago. And that golden cross. The one Lonnie always carried in his pocket to protect him from his sins. She hugged the arrangement to her chest, bowed her head, and wept.

"Lorna?" Gunn wrapped an arm around her and gently pulled her closer. "What is it? Do ye ken who left it here?"

"I do," she whispered.

"Why did they not bring it to the keep? Visit with ye?"

Struggling to speak through her sorrow, she shook her head. "Because they couldna find the way."

He gently brushed the tears from her cheeks, his expression reflecting her grief. "When ye say they couldna find the way..." His voice trailed off, but his meaning was clear.

With trembling fingers, she traced the gold outline of the poppy pinned to the heart of the largest white bow. "Aye. My friends wouldna ken how to make their way here any more than I did when I came. They were the only family I ever had back in my time."

"We shall set a cairn here," Gunn said quietly. "And torches that shall be kept burning bright each night." He gently hugged her closer. "That way, if they ever find a way to join ye, they willna arrive to darkness." When she didn't answer, he lifted her face to his. "But swear ye will never use this place to try to return to them, aye? I couldna bear it."

She stretched on tiptoe and brushed a tender kiss across his lips. "I will never leave ye, *mo ghràidh*. Ye are my home, my heart, my all."

"As ye are mine, m'love. As ye are mine."

About the Author

If you enjoyed LOVING HER LONELY HIGHLANDER, please consider leaving a review on the site where you purchased your copy, or a reader site such as Goodreads, or BookBub.

If you'd like to receive my newsletter, here's the link to sign up:
maevegreyson.com/contact.html#newsletter

I love to hear from readers! Drop me a line at
maevegreyson@gmail.com

Or visit me on Facebook:
facebook.com/AuthorMaeveGreyson

Join my Facebook Group – Maeve's Corner:
facebook.com/groups/MaevesCorner

I'm also on Instagram:
maevegreyson

My website:
https://maevegreyson.com

Feel free to ask questions or leave some Reader Buzz on
bingebooks.com/author/maeve-greyson

Goodreads:
goodreads.com/maevegreyson

Follow me on these sites to get notifications about new releases, sales, and special deals:

Amazon:
amazon.com/Maeve-Greyson/e/B004PE9T9U

BookBub:
bookbub.com/authors/maeve-greyson

Many thanks and may your life always be filled with good books!
Maeve

Ingram Content Group UK Ltd.
Milton Keynes UK
UKHW020644140423
420171UK00014B/380